THE LIAR'S DAUGHTER

MEGAN COOLEY PETERSON

DISCARD

HOLIDAY HOUSE • NEW YORK

Library of Congress Cataloging-in-Publication Data

Names: Peterson, Megan Cooley, author.
Title: The liar's daughter / Megan Cooley Peterson.
Description: First edition. | New York : Holiday House, [2019] | Summary:
Desperate to escape deprogramming after being rescued from a cult,
seventeen-year-old Piper wants to rejoin her family, but the truth about
that family, her past, and herself cannot be denied.
Identifiers: LCCN 2019014092 | ISBN 9780823444182 (hardback)
Subjects: | CYAC: Cults—Fiction. | Family life—Fiction. |
Kidnapping—Fiction. | Brainwashing—Fiction. | Memory—Fiction.
Classification: LCC PZ7.1.P456 Li 2019 | DDC [Fic]—dc23
LC record available at https://lccn.loc.gov/2019014092

ISBN: 978-0-8234-4418-2 (hardcover)

For my daughter,

the map of my heart,

and for anyone who has ever felt lost

and needed to be found

1. AFTER

A bed.

A window seat.

A chipped desk with daisy stickers on the drawers.

These things belong to me, I'm told.

The woman takes me from the room and down a hallway, the walls so close they almost crush me. She wears all beige and not a stitch of makeup. My bladder strains, and I can't remember the last time I peed. Her shoes squeak against the floor; her skirt rustles. My ears ring from the roar of it all.

The woman nudges open a door. The white walls and floor blind me, and I blink until my eyes adjust. It smells faintly of bleach. "There are clean towels in the cabinet and soap in the shower. Use whatever you like. This is your bathroom now. You're safe here."

She looks at me expectantly. I say nothing.

Finally, the door closes, and the click echoes around the room. The urine bleeds through my pants before I can get to the toilet.

I jut out my chin in defiance, make sure whoever's watching can see it.

Father and Mother told me this might happen. "The world can be an evil place," Mother warned. "I'm the only one you can trust. Me and your father. Never forget that."

Cold water surges from the faucet, pummeling the bottom of the tub. I twist the knob to the left, to the right, but there's just cold, no warm. My reflection in the metal is distorted, inhuman.

They fixed it so I have to bathe in ice-cold water. They think I'm weak. They think I'll break.

My pants cling to my legs as I pull them off. I unhook my mother's necklace with the green stone and set it on the counter—but then the stone catches the light, and I put it back on, listening for sounds outside the door.

When I face the mirror, I barely recognize the girl looking back. My collarbones stick out, shadowed underneath. My breasts are smaller, my stomach shrunken in. My hair falls out when I pull on it.

They told me I'm safe here. They told me this is my family now.

But I don't know these people. And this is not my home.

Voices come from behind me, warped, like a recording played backward. When I turn toward the door, they snap off.

"The world can be an evil place."

I conjure Mother's voice. It comforts me. We'll find each other again, like she promised.

The water scalds my foot, so cold it circled around to being hot.

The tiles on the floor are tiny hexagons slithering underneath the bathtub, flat and cracked. Bottles line the sides of the tub with promises of better hair, softer skin. My mother's fancy soaps smelled of lavender and lemon.

I drag a rag across my body, over and over until my skin turns pink.

I'm the only color in the room.

2. BEFORE

The kitchen reeks of bleach.

I hold my finger up to my lips and smile at Beverly Jean, who sits on a stool next to the kitchen sink. The Aunties have a towel wrapped around her small shoulders, secured in the front with a clothespin. Auntie Barb combs through her hair while Auntie Joan mixes up a bottle of hair bleach.

Beverly Jean's eyes swing like a pendulum as she watches Auntie Joan jolt the bottle back and forth.

"Can I hold her hand?" I ask. As the oldest daughter, it falls on me to help take care of the younger children. Auntie Barb and Auntie Joan aren't exactly maternal, and they expect me to make up for that.

Auntie Joan plunks the bottle down on the table and sighs. Her long, graying hair is gathered in a tight bun that pulls her crepe-paper skin back sharply.

"Do what you like," she says. "But keep her quiet. You know how your father hates it when you children cry."

I rush to Beverly Jean and squeeze her hand with mine. "It'll be over before you know it," I whisper. "Just close your eyes and hold my hand, and it'll be okay."

Beverly Jean does as I instruct, and Auntie Joan squirts the dye onto her scalp. Almost immediately, it turns the skin red. I've asked for less-harsh dyes to be used, but the Aunties say this is all that's available.

Beverly Jean whimpers. I hold her hand even tighter and hum "Hush, Little Baby," the same lullaby I sang to her when she was little.

When Auntie Joan finishes, Auntie Barb snaps a plastic shower cap over Beverly Jean's burning head and sets a timer. Auntie Barb wears a long denim dress and compression socks. Every day, the same. "Fifteen minutes," she says. "Not a second less."

The Aunties disappear down the hallway, and Beverly Jean opens her eyes. "After your wash, I'll rub ice cubes on your scalp, okay?" I promise. "That always helps."

When the timer rings, I put my hand in the sink water and touch it to Beverly Jean's arm. "Does this feel too hot?" I heated up a pot of water on the woodstove an hour ago, and I hope it hasn't cooled too much in the sink. We don't have running water, but the pipes still work for drainage.

"No, it feels good. Thanks, Pip." When Beverly Jean was little, she couldn't say my whole name. So she said Pip instead, and it stuck. It's all she calls me.

She leans back, and I peel off the cap and wash the bleach from her hair. Her once-dark roots have turned as bright as the goldfinches that feed on Mother's sunflowers. I massage toner into her hair, and soon she is a perfect blonde again. Just like Mother.

After I towel dry her hair, I grab an ice cube from the icebox and rub it along the angry patches on her scalp. "You deserve an ice pop," I say. "What flavor?"

"Grape!"

I pry one out of its mold. "Father and Mother will be here in a few hours," I tell Beverly Jean. "They'll be so happy to see you looking your best."

She scrunches up her nose. "How come you and Henry don't have to get your hair dyed? It doesn't seem fair."

I touch my long ponytail. "Because our hair is already blond. Mother just wants us to look like a family. She doesn't want anyone to feel left out, or unloved, or different."

"But what about Caspian and Thomas?"

"Father took them in, but they're not our brothers. It's all right if they're not blond. Does that make sense?"

"I guess so." Beverly Jean bites into her ice pop.

I kiss her cheek. "Good. Now finish up your ice pop. I've got to help with Samuel's hair next."

✘

After we finish the bleachings, I go outside looking for Caspian.

The lake laps against the shore, and pieces of seaweed bob along its surface. A few of the younger children are trying to catch a frog in a bucket. Their laughter washes away the stench of bleach trapped in my nostrils, and I smile.

The old roller coaster rises above the trees. Our property includes a derelict amusement park that's been abandoned for forty or fifty years. Father's torn most of the rides down, but a few remain. He said this was the perfect location for his children, far from cities and towns.

We live in the old caretaker's house. It has two stories with lots of windows and hardwood floors. The roof over the boys' bedroom needs to be repaired, so for now it's covered with a big piece of blue tarp. Father prefers to keep us "off the grid," so we don't have electricity or running water. But we have a pump, generators, candlelight. We have all we need.

The Aunties are nowhere to be found. They must be resting before lunch; they're always telling us how vexing we are.

I stop in front of the old oak tree. Nailed to its trunk is the sign Father carved from a piece of balsam wood.

The Community is truth.
The Community is loyalty.
The Community will keep you safe.

It's our creed, everything the Community stands for and believes in. Every time I'm feeling sad or frustrated, I read the sign. It fills me with light and hope.

When I reach out to touch it, a spark of magic pricks my finger.

I find Cas working in a row of corn, hacking at weeds with a hoe. Our garden is large, at least twenty feet long, with corn bordering the far end. We grow many different crops: artichokes, lettuce, tomatoes, cauliflower. My favorites are the root vegetables, the carrots and beets and radishes that hide themselves away until they're ready.

Cas wears a white T-shirt, and his wide shoulders press at the seams as he works. I grab the handle right out of his hands.

"Hey!" he says, trying to snatch it back. "I'm using that."

I jump away, keeping it just out of his reach. "You've worked long enough today. I need you to time me."

Father put a buoy a hundred feet from shore, and I've been practicing swimming out to it and back. When war comes, I have to be as strong as possible. All those extra push-ups I did this week must've made me at least a second faster.

Cas's eyes meet mine, blue like the sea he was named for. I've never seen an ocean in real life, only in a book, but the photograph stuck with me, and someday I'll swim in one. Cas's eyelashes are so dark and thick it looks like he's wearing mascara. He's the only one of us with dark hair; his brother Thomas has brown hair, but Cas has black hair like he says his father had. "I think you've just about perfected your swimming by now," he says.

"Come on," I wheedle. "It's been two weeks since anyone timed me. I'm sure I've gotten faster since then. I want to show Father when he gets here. Prove that I'm ready to be initiated."

"You know Curtis is proud of you no matter what, Piper. You're his favorite."

"That is totally untrue."

Cas nudges me with his shoulder. "Oh, please. You were so afraid he'd love me more than you when I first got here that you told me I could eat as many strawberries from the patch as I wanted. I got in a lot of trouble for that."

Father took Caspian and Thomas in a few years ago when they had no place else to go. He was forced to expel their parents from the Community when they brought drugs into the compound, but of course he allowed the boys to stay—it would have been too cruel to let the Outside have them. Thomas has been at the main compound with Father and Mother these past several months, ever since he was initiated into the Community, and I'm itching to hear all about his new life there.

"I never told you to eat those strawberries, and you know it! If you're going to lie, at least come up with something interesting."

He gives me a playful shove, and I shove him back. My stomach flutters, but I ignore it.

Then he goes for my weak spot—the soft skin of my inner arm. He tries tickling it, and I squeal and run toward the lake, kicking off my sandals. The smaller children laugh and chase after us, and soon we're all splashing water at one another. The sun warms my shoulders, and the cool water is a salve, taking away the sting of Beverly Jean's burned scalp, the sting of missing Father and Mother.

"Get out of that filthy lake water this instant!"

Auntie Joan stands on the shore, hands on hips. We immediately fall into line, youngest to oldest, and march toward the house.

We're good at following orders.

"You're lucky I don't take a switch to each and every one of you," she says. "You need to get cleaned up and dressed."

When she's not looking, I reach back and smack Cas on the arm. He catches my hand and holds it, just for a moment, before letting go.

3. BEFORE

The last time Father and Mother came to stay, Millie hadn't started walking yet.

It was an easier time.

She wiggles out of my grasp now, naked, and takes off down the hallway holding her favorite stuffed animal, a giraffe missing an ear. "Millie, get back here!" I chase after her, freshly washed diaper in my hand, and find her at the large hall window overlooking the lake. She always waits there for our parents, who're due to arrive any minute.

"Millie," I coax. "Don't you want to look pretty for Mommy and Daddy?"

She pops a thumb into her mouth. "Where's Mommy?"

"She and Daddy are on their way. Let's get you dressed, and then they'll be here."

I lead Millie back to the girls' bedroom. Beverly Jean is already dressed, immaculate in her burgundy dress with the white sash. She sits on her bed, dressing one of her paper dolls in a purple ball gown.

Carla slumps over the desk, drawing in her sketchbook. She's got her dress on, but not her sash. She's a few years younger than me and recently decided dresses are evil.

"Carla, where'd your sash go?" I try peering over her shoulder, and she blocks her drawing with her arms.

"Beats me."

"Look through the closet. You don't want the Aunties to see you without it."

Carla grunts, closes her sketchbook, and yanks open the closet doors. She kicks aside a basket of dirty clothes. "Not here."

Millie lies on her back, and I lift her bum and slide the diaper under it. Once it's secured with safety pins, I slip one foot into her tights, and then the other. Her tights stretch against her meaty thighs, and I'm afraid they'll tear. Whoever invented tights for babies should be locked up. "You barely looked. Please, Carla, just do as I say."

"You're not Mother, you know," she reminds me, but then she immediately locates her sash on the shelf and ties it around her waist.

"Was that so hard?" I ask. Carla ignores me.

"You look so pretty," Beverly Jean tells her.

"I look ugly." Carla sags onto on her bed, which is across from mine. "I'm all broken out."

"You both look lovely," I remind them. Once I've changed Millie into her dress, I hand her off to Carla. "Try to keep her from getting naked again," I say, slipping out of my bell-bottoms and crocheted peasant top and into my dress. Auntie Barb made us matching burgundy dresses a few months ago, and mine is already a little looser. All that swimming has made my body leaner, more streamlined. But I don't complain. Mother loves it when we're all dressed up. Father doesn't care for vanity, but he indulges her.

Auntie Barb sticks her head in our room. "Hurry up, now. Let's get lined up outside."

Once she's gone, I take Millie back. "I hope you read your pages," I tell Carla. She rolls her eyes as she lifts Father's book from her desk and shakes it at me. All of Father's teachings are hand-typed and bound in leather. He'll know if we've fallen behind in our reading.

For once, the boys beat us outside. They stand on the front lawn in a perfect row. Caspian adjusts his burgundy tie and straightens his hair. A lock falls over his forehead, and I want to brush it away, to touch him, but the Aunties are watching. They don't seem to approve of our closeness anymore. Next to Cas is Samuel, eleven, and then Henry, eight. Their matching corduroy suits and ties are darling, and I waste no time telling them so.

Samuel sticks his tongue out at me.

"I saw that," Auntie Joan warns.

The girls line up next to the boys as the Aunties inspect us. Auntie Barb passes a lint roller over Samuel's jacket, then moves on to Caspian's. Auntie Joan orders Henry to take off his cowboy hat.

"Me hungry," Millie whines before chewing on her giraffe's arm.

"We'll eat soon. Now quiet, please," I say.

Tires crunch on gravel, and then a sleek black limousine rolls up the drive, stopping right in front of us. The driver steps out, races around to the back, and whisks open the door.

Mother puts one foot out; she's wearing silver high heels, and I can't wait to try them on later. Blue gauzy fabric tumbles over her leg as she takes the driver's hand and emerges into the sunshine.

She wears a straw hat and large sunglasses. Her wavy blond hair flows down her back.

Mother is the most glamorous woman I've ever seen. She puts the Hollywood movie stars to shame. We've watched a few films together, films like *Casablanca* and *Meet Me in St. Louis* with beautiful actresses. She outshines them all.

She stops when she sees us and throws up her arms. "My darlings!"

Samuel and Henry tear off toward her, Millie toddling close behind. Beverly Jean looks at me, as if she's not quite sure it's "cool" to show affection now that she's seven.

"Go on," I whisper, and she skips ahead.

Mother crouches in her dress as the children tumble into her open arms. She plants kisses on their faces, and her laughter flows over everything like honey.

It is always better when she's here. I swear, even the sky is bluer.

Caspian, Carla, and I hang back by the Aunties. We'll get our time with Mother. Right now, the little ones need her most.

Mother glides toward us with Millie on her hip, the others trailing behind her like ducklings. "Oh my goodness, how I've missed you all." She takes off her sunglasses and kisses us on the cheeks. Her perfume is new. I'll ask her later what it is. Maybe she'll let me wear a little.

"I've brought presents," Mother coos, and Henry and Samuel jump up and down with giddy excitement.

"Did you bring me a gun?" Henry asks. Blond curls frame his soft face, and his eyes are as big and brown as a fawn's.

Mother drops to one knee. "A gun? Whatever do you need a gun for?"

"I need it to shoot the bad guys."

She smiles. "When you're older." She turns to Samuel. Freckles spatter his wide nose, and he's missing his two front teeth. "What about you, Sam? What are you hoping for?"

"New cartridges! *Pac-Man*! Or *Super Mario Brothers*!" His voice breaks, and Carla rolls her eyes.

"Kindness, Carla," Mother reproaches.

Auntie Joan steps in next to Mother. "We've got coffee and tea ready in the living room if you'd like to go inside."

"Give me a moment with my children." She takes both of my hands in hers and pulls me close. "I think I've missed you most of all," she whispers in my ear.

My eyes well up, and she wipes away my tears. "I'm so happy you're here, Mother."

"Me too, my darling. I've brought a bag of new yarn for your crocheting. Remind me to give it to you later—I found the most gorgeous yellows and greens."

She gives Carla a hug, then Caspian. It feels selfish to show her how much I miss her. Mother helps Father with the Community—she runs companies and does so much charity work. She's busy from morning until night and hardly ever sleeps. We know she wants to be here more, but she's far too important.

Still, I won't waste a single moment of this visit being sad.

Once Mother has hugged all of us, she steps into line as well. She nods at the driver, who scurries to the other side of the limo. He opens the door, and Father's head rises above the shiny black roof.

Light streams through the trees, illuminating Father's shaggy brown hair. He seems to float around the back of the car, wearing

13

linen pants and a matching shirt, and—as usual—no shoes. His gait is languid and serene, and I envy how self-assured he is. I wish I had half his poise.

Father stops a few feet from us. We straighten our shoulders, a synchronization perfected over years. He drinks in our faces, checking for something I've never been quite able to put my finger on.

"Children," he says after a while. No one responds, and even Millie manages to stay quiet. "I expect you've all been well in my absence, and listening to Joan and Barb. When I speak with them later, I don't want to hear anything but a glowing review. Is that understood?"

"Yes, Sir," we say in unison.

He relaxes his face a touch. "Good. I'm exhausted from the trip." Father steps toward me. "How are you, Piper? Been practicing your swimming?"

"Every day. And I crocheted a new blanket to donate." Father does a lot of philanthropic work, including donating the Community's handcrafted blankets and scarves to shelters. I try to make at least one or two a month. It makes me sad that people on the Outside don't take care of each other, that they need shelters at all.

He kisses the top of my head. "I'm glad to hear it. While I'm here, we'll go for a walk, just the two of us, and you can tell me what you've been up to."

Then Father moves toward the house like a king returned to his castle.

After a moment, Mother comes out of the stupor Father sometimes puts people into. "Come along, then, Mommy needs a drink!"

As everyone follows Mother up to the house, Thomas emerges from the limousine. Cas and I hang back, eager to see him. He wears all black, and there are dark circles under his eyes. His brown hair has grown out a little. He is handsome like Caspian, but sharper, somehow.

"We missed you," Caspian says, giving his brother a hug. "Glad you're back. It's not the same around here without you."

"So? How is the compound?" I'm practically jumping up and down. "Tell us everything about it! Leave nothing out! We're so proud of you!"

Thomas's usual smile is gone. "It's fine," he says, his voice flat. "We better get inside."

I tug on his sleeve. "Come on, Thomas. You've got to tell me more than that!"

"I will later. I'm pretty exhausted right now."

I glance at Caspian, confused, and he grabs hold of my hand. He always does this when he's nervous, kind of like how I chew my nails. A habit, nothing more. But when he brushes his thumb across mine, it feels like it *could* mean something more. My skin tingles, and I don't know if I should hold on tighter or let go.

I let go.

It's what Father would want.

Thomas yawns. "I got something for you, Piper." I must have a surprised look on my face, because he finally smiles. "I'll bring it to your room after lights-out, okay?"

I throw my arms around him, and he gives me a huge hug back. "Thank you, Thomas. I'm so glad you're home."

"What about me? Did you forget *my* gift?" Cas juts out his bottom lip and pretends to be sad. Thomas rolls his eyes.

We slip into the living room, where the Aunties have coffee, tea, and pastries waiting. Auntie Joan brings Mother a martini with three olives, her favorite.

Mother sinks into a plush armchair and takes off her hat. "This is exactly what I needed. Thank you." She holds the glass up to her nose, closes her eyes, and takes a huge whiff. Then she hands the glass back to Auntie Joan, who takes it outside and dumps it into the grass. Mother used to drink before she joined the Community, and Father allows her this indulgence once in a while, to test her resolve. Drinking alcohol is forbidden. Father says alcohol dulls our senses, makes us weak, and opens up our bodies to disease.

The Aunties motion for us to sit, and we move onto the sofas. Millie tries to climb into Mother's lap, but Father picks her up. "Your mother needs a break," he says sternly, but Millie kicks and cries anyway, and her sash comes undone. Father puts his hand on her forehead and closes his eyes, trying to calm her, but it doesn't work. Mother lifts Millie onto her lap and reties her sash.

"So," she says as Millie burrows against her, "what have you all been up to since we've been away? Spare no details."

Father's jaws clench as he folds himself into the chair next to her. He rolls his head on his neck and shifts, as if he can't get comfortable. I try not to watch him, but I'm alert to his every mood. Cas and Thomas watch him, too, but the little ones are oblivious.

Henry and Samuel tell her about the frog they caught on the beach and are now keeping in a terrarium in their room. "We named it Captain John Wayne!" Henry tells her. Beverly Jean says she learned to make an apple pie from scratch, and that we'll have it for dessert after supper. She also made a macramé plant holder. Carla has hand-beaded some necklaces.

Mother beams. "I am just so proud of all our children. How did we get so lucky?" She looks at Thomas. "And our Thomas, back for the first time since he was initiated. I could cry, I'm so proud."

Father nods, walking over to Thomas and patting his back. "Thomas is a true asset to the Community. He's here for a special project, children, which I'll explain later."

"Thank you, Curtis," Thomas says, keeping his eyes on the floor.

"I hope your aunts haven't been too hard on you in our absence," Mother says.

Caspian and I exchange a glance. They are always too hard on us. But we can't tell that to Mother, and especially not to Father. The moment they're gone again, they'll make us pay for it.

"Not at all," I say, and smile at Auntie Barb. She looks away.

Father rubs his temples. "It's been a long journey, children, and your mother and I need a rest. We'll see you all for supper." Father takes Mother's elbow and guides her upstairs to their bedroom.

"Keep those outfits spotless," Auntie Joan says, clearing away the pastries before any of us can take one. "Dinner's not for a few hours."

"But the little ones need to get outside and run off some energy," I say. "Can't they change into regular clothes until then?"

"You know your mother wouldn't like that."

"Can't they at least go outside? I'll make sure they're careful and clean."

"Fine, but if I see any stains, I'll hold you personally responsible."

I stand and shake her hand. "Deal."

No one moves until the Aunties leave the room.

4. AFTER

The woman waits outside the bathroom door, speaking with someone. I'm wrapped in a towel and lying on the bath mat, wanting desperately to suck my thumb, to transport myself back to Mother and Father and my brothers and sisters.

A knock on the door, and she's inside again, taking away all the oxygen in the room. Behind her, the outline of a man vanishes.

"I don't mean to barge in," she says. "But you've been in here for over an hour."

I try to wipe my eyes without her seeing. I refuse to speak.

The woman sets a bundle next to me on the floor.

"Fresh clothes," she says, patting them. "Come on downstairs into the kitchen when you're dressed, and we'll have breakfast. I made blueberry pancakes and toast with strawberry jam."

She smiles, but I don't smile back.

Once she leaves, I get dressed. The shorts sink down my hips, and the T-shirt falls off my left shoulder. It says NO LIMITS across the chest in obnoxious pink letters.

She never bothered to check my size—to get me something that fits. Maybe these were someone else's clothes.

My hand rests on the doorknob, but I'm afraid to turn it. The smell of bleach returns, stronger than before. Shimmers and zig-zags of light slash my vision.

I can't remember how I got here.

These gaps make me feel stupid and weak. Father says knowledge is power. I have no knowledge, and no power.

I step outside. The hall is a dark tunnel, so I feel my way along, unsure of where to go. Closed doors line the walls. I turn one of the knobs, but the door is locked.

They all are.

Stumbling down the stairs, I end up in a wide-open room, with more white walls, white furniture. It reminds me of a hospital.

A red prism hangs in a picture window, tossing a colored gash on the opposite wall. This place is nothing like home, where the windows were lined with old Coke bottles holding wildflowers.

"Are you hungry?" The woman's voice comes from my left. She stands in a room separated by a wide archway, her hand resting against a refrigerator.

My stomach snarls, a feral thing, and I follow the smell of breakfast to a wooden table. A single placemat sits on its surface. Two white pills wait on a napkin next to the plate.

I push them aside.

But I always was a sucker for toast with strawberry jam. Mother makes the world's best strawberry jam. She even won a blue ribbon for it at a fair when I was little. Her smile that day was my entire universe. She held me in her arms as Father took our photograph, the envy of everyone there.

I haven't eaten in so long, spots dance in my peripheral vision. I want to ask if the blueberries are organic or if the strawberries have been poisoned with DDT.

I eat anyway.

I'm going to need my strength. They don't know it, but I'm leaving.

✘

After breakfast, the woman orders me to come to the living room. She says there's a doctor who wants to help me.

Frames clutter the mantel above the fireplace. Locked inside are photographs of smiling little girls. In one, a girl rides a bike; in another, the same girl hugs a doll. She's missing a front tooth.

The remaining photo is yellowed and grainy. An out-of-focus girl splashes in a kiddie pool.

The woman stands behind me, her breathing and the ticking clock the only sounds in the room.

She clears her throat, then gestures to the man seated on the sofa. "Are you ready to begin, Piper?"

The man licks his lips, which are topped by a mustache. "Hello, Piper. I'm Dr. Lundhagen, but you can call me Oscar if you'd like." He wears a turtleneck and a dark gray blazer and adjusts a thick gold watch wrapped around his wrist.

Father says only fools covet wealth.

The woman takes a hesitant step toward me. "Oscar is here to talk with you, Piper. Just the two of you. About how you're feeling."

"Would that be all right with you?" he asks. A few dark nose hairs dangle into his mustache.

I shrug, but I don't move.

The man looks at the woman. She disappears from the room. A door opens and closes in the hallway.

I am alone with another stranger.

He clears his throat. "Would you like to take a seat?" He points to the opposite end of the couch. A shelf of porcelain figurines takes up most of the wall next to it.

Their eyes are dead.

I drag a high-backed chair across the room, positioning it so I am seated directly in front of him. I sit up as tall as I can. He is sunk into the couch, lower than I am. Weaker.

"Thank you for speaking with me, Piper. I know this can't be easy for you."

My response is to stare and remain silent, though I want to point out that I have not, in fact, spoken a single word to him. I wrap a hand around my necklace and rub my thumb over its green pendant. Mother told me the amazonite stone stands for courage. It's cool to the touch, like always.

He clasps his hands. Black hair grows from each thick knuckle. I burp up a little of the pancakes, but swallow them down without blinking. The ingredients were probably full of preservatives, leaching all the nutrients from my cells, poisoning me.

"How are you adjusting?" His eyebrows rise up his forehead with feigned concern. "You've been here for a little over a week now."

A week? Have I?

He scratches the back of his head. "Jeannie says you haven't been eating all that much."

Jeannie. The woman. I hate the sound of her name, a choking of consonants and vowels and lies.

"Your appetite will come around again. You've been through quite an ordeal, Piper. It's normal to feel disoriented and fearful. Everything here is different, and probably quite strange. You're shell-shocked."

He stares, waiting for me to say something. Finally, he sighs. "I must seem strange, too. I get it. Maybe we can chat again another time, when you're feeling better. I'd love to help you, Piper. Anything you say to me will be kept just between us."

The floor in the hallway creaks. She is listening.

5. BEFORE

A goldfinch skitters in the weeds, sunlight dappling its yellow feathers. I lean against a bumper car and watch as it pecks the ground. When we first moved here, the cars sat on a metal platform, but Father tore it down after a lightning strike. Now they're rusting in the grass.

We all come here sometimes, using the cars as places to talk or read. Henry and Samuel pretend they're rockets and fly them to space. Beverly Jean turns them into houses for her paper dolls.

Moving away from the car, I scan the forest floor. Mother seems more tired than usual, and a bouquet of wildflowers might cheer her up. A poppy, bright as a pumpkin, cuts through the green, and I add it to my handful of baby blue eyes and buttercups. I wipe the dirt from my hands as Cas joins me.

"Picking flowers for Angela?" He's no longer wearing his jacket, and the sleeves of his white dress shirt are pushed up his hard and sinewy forearms.

I force myself to look away. "How'd you know I'd be out here?"

I can feel the smile in his voice. "Because I know you, that's how." He climbs into the lime-green car and leans back. "Can I admit something without you getting upset?"

"That depends, doesn't it?" I slide in next to him, same as always, but leave a little extra space between us.

The air snaps with electricity, most likely from Father's return. Anything feels possible today.

He turns toward me, his eyebrows crinkled together. "I'm not as happy as I thought I'd be now that Curtis and Angela are back."

His eyes search mine, like he's waiting for me to agree or argue or tell him why he's wrong. Like everything depends on what I say.

I've never lied to Caspian before, and I don't plan to start now.

"Cas," I say, trying to keep my voice steady. "I know it's hard being here without them, but Father and Mother have done so much to keep us safe and happy. Showing them gratitude is the least we can do. A grateful heart starts with good thoughts. We have to weed out the bad ones, just like your garden, or they'll poison us."

He nods and looks away. "You're right. I know you're right."

"You know you can tell me anything, don't you?"

He reaches for my hand out of habit, but doesn't take it. "I know."

Energy sparks off him. He's like the lightning that struck the bumper-car ride. I want to touch him, to see if an arc of light might flash between us.

"Can I tell you something funny, then?" he asks, hesitantly. "I had a *huge* crush on you when Thomas and I first moved here."

My heart pulses. "You did?"

He glances at me. "I was too afraid to talk to you. Every time I tried, I got all tongue-tied. Thomas made so much fun of me."

"I thought you hated me!"

"Nope. And now you're stuck with me for life." He takes the bouquet from me. "We need more flowers. This is looking kind of sad." He goes ahead and grabs my hand. "Come on. Let's go for a walk."

We head deeper into the woods. Cas leads us around trees and over moss-covered rocks and logs. He keeps his eyes trained to the ground, looking for pops of color. It's like magic back here, and I am grateful for this world Father has given us.

"Is that a flower?" I ask, kneeling to pick a strawberry-shaped burst of red.

"Don't touch that!" Cas warns. "It's a red thistle. They have prickers."

"But it's so red. Have you ever seen something so red?" I gently touch its stem with my finger, and it doesn't sting me. "Mother would adore it."

"You'll cut up your hands. Let me pick it." He squats next to me and pulls a couple from the dirt, adding them to the middle of the bouquet.

"They're perfect, Cas. Thank you."

He gives me a lopsided smile.

We continue our walk, venturing deeper into the shade of the trees. Ferns and weeds edge our path, and pine trees rise above us. Cas stops and picks a pine cone off the ground. He studies it for a moment. "I think this is a Coulter pine. See how its pine cone looks like a pineapple?"

"You know more than anyone should about trees."

He tosses the pine cone with one hand and catches it. "Not much else to do around here but read and hoe corn."

When he tosses it again, I try to catch it but knock it to the ground. It rolls ahead, and we scramble for it, our laughter and the cicadas the only sounds. Cas gets to it first, and when I push back my hair, I gasp.

We're standing at the chain-link fence. It runs the perimeter of the property, topped with coiled barbed wire.

"Cas," I whisper. "We should go."

He walks toward it and grabs it with one hand, gives it a shake. "It's only a fence," he says. Mother's bouquet quivers in his other hand.

"The Outside isn't safe. I'd feel better if we went back to the house."

He turns to me. "Have you ever thought about climbing over? Just to see what's out there?"

I back away. "No, never. Please get away from there. You're scaring me."

Cas gently sets the bouquet on the ground. "I wonder if anyone's ever tried to climb it?"

"Cas, stop. The fence is there for a reason. We're wasting too much time out here; I should be back with the littles to make sure they stay clean."

"It'll be fine," he says. "I just want to see if I can." He grips the fence and hoists himself up, shoving his feet between the chain links.

"Cas, no! What are you doing? Stop!"

"It's okay! It's easy!" he says, getting dangerously close to the top. To the Outside.

My hands grow slick, and I wipe them on my dress. Something rustles in the brush beyond the fence, and suddenly the trees are closing in on us.

"Enough! Cas, I'm coming up!" I rush forward and pull myself onto the links, keeping my eyes on the fence as I climb, trying to ignore the danger beyond. I sweat; my arms burn. When I'm close enough, I use one hand to grab for him, but my foot slips.

I plummet to the ground, and my teeth clatter when I land on my tailbone.

"Piper!" Caspian jumps down. "Are you okay?" He gives me a hand and pulls me up, worried. "I'm sorry, Piper. I was just fooling around. I swear."

I squeeze my hands together to keep them from shaking. "Please never do that again." I wipe the dirt from my dress—it's not stained, thankfully—and pick up the bouquet. One of Mother's buttercups is broken, and I ease it from the bunch. I must have fallen on it. "This one's ruined."

Cas takes the buttercup and tucks it behind my ear. "No, see? It's not ruined. It's perfect."

I touch it and smile, my heart still racing.

The Outside can't harm us here. The fence is strong.

We just have to stay on the right side.

6. BEFORE

Father says people don't believe with their heads or their hearts.

They believe with their eyes, and we help them to see.

Father and Mother emerge from their bedroom an hour before supper. "Let's make a film!" she says.

Mother loves making home movies of all of us. She watches them almost every day at their compound. She shows them to the Community, and she tells me they even help Father bring in new members.

"Everyone loves a happy family," she always says.

I check to see if everyone is clean. Henry and Samuel have been carefully playing in the sand with twigs; I give them a quick once-over, and to my relief they're dirt free. I put a huge bib on Millie the second our parents went to sleep—the bib is a mess, but at least her outfit's spotless. Everyone seems presentable.

Thomas has changed into his suit. I tried to get him alone so we could talk about his life at the compound, but Samuel and Henry wouldn't leave his side.

Father balances the camera on his shoulder as Mother arranges us on the lawn like dolls. "Let's try for a playful game of tag," she says, looking to Father. He nods his approval. "I want smiles and laughter. Positive, upbeat energy!"

Mother fusses with Carla's hair, brittle from the bleach. Combined with today's humidity, it's a giant ball of fluff on her head.

"Piper!" she calls. "Go get Carla a ribbon and tie back her hair. It's a wreck."

Hurrying inside, I scrounge around our bedroom for a white ribbon. Mother will want it to match Carla's sash. Carla's sketchbook sits on the desk, and I flip open the cover, knowing she'd kill me if she caught me snooping. She's been so secretive and moody lately, and I expect her drawings to match. But they don't. Each one is beautiful—Millie's profile, the lake with figures dancing on the beach. My favorite is of a single lily; the shading is impressive, and I reach out to touch it, half expecting a real flower to bloom from the page. When Carla was little, she used to paint flowers on rocks and hide them around the yard for us to find. I carefully close the book and smile, glad my sweet, dreamy Carla is still in there somewhere. I haven't lost her.

As I head downstairs, the Aunties are gossiping in the kitchen. It must be hard for them, taking care of someone else's children. They're not even our real aunts, just members of the Community. Most of Father's followers live with him and Mother at the compound, hours and hours from here. I've often wondered if Auntie Joan and Auntie Barb chose to be our caretakers, or if the job was forced on them.

"He's found another one," Auntie Joan whispers.

"Where'd he get this one?"

"I don't know, but we're cramped the way it is."

When I enter the room, they snap their heads toward me. "You need to be outside, Piper. It's filming time." Auntie Barb snuffs out a cigarette.

Smoking isn't allowed. She shouldn't have those cigarettes. I'll bring it up with Father later.

"Mother sent me. Carla's hair is messy." I hold up the ribbon.

"Then what are you standing around here for?" Auntie Joan shoos me outside.

Back in the hot sunshine, I carefully smooth Carla's hair and tie it with the ribbon. "You should wear it like this more often," I say. "I can actually see your pretty face."

She touches a pimple on her chin. "Get real, Piper. I know what I look like."

"Pretty, like I said."

"I'm not like you and Mother, and you know it."

I wish she could see herself the way I do.

Father calls "Action!" and we begin our game. Mother lunges for Millie and pretends to miss her, grabbing her giraffe instead. This sends Millie into a fit of giggles. The game doesn't last long, and soon we're all sitting around Mother, the littles hugging and kissing her. Mother's smile is radiant.

Cas moves close and wraps an arm around my shoulders, like he always does, and that same flutter returns. His face is too close to mine, and when I glance at him, he's already looking at me. I smile and focus back on Mother, but my attention is really on the heat of his skin.

I should want to shrug him away, shrug these new feelings away. Father says romance, masturbation, and sex are distractions from our cause. He arranges marriages within the Community, and love doesn't factor in. These feelings can't be right, whatever they are.

I check to see if Father can read my thoughts, but he's bent over Henry.

"Wait, wait." Father pushes a button on the video camera and touches Henry's shirt. There's a smear of dirt on it. "What is this?" he demands.

"I was playing with Sammy," Henry says, his voice quivering. "Down at the beach."

"Piper, did you let this happen?" Father barks at me.

My heart sinks into my shoes, and I quickly move away from Caspian. "I'm sorry, Father. I told them to be careful." It was unfair of me to ask Carla to watch them while I picked Mother's flowers. I knew this could happen.

Thomas approaches Father. "It was my fault," he says loudly. "Piper asked me to watch the children for a minute, and I got distracted."

"Thomas," I murmur, but he shakes his head.

Mother touches my arm. "Curtis, no one will mind the stain, will they?"

Father takes a deep breath. "I need these movies to be perfect, Angela. You know that."

Mother finger-combs her hair. "I'm sure they didn't mean any harm." Father gives Mother a look, and her neck turns blotchy red. "I've got a headache," she says suddenly, and wobbles toward the house, not stopping even when Millie cries for her.

I pick Millie up. "Bad, Piper," she says as she lays her head on my shoulder, snot running out her nose.

Father opens the side of the camera and pulls out the tape. "Thomas, you need to be more responsible. Especially on these visits. You know how important they are—to me, to your future, to our cause. I need to be able to rely on you when the time comes.

You look away for one minute, *one second*, and this could all come crashing down."

Thomas nods and pushes back his shoulders. "It won't happen again."

"It better not," Father says. "Tonight, you'll dig holes as punishment. Then you can see the consequences of your mistakes. One for each of the children, and one for yourself. I want them completed by sunrise."

"Yes, Sir."

I don't speak. The Community does so much important work, helping give back to people in need, developing sustainable organic farming practices, offering the wisdom of Father's teachings. Father has even pioneered a meditation technique that prevents psychic attacks.

He's saving the world, and that's what I want to do. I've been seventeen for half a year now, and Cas turns eighteen in two months. Father hasn't once mentioned our initiations, but it's all I can think about. If I can't convince Father I'm ready now, I'm afraid I'll never get to join.

If he thought *I* had made the mistake today...

Father leaves without another word and goes into the house. I hand Millie to Carla, who takes her and Beverly Jean inside. Caspian takes Samuel's and Henry's hands and follows Carla. Thomas stands frozen on the shore.

"You didn't have to do that," I say to him, though part of me is relieved.

"I did what I had to do." He stares out at the lake. I've barely seen him smile since he got back.

"Are you all right, Thomas?" I ask quietly.

He snaps his head toward me. "What do you mean?"

I swallow. "You just seem so…heavy. Like you're mad at us or something. I'm sorry about just now. Can you forgive me, Thomas? I don't think I could stand it if you were mad at me."

He sighs. "I'm not mad at you, Piper. I could never be mad at you."

"I was worried." I exhale. "What should we watch tonight? It's Sunday. I'm thinking we could start *Mork and Mindy* over, if you want."

Thomas and I had a Sunday night ritual. After we put the littles to bed, we would watch one hour of TV. Father has a bunch of shows on tape—*Happy Days*, *All in the Family*, *The Facts of Life*—and we got to choose whatever we wanted. We didn't want to waste too much of the generator's power, so we were careful never to go over our time limit. Cas wanted to watch with us, but the Aunties always seemed to put him to work weeding in the garden or canning in the basement.

We'd just finished up *Perfect Strangers* when Thomas moved to the compound. Caspian tried to watch with me when Thomas left, but it wasn't the same. He asked too many questions about the characters, and he didn't think Robin Williams was that funny. Besides, I liked that Thomas and I had something that belonged just to us. Thomas is like a brother to me, and I feel safer when he's here.

Thomas pinches the bridge of his nose. "I'm tired. How about next Sunday, okay? I'll still be here then."

I force myself to smile. "Of course. I'm just glad you're home." I give him a hug. He squeezes back and doesn't let go for a long time.

7. BEFORE

Mother sleeps through dinner, and we eat in silence. The table's open place setting is like a smile missing a tooth.

I hate disappointing her. If only I had been more careful with Henry.

Caspian spoons some extra green beans onto my plate. "I picked these today. What do you think?"

I take a bite, my teeth sinking into the crisp warm vegetable. "These are groovy, Cas. You have a green thumb, that's for sure."

"You should help me tomorrow in the garden. There're a lot more of them to harvest."

"You sure about that? I can kill a plant just by looking at it. I mean, you've seen me do it."

A dimple forms in his cheek when he smiles, and I touch it with my finger, same as always. I used to tease him that he had a belly button on his face. But the gesture feels different now, and I put my hands back in my lap, my face burning.

Father slurps his tea. "Less talking, more eating," he says. "The rules are too lax around here."

Millie cries, and Thomas feeds her a bottle. When he catches me watching him, he smiles. But his eyes don't crinkle the way they normally do.

Father sets his fork on his plate. "Tomorrow, children, you need to start putting another coat of shielding paint on the house. The cell phone radiation is stronger lately. The government must've put up another so-called cell phone tower close by."

I've never seen a cell phone, and I hope I never do. They cause electromagnetic radiation poisoning, but Father has tricks to keep us safe. Last year we put up special fabric on all the interior walls to block the radiation.

"Good idea, Father," I say, which elicits a smile. I notice Samuel hasn't eaten much. "How's your tooth?" I ask him. "Any better?"

Samuel touches his cheek. "It's been hurting all day."

"We'll put more clove oil on it after dinner. I made a fresh batch last week that should be ready."

✖

After dinner, I dab the oil onto Samuel's tooth as Cas and Carla clear the table. The oil helps numb the pain. "Thanks, Piper," he says before joining the others outside to play badminton and croquet on the lawn.

I fill a tin pail with water from the pump and place it on the woodstove until it just starts to boil. Then Cas plugs the sink and pours in the water and soap. We have a lot of dishes to wash.

"Did Angela like her flowers?" he asks.

"I put them on her bedside table, but she was pretty groggy. I don't think she noticed them yet. It was probably a dumb idea anyway."

Cas takes my hand in his. "It's not dumb, Piper. You're the most caring person I know."

I flush. I can't stop thinking about what Cas said—that he used to have a crush on me.

Before I can say anything, Auntie Joan taps my shoulder. "I'd like a word."

Cas quickly drops my hand, and I follow her into the basement. The Aunties' bedrooms are down here, along with a small sitting area and sewing room. It smells musty, and the lights are always low.

Auntie Joan stops at a side table in their sitting room. "You said you would look after the children, and not let them get dirty."

I swallow. "Yes, I did."

"I said I would hold you personally responsible if any of them dirtied their outfits. Do you remember that?" She picks a belt up off the table. "Pull up your dress and turn around."

"Please, Auntie Joan, you can't be serious. I'm not a child anymore. Plus, it was Thomas's fault, not mine."

As soon as the lie about Thomas leaves my mouth, I know I deserve the beating. I run my tongue over my cracked tooth, a souvenir from my last trip to the basement.

She sighs, watching me. Then she carefully sets the belt on the table. "If anyone asks, I was very hard on you. Now go on. Get out of here before I change my mind."

Upstairs I find Mother alone in the dining room, eating cold chicken. Beverly Jean's pie sits untouched on the table.

"How are you feeling?" I ask.

Her makeup is smudged, and there are lines on her face from the pillow. "A little better. The trip was horrible this time. It's so hard juggling work and family and helping your father with the Community. I am paper thin, about to be blown away."

I sit next to her and take her hand. "You're doing the best you can. Don't talk like that."

She smiles. "What would I do without you?"

I take a deep breath and hold it for a second. "Have you thought about living here full-time? Or visiting more often? It's so peaceful here. I bet it would be good for you. And for Father."

"Piper, darling, you know that's simply not possible. I've got my companies to run, and your father has the Community to lead. Who do you think keeps all of this going?" She gestures around the room.

"You and Father do."

She takes her hand from mine and cuts her chicken into smaller and smaller pieces. "I know it can be hard to understand, but this is the way it has to be for now. We can't travel back and forth on a whim. Weeks of planning go into each and every one of our visits here. We must be very careful not to be followed. We can't risk leading anyone from the Outside to our children."

"What if we came to live with you? I know the younger kids would really love that. Millie cries for you in her sleep sometimes."

Mother sets down her knife. "You're trying to make me feel guilty." She takes a sip of her water. "Our children can't live at the compound; the government would find you too easily. Here you have sunshine, the lake, privacy, the best tutors money can buy. Everything a child could ever want or need."

"I would help with the children. They wouldn't be a burden."

"Is that how you see me, Piper? As a mother who views her children as burdens?"

"We just miss you, is all."

She touches my cheek. "That's why we must make the most of our time together, instead of dwelling on things that can't be changed. Live in the moment. Does that make sense?"

I nod, then pause. "Mother, is Father happy with me? I feel like I'm always disappointing him."

She drops her fork, which clanks onto the plate. "Why would you say such a thing?"

"I ruined the video today. I just…I feel like I'm always letting him down." I chew my thumbnail. "And he hasn't mentioned my initiation. Not once."

She touches my hand. "Your father is not like anyone else, Piper. I wish you could see him with his followers. They yearn for him like children for a parent, and he offers them so much guidance and hope and assurance. You don't see it, living in a place so serene, but the world's gone mad. The fact that you're here, safe, is a testament to how much your father loves you. If you can't see that, then I feel sorry for you."

8. AFTER

This house breathes.

It waits.

The rooms change positions. Doors appear in new spots, stairs where only a wall was before. Sometimes, if I listen close enough, I can hear its heart beating.

Each time the house shifts, the woman says it's a big house, that I'm not the first to be confused by it. "You'll figure it out in time," she insists. "And I'm always here to help."

Most days I keep to the room she gave me, leaving only when she fetches me for meals. I pretend the daisy stickers on the desk are from Mother, a secret message just for me. I haven't seen her since They took all of us children away.

I can still hear Millie's cries. I wish I could just forget.

I rub my fingers across the sticker, wiping the tears from my face. I never know when the woman will return, and I don't want her to see me crying.

I find paper and pens in the top desk drawer and start sketching out a map of this place. If I can keep my thoughts clear, I'll find a way out.

Here is what I know:

My name is Piper Blackwell.
I'm seventeen.

My parents are Curtis and Angela Blackwell.

The government took me, Mother, and my siblings away from our home three weeks ago.

I haven't seen or heard from my parents or anyone else.

I've been locked away by a woman named Jeannie in Northern California. At least I think it's California; that's what her newspaper said.

Sometimes I wake up in strange places. Either I go to these places, or someone puts me there.

I move to the window seat. Somewhere out there is my real family.

Waves of green grass roll up and down the hills. Pine trees frame the horizon. Most of the other houses are far away, past a long driveway leading to a gate that's always closed—locked, I'm sure, just like this window.

The closest house is white with black shutters. Its fence butts up against this house's, but I haven't noticed any people in its yard. Or its windows. Or its driveway. It might be abandoned.

Footsteps move outside my door. They are the quiet, measured steps of the woman.

She knocks. "I'm going to the grocery store. Be back in an hour, okay? Stay inside."

Once she's gone, I try the window's lock again, but it doesn't budge.

Cold air is blasting through a vent in the wall, and I cross the room to a closet loaded with clothes that don't fit. There are jean skirts, T-shirts, jumper dresses—everything looks new, unworn, sterile. I ease into a sweatshirt that's too short—it sits just above the waist of my shorts and says STRANGER THINGS in red letters.

I'm not sure if that's a movie or a brand name. I peel it off and find another sweatshirt. It's also too short, but I give up and leave it on.

I resume my spot at the window seat as an impossibly shiny black car rolls down the driveway to the gate. The woman gets out, opens a box, and waits as the gate opens. She looks up at my window before driving away, the gate closing behind the car.

My door creaks as I enter the hallway, map and pen in hand.

The room across from mine is locked. The next door's handle won't turn, either.

The staircase has moved again, waiting for me at the end of a new hallway. My throat seizes, and I quickly add it to my map and scurry down the stairs to a front room. A door with a stained-glass panel burns with sunlight. It must lead outside, but the knob won't turn and the deadbolt won't yield. I squat and stare out the keyhole. The woman locked me in.

Or maybe the house itself is keeping me prisoner.

A pair of men's boots lay on the floor, one upside down, laces untied. They look like Cas's boots, and I kick them away.

The kitchen looks the same as the last time I was here. I rifle through drawers, but there's no skeleton key. I find some dull knives, though, and run to the front door with a handful. The first knife is too big to fit inside the keyhole. I try another, then another. All are too big.

I decide to keep one of them under my mattress, just in case.

The window above the kitchen sink is locked. The windows in the living room are locked. I move from room to room, trying to flip latches, straining against frames, always looking behind me in case someone is there.

When I go back upstairs, trying every door again, the room across from my bedroom opens this time. The room is piled with junk: a sewing machine, fabric, old games, photo albums.

And a phone. A black rotary phone, on a shelf. We had one at home, though Father had it shut off years ago. My hand shakes as I lift the receiver and hold it to my ear.

There is no dial tone.

I hang up and try again.

Nothing.

I slam the receiver down.

My stomach growls, and I race into the kitchen and pull open the refrigerator. Inside, vegetables sit in neat rows in a plastic drawer, and jugs of milk, arranged like sentries, hide a half-eaten apple pie. I scoop out a piece of pie with my fingers and eat it over the sink. The sticky sweetness drips down my chin.

I am so hungry. My stupid dizzy spells make a hunger strike impossible. I've gotten them all my life if I don't eat every couple of hours. The Aunties always said they were nothing to worry about.

But today I'm worried.

After I rinse my face, I glance outside.

There's a girl framed in the neighbor's upstairs window.

My first thought is to duck away, but I don't. The girl just stands there, still as a statue.

Maybe she can help me. I flap my arms at her in exaggerated motions.

"Help!" I scream. "Help me!"

The girl doesn't move, and I wonder if she's real at all. When I pound on the window, she pulls the curtains closed.

She's gone.

"Mother," I whisper, choking up. "Where are you?" I am having a harder time remembering the sound of her voice, the warmth of her hugs.

A hallway appears on the other side of the kitchen, one I don't remember. I draw it on my map and circle it, afraid it might swallow me away. Every room in this house has the same locked knob as the stained-glass front door.

And then the stained-glass front door opens.

The woman enters, carrying a brown bag. "I'm glad to see you're up and about," she says. She locks the door behind her and tucks the key into her pants pocket, patting it twice. "Are you hungry?"

She smiles too much. Tries too hard to seem nice.

She carries the bag into the kitchen. Chunks of pie remain in the sink. I should have thrown them away.

"I'm making hamburgers and corn on the cob for supper." I don't say anything. "My sister sent me something today." She takes a brown box from the cupboard and lifts out another porcelain doll. This one has wings and a halo. "Where should I put it on the shelf?"

I shrug, my silence my only weapon—that and the dull knife in my pocket. I pat it twice.

She puts the figurine back in the box. "It's eleven," she says. "*The Young and the Restless* is on. Want to watch with me before lunch?" When I don't answer, she fishes two cans of soda from the fridge and gives one to me. "I refuse to take no for an answer. Come on, it'll be fun."

She sits on the sofa, but I remain standing. She explains all the characters, who's been married to whom, who's died and come back to life and died again.

I am my parents' daughter.

I don't give in. I say nothing and retreat to my room.

To the only door that doesn't lock.

I wait a few minutes for the girl to come back to the window, shutting my curtains when she doesn't. Then I crumple up my crudely drawn map of this place and toss it in the trash can.

9. BEFORE

Father asks us to gather at the benches for an emergency teaching before lights-out.

The benches are made of planks of wood set over cement blocks, and they form a half circle around the big oak tree. Thomas drags Father's platform in front of the benches as I sit next to Caspian with Millie in my arms. Cas is wearing a T-shirt with the sleeves cut off, and my eyes linger on the curve of his shoulders, the hard, high lines of his cheekbones, the soft sweep of his lips. Sometimes I wonder if he ever looks at me the way I look at him. I bounce my heel off the ground and chew my nails, and Mother reaches over to pull my hand out of my mouth the way she always does.

"Bad habits," she mutters.

Father steps onto the platform. "Blessings to everyone, my dreamers of dreams, my makers of music."

"Glory be," we answer in unison.

"Bounty and freedom have been bestowed upon us, and we are grateful."

"Glory be," we say again.

"The end of days. Armageddon. The apocalypse. All synonyms for the same thing—man's destruction of himself. You, my children, will be the hope of all mankind—you and the Community."

I sit up straighter. Beverly Jean grabs hold of my hand. I squeeze back. Father's teachings can be frightening for the littles.

"Our bodies are pure, free from pesticides and radiation poisoning. We have survived, and we will continue to survive, without the help of a diseased society." His eyes flash. "On the Outside, despair falls down like rain. Consumer culture turns people into mindless drones. Divorce turns families into strangers. Women reject their natural femininity, brainwashed into thinking raising children and caring for husbands is a weakness, that a woman only has value if she rejects her womanhood. A man's strength, his desire, his natural ability to lead are all suppressed, twisted into guilt and shame. Men become weak and impotent, forbidden from leading their families with a firm hand. People inject their bodies with poisons, carve up their faces to appeal to vanity, rot their brains with mindless technology. This place I have built for you is free from all that. I'm the only one who can keep you safe. But it takes work and dedication, and nothing comes for free. This sick world is coming to its end. Are you prepared to do whatever it takes to save mankind?"

"Yes, Sir," we say together.

"Do any of you know what this is?" Father holds a plastic sandwich bag filled with white powder.

Millie cries on my lap, and I hum a song in her ear to calm her down.

"This is DDT, a highly toxic chemical insecticide. The government first used it during World War II, when soldiers in the field were catching diseases from flies. So they doused their sleeping bags in poison. Sprinkled it where they slept and dreamed. Then they allowed our farmers to spread it on their crops. Planes dropped this nightmare over entire neighborhoods to control the insect population."

Father opens the bag. "Your government would tell you to eat the DDT, convince you it's safe, and then blame you when you're lying in your sickbed, riddled with tumors. And, in fact, that's *exactly* what they did. Scientists let their ethics be compromised by Congress and the chemical companies, and assured the public that DDT was safe. But it wasn't.

"Do you see, my children? The government is not for the people. It never was. And I'm the only man who sees this truth and isn't afraid to tell it."

Auntie Joan gives Father a slice of bread. He takes a pinch of the DDT from the bag and sprinkles it on the bread like salt.

"I can keep you safe from the poisonous chemicals this world is drenched in, but I need you to trust me. We cannot afford failure, as we failed with our video today. I know it seemed a small thing, but small mistakes lead to bigger mistakes. I can't stand the thought of losing any one of you. I need you to be diligent. Henry, your youth does not excuse your mistake. You were ordered to stay clean, and you disobeyed that order."

Henry whimpers, and Mother gathers him into her arms.

"Faith. That is what you need to survive. Faith in me. Faith in my abilities." He pounds his fist against his chest. "Faith can be a hard pill to swallow. Trusting in something you can't always see or touch or smell, but knowing it's there anyway, guiding you, protecting you. For I will always protect you." Father brings the bread close to his face, examining it. "If I eat this bread, I will not be harmed. I have faith in my abilities because I've witnessed them firsthand. Many at our compound have. But you, my children, have not."

"Curtis," Mother says, then falls silent.

"Unless one of my children has the faith required to take a bite?"

"I'll eat it!" I say without thinking. Caspian looks at me, but I keep my eyes on Father.

"Are you certain, Piper?" Father asks. "Do you have the faith required to walk with me on this path? It's not an easy one."

I sit up as straight as I can, flexing my muscles until my spine cracks. "I have faith in you, Father. I always have."

He nods, once, and I hand Millie to Carla, then rise to take the bread from him.

"Don't be afraid," he whispers.

I lick my lips, fighting the urge to look back at Cas. Father always keeps his promises. I have always been safe under his care.

He will always protect us.

I will not die.

I expect the powder to burn my tongue or fizz on my lips, but it doesn't. The bread tastes like it always does, maybe a little bit sweeter. Each bite brings me closer to Father, closer to the Community, closer to initiation, to my purpose.

When I'm finished, Father steps down and embraces me. "Do you see, children, how Piper trusts in me? This is what I expect of all my children. Do you understand?"

As the others nod, Father whispers in my ear, "It was only powdered sugar. You passed the test, Piper. Good girl."

"Thank you, Father," I say, out of breath.

I feel sorry for people who have no faith in anything.

10. BEFORE

At midnight, I peel away the covers, my body entombed in sweat.

The house sleeps. The sticky air moves away from me. My parents don't stir as I tiptoe past their room.

Outside, I fill a mason jar with water from the pump and pick strawberries from our garden, wrapping them carefully in a napkin. Knowing Caspian, he'll notice some missing, but I'm taking them for his brother. He'll understand.

The sky is black, and each star shows off her light. I tilt my head back and count as many as I can.

There is so much beauty here.

I walk into the woods. The roller coaster is almost invisible at this time of night, blending with the trees. A camping light flickers ahead, and as I get closer, Thomas's grunts interrupt the crickets' songs.

Thomas has been cut in half, only a torso now. He stands in a hole, plunging his shovel in and out, dumping more earth onto a pile. Again and again he does this, fulfilling the punishment Father gave him. Mounds of dirt surround him like a fortress.

All because I was too much of a coward to take the blame for my mistake.

My footsteps startle him, and he looks out into the darkness. "Who's there?"

"It's just me," I whisper, stepping into the lantern's light.

He wipes his brow, his face slick with sweat. "You shouldn't be here, Piper. You could get into a lot of trouble."

I hold out the jar and napkin. "Here, I brought you these. I thought you might be thirsty and hungry."

He looks at the water and licks his lips. "I can't. Curtis said no food or drink until I'm done."

"Take them, please. I won't tell Father."

"He'll know. He always knows." He leans against the shovel and sighs.

A toad chirps nearby, and I jump. Some strawberries tumble from the napkin into the dirt. I drop down to scoop them up, and Thomas climbs out of the hole. He takes the napkin from me and eats one of the strawberries.

"I'm so sorry, Thomas. It should be me out here, not you."

"I knew the risk." He sits in the dirt and takes the jar of water, emptying it in a few gulps.

For a minute, we sit together in silence.

"Tell me about the compound," I say. "Was it everything Father said it would be?"

Thomas sets the jar down. "It wasn't anything like I thought it would be."

My heart thumps. "Better than you expected?"

"No, Piper. Not better."

He sounds tired. Flat. My dream of a perfect life at the compound fades. "Thomas, you're scaring me."

The compound is a place where Father's love touches everything, where clean food is bountiful, where we can learn from him and prepare for the future. It's a place where people matter, where *life* matters. Where everyone pulls together for the good of the world, to ensure mankind's survival.

It's not possible to be unhappy at the compound. So why is Thomas acting unhappy?

He stands and wipes the dirt from his hands. "You should go back to bed before they catch you. Don't worry about me, I'll be fine. I'm almost finished."

"Why won't you tell me what it's like there?"

There's a pause.

"Curtis has a cell phone," he says finally.

The crickets go silent.

I shake my head until I can hear their chorus again. "That can't be right. The radiation."

"He has one. I saw him with it."

"I don't believe you. Stop kidding around."

"I saw it, Piper," he says, his words drawn out. "With my own eyes. My parents had cell phones before we came here, so I know what they look like."

"Then he must have his reasons. Father knows what's best. He probably has one so he knows what we're dealing with. It's not your place to question him."

He looks at me. "Sometimes there isn't enough food."

My muscles tighten. "No. That can't be true. The fields at the compound go on for miles."

"That's what he told us, but they don't. We have crops, but the compound is a lot smaller than he said it was. Sometimes we only get one meal a day. A small one. Rice and corn porridge and almonds. Piper, once we had to eat expired crackers crawling with weevils." He swallows. "But Curtis *always* gets enough to eat. *Real* food."

Sweat dots my upper lip. "He's our leader, Thomas. We need him to stay strong. Otherwise he won't be able to keep us safe."

"Is that what you think?"

I stand. "Of course it is! Why are you being like this?"

Thomas shakes his head. "I don't want to fight with you."

"Then maybe you shouldn't cut Father down like that, Thomas. It's hurtful, what you're saying about him."

"I thought I could talk to you," he says lifelessly. "My mistake."

I ball my hands into fists. "You can, Thomas, but *not* when you're talking nonsense. How can you accuse Father of *lying* to us? That's exactly what the Outside wants you to think!"

"If you say so."

"I can't believe what I'm hearing! You more than anyone know the power of Father's plan. Didn't he give you a better life than the one you had before? You yourself have told me so many times how grateful you are to him. That he's the father you never had. That you were *glad* to be rid of your birth parents!"

"And I used to mean all of it."

I sigh. "You know what? I'm done with this conversation." I turn on my heel.

"Don't tell Cas about the compound," he calls out after me. "It's better if he doesn't know."

I'm almost out of the lantern's light when I stop and look back. As Thomas climbs into the hole, I finally realize what he's digging.

Graves.

11. AFTER

It's the noises that are most different from home. The noises I can't shut out.

A dog's barking.

Cars driving by.

The whir of a coffee grinder, as if the woman is chewing up bones and spitting them out.

She appears at my door. "Want to help me in the garden? It's a lovely day." When I don't answer, her smile slips. "I'll be outside if you want to join me."

She leaves, and a door slams from somewhere deeper in the house.

We didn't slam doors at home.

And we never locked them.

I pull on a pair of jean shorts and a white T-shirt with holes at the shoulders, showing my skin. Mother would be appalled by the clothing the woman has given me.

When I go downstairs into the living room, the front door sits open, its stained-glass panel twinkling in the daylight.

It might be a trick, a test of some kind.

But.

I tiptoe forward and slip into the sunshine.

This is the first time I've been outside since They brought me here. Closing my eyes, I listen to the birds sing and the katydids chatter. It's almost as if I'm home again, picking wildflowers with Mother or meeting Caspian in his garden for a chat.

My eyes fly open.

I cannot think of them.

I must focus on what's in front of me.

The front porch runs the length of the house. Wrought-iron fencing along the perimeter of the yard connects to the large steel gate at the end of the driveway. I glance at the white house with black shutters where I saw the girl in the window.

The road beyond the gate is void of cars.

I step from the porch and approach the woman. Knees in the dirt, she appears smaller than normal. Weak and exposed. I could knock her out, climb the fence. I think of the knife tucked under my mattress.

She sits back on her heels and holds out a spade. "We're plant-ing our winter garden. Turn some dirt with me."

I take the spade, careful not to touch her hand, and sit a few feet away.

"Do you like broccoli?" she asks.

I touch my necklace.

"We're planting broccoli and cabbage. It's always nice to have fresh produce in winter. One of the perks of living in Northern Cal-ifornia, I suppose."

She stabs at the earth, claws it, rips into it with vigor. Mother and I loved helping Caspian in the fruit and vegetable garden. Every fall we'd pick the strawberries and tomatoes and eat some on the front steps. We canned the rest.

"And I'm planting strawberries, too, of course," she says. "They'll be ready in time for my Christmas pies and jams. You can help me make them, if you want. I'll teach you all my tips and tricks."

Strawberries belong to Mother and me. I flick my spade into the dirt.

"You don't want to garden?" the woman asks. When I shake my head, her face falls. "That's fine. But stay in the yard, okay? It's not safe by the road. Drivers don't pay enough attention on these back roads."

As if I have anywhere else to go.

I wander. Around the side of the house, a grouping of maple trees stands guard near the fence. Under their shade is a stone bird-bath. A robin sits on the moss-covered rim, her orange breast quivering with her song. She lets me watch for a few minutes before she flies away.

There is also a garden shed, painted blue to match the house. A combination lock hangs from the door. I yank on it, but it doesn't open. The feeling that I'm being watched prickles my neck, but when I turn around, the woman's still digging in the ground.

I move off, making my way along the fence. The posts are spaced about ten feet apart. The dirt is freshly turned where they have been jabbed into the ground, and clumps of dug-up grass are everywhere, brown, dying of thirst.

This fence is new.

At the edge of the yard, I find a section of fence that belongs to the neighbor's house, worn from years of sun and rain. It still smells like cedar, and the smell transports me home. Cas appears, smiling. He reaches for my hand. Up the rickety roller coaster we climb, easy smiles on our faces.

Poof.

He's gone, and I'm a prisoner again.

My eyes snap from window to window, looking for a fluttering curtain or a human shape. Where is the girl? I know I didn't imagine her, but the window upstairs remains empty. The house seems dead, somehow.

I move closer to the fence. A knot in the wood has rotted away, leaving behind a peephole.

I stick my eye up against it.

The neighbor's yard is sparse and empty.

Then, a flash of color.

A girl's face follows. "Hey there," she says.

My heart pounds. "Hello," I creak, my voice hoarse.

"You must be my new neighbor."

"I-I am. Who are you?" My mind whirls with possibilities. She might have access to a car, or money. She could help me get back to my parents.

But the girl turns away. "Shit," she says. "My folks are home. Gotta go."

"Wait!" I say, pressing my hands against the rough wood.

But she's gone.

I sense different eyes on me, suddenly. A growl from behind me reveals a mass of black muscle. It's the dog. The dog I've been hearing from my room.

It bares its teeth, white and pointed, and tugs on its chain, but it can't break free. Spittle bubbles up on its lips while it watches me.

My whisper for help dies on the breeze.

The dog barks, and the woman turns. She stands, throws off her gloves, and runs across the yard.

"No, Daisy," she scolds. "No bark! No!"

The dog cocks its head. It sits, and its face relaxes.

"Sorry about Daisy. She's very protective. We had to get her after…well, it doesn't matter. We keep her outside now." The woman pets the dog's head. "Daisy, this is Piper. She lives here now; she's one of us." She moves next to me and puts an arm around my shoulder.

The feeling is both strange and familiar. The scent of Mother's perfume blows off the woman, and I look at her. When I inhale, the smell is gone.

"See, Daisy?" she says. "Piper's a nice girl."

Daisy's tongue lolls from her mouth as she begins to pant.

"Would you like to pet her?" the woman asks me.

I shrug.

But if I can gain the woman's trust, she might let me outside unsupervised. And I'm certain I can bust through the fence. So I lean forward to pet the dog.

"Just move slowly. Let her sniff your hand."

I reach out slowly, expecting to lose a finger or two, but the dog licks my hand instead.

"She likes you!" the woman says. "I knew she would. She's very good at reading people."

Daisy rubs her head against my side, and I sink to my knees. She licks my face, and I smile. I wrap my arms around her, the first hug I've had in ages, and that's when my necklace's chain slithers off my neck. The green stone falls into the grass, and I scoop it up and hold it against my chest.

"Your necklace," she says. "I can take it to a jeweler and have the clasp fixed."

I shake my head and turn away from them, holding the stone so tight I'm afraid it will crumble in my hands.

12. BEFORE

My sisters make noises when they sleep. The sounds are like fingerprints, easily identifiable.

Carla snores and smacks her lips.

Beverly Jean talks while she dreams, nonsense words that don't make any sense.

Millie thrashes in her crib, her feet hitting the bars in a haphazard rhythm.

I wonder if I make any noises. Right now, I hover between awake and asleep, not quite able to shut down my brain.

Maybe silence is my noise.

I sense Father in the room before he whispers my name in the dark.

"Ready for that walk?" he asks, a warm smile on his face. His breath smells like coffee and toothpaste.

I squint. "What time is it?"

"Almost sunrise. We can watch together. Now come along—I'll meet you outside."

I can't remember the last time I watched a sunrise. Of course Father would suggest it. He sees the beauty in what everyone else chooses to forget or ignore.

As I grab my brown suede skirt and knee socks from the closet, my foot brushes against a small cardboard box on the floor. I open the folded piece of paper taped to the front.

I brought these back for you. Some of the women said they could spare a few. —Thomas

Inside the box are a bunch of tampons. It's been nearly a year since we had any here—Father says they're not biodegradable and prefers we don't use them. But the sanitary napkins I make out of fabric scraps are messy and never fully come clean.

"Thank you, Thomas," I whisper, hiding them under my mattress. The Aunties wouldn't approve…but I keep the gift anyway. We really need them.

Father's already down at the lake skipping stones when I come outside. It's that hazy gray-blue time just before dawn, and the pine trees on the other side of the lake look painted, their edges softened.

On the beach, I follow his sunken footsteps, placing my foot inside each one. I want to surprise him, but he turns around before I get too close.

"There you are, sleepyhead."

"Is Mother feeling better today?"

He nods. "Much better. It's good for her, being here with you children. She'd been coming down with awful headaches all week, but when she arrived here, she healed." He skips his last stone. "I saw Beverly Jean's scalp last night while we were brushing teeth."

I can't tell if he wants me to comment or not, but I do anyway. "It's getting worse every time."

"I suspected as much. I think it's time to do away with that tradition. You know you're family. And I see how much you love each other. A hair color can't change that. I'll talk to your mother about it. She can be so terribly insecure sometimes, but I've given in to this indulgence for far too long."

I hug him, squeezing extra tight. "Thank you, Father. Everyone will be so happy you've made this decision."

"How about that walk?" he asks, taking my hand.

We move down the beach, past the stone circle where we build bonfires and roast marshmallows, into the woods on the other side of the drive.

"Your mother and I had a good talk last night," he says. "She told me you want to live with us at the compound. That you are ready to be initiated."

My chest tightens. "She did?"

He stops and faces me. "I keep you and the others here for your own protection. The Outside is a dangerous place. You remember when Thomas and Caspian came to live with us? I never wanted to disparage their parents in front of you, but they were incredibly troubled people, addicted to drugs and living in a car with their children. I hoped my group could save them, but it couldn't. They chose addiction over their own sons, can you imagine? That's the world I'm saving you from." His gaze burns into me. "Initiation is not for children or the faint of heart. It puts you on the front lines. But maybe you're ready now to face evil head-on?"

"I am ready, Father. I only want to make you proud."

He kisses my cheek. "We have a special bond, the two of us. When you were a baby, you had terrible colic. Cried and cried, all hours of the day and night. The only thing that made you happy was when I would carry you around the house and tell you stories."

"I had colic? You've never told me that."

"Oh, yes. You inherited that from me. My mother, your grandmother, used to put whiskey in my bottle to calm me down. Times were certainly different back then. And I'm sure they'll be different when you become a mother."

We start walking again, moving down a well-worn path through the trees. "That's a long way off," I say, not able to imagine having my own child.

"It's closer than you think. You're seventeen, and life's going to move much more quickly going forward. In fact, I've chosen a husband for you."

I stop walking. "A *husband*?"

He lets go of my hand. "We need new members. Members with pure blood, children of true believers. Your marriage will be celebrated by everyone in the Community."

I don't know whether to feel happy or sick. If he wants me to marry a Community man, it must mean I'm going to be initiated. But I've never even been kissed. I always knew Father would choose my husband, but now that he has, I'm afraid. How can I marry a man I've never met?

"I'm nervous," I admit. My vision dims, and I realize I haven't eaten breakfast.

"You trust me, don't you?"

"Of course I do, it's just that—"

He stumbles against a tree, jams his fingers into his temples, and closes his eyes.

"Father?" I reach for him. "Are you okay?"

"I've had a vision," he pants, out of breath. "Of you and me, working together, side by side in the Community." He opens his eyes. "I've been meditating on this for a long time, but now I'm certain."

"Certain of what, Father?" My insides twist and tighten. If he is certain I'll be initiated, then my life will finally have purpose.

He touches my hair. "We'll talk more after my morning teaching. For now, let's go catch that sunrise."

13. BEFORE

There's a room at the end of the upstairs hallway that's always locked. No one ever goes in or out, not even the Aunties. When I was little, I used to squint through the keyhole.

But the room never shared its secrets with me.

Until today.

Father unlocks the door and invites me into his private office after his teaching.

He throws back the curtains, illuminating the pale green walls. I admire the typewriter sitting on a worn wooden desk, an Underwood Five. Black keys and a matte gray body.

"You can touch it, if you'd like," he says.

The keys are smooth and cool, and when I push one—

Clack!

The sound snaps back on itself. It ricochets off the walls. Then, stillness.

The spark of the key and its power make my body tingle.

"I can't use a computer," he explains, stepping next to me. "The government would see my work. They have eyes everywhere. They're even having me followed, I'm certain of it."

"Why would they do that? Is that even legal?"

"The government can do what it likes. We reject blind worship of those in power, Piper, and the government isn't too keen on that." He takes a deep breath in and out. "I'd like you to help me, to be more involved in the Community."

"You want *my* help?"

"You're ready now." He studies my face. "You're like me, looking for what no one else can see, searching for truths that might be uncomfortable. And you're patient. Infinitely patient. I don't often let women take on this kind of role. Most are too emotional to think rationally about hard decisions. But you're not like them. You're special."

I beam.

Maybe I have finally found my purpose in the family. Cas has his gardening, Thomas his carpentry work at the compound. The children learn through play, and all I do is clean up after them. I'm not complaining, but I want something of my own.

"The husband I've chosen for you is one of my most trusted men in the Community."

I nod and force a smile on my face, afraid to blink. Moisture sits on the rims of my eyes, and when Father turns his back, I quickly wipe it away.

Grow up, Piper, I tell myself.

Father turns and studies me for a moment. "It's Thomas."

"Thomas?"

"Yes. You and Thomas are a perfect match. You complement each other. You will be an excellent helpmate to him."

My body breaks out in a cool sweat.

I can't marry Thomas. It's all wrong. *He and I are all wrong.* When I imagine becoming a wife and a mother, there's only one face I see.

But I say nothing.

I must have faith in Father. I *must*. I suck in a breath and hold it, wishing my heart would slow down. I'm wrong to want something different than what Father has decided is right for me.

He paces the room, motioning for me to take a seat at the Underwood. "You'll transcribe for me, Piper." I obey, guiding in a sheet of paper with shaking fingers.

Suddenly he stops. "It's time to recruit," he informs me. "I have felt this coming for some time, and now the time has arrived."

My fingers are poised over the keys, each one a stepping-stone to where I need to be. I will trust in him. "I'm ready when you are," I say, as quietly as I can.

He clasps his hands and brings them to his mouth. "The title is 'Pharmacology and Its Failings.'"

I type quickly, each finger hitting the correct letter.

With just a title, the page seems to glow with magic.

Father's magic.

"Paragraph one," he says. "The development of psychotropic drugs has been catastrophic for the human race. Mental illness has affected civilizations for thousands, if not millions, of years. In fact, the ancient Greeks were aware of it, and the physician Hippocrates was one of the first to propose that mental illness was caused not by external factors, but by internal factors. An imbalance of the 'humors.'"

He pauses, and I can hardly keep my hands steady. His brilliance leaves me dumbstruck.

"Okay," I whisper. "Got it."

He paces again, venturing deeper into a darkened corner of the room. When he speaks, his voice comes from many directions at once.

"Paragraph two. It is a narrow-minded view of mental illness that sped up the development and overprescription of psychotropic drugs. Most mental illnesses can be cured with natural medicines and lifestyle changes. Yet children as young as two are being given antidepressants and antipsychotic medications. The effects of these drugs on young, growing brains, and even the effects on adult brains, seem to be of little importance to the drug companies. They have picked up Hippocrates' hypothesis and turned it into a money-making scheme. How else can it be explained that first-world countries, with all the so-called comforts of modern society, are prescribed the most antidepressants?"

My fingers still. "Is this true, Father?"

He steps into the light. Tears stream down his face. "Yes, I'm afraid it is, Piper. Not everyone is as blessed as the Community is."

I rise to comfort him, but he holds up a hand. "I'm all right, Piper. This is difficult, but we must be strong."

I resume my place, and he continues, expounding on the virtues of nature, of living closer to the way early humans lived to cure mental illnesses. Physical labor, meditation, a diet rich in fresh fruits and vegetables free of pesticides. Living in small groups and villages instead of congested, polluted cities.

Living free.

"People say they want to be free," he goes on. "But they continue to shackle themselves, to become *un-free*. A house, a car, technology, it all has to be paid for. Options become more and more limited. People feel trapped. They turn to drugs, alcohol, gambling, and sex to numb away their increasing discomfort. They walk into a doctor's office and walk out with a bottle of pills instead of changing the very circumstances that are making them sick in the first place. The cycle repeats itself, creating an even sicker society."

He sinks to the floor, crosses his legs, and hangs his head. Above him a replica of da Vinci's *Last Supper* hangs in a gold frame.

My eyes flick to the paper. I read the last sentence and gasp—I've made an error. I typed "slicker" instead of "sicker."

He looks up. "What's wrong?"

My chin quivers, my initiation moving further out of reach. "I ruined it," I admit. "I misspelled a word."

He rises, digs through papers on the table, and hands me a small bottle. "Everyone makes mistakes, Piper. It's how you deal with the fallout that defines you."

I hold the bottle under the lamplight.

It's Wite-Out.

"There's always a way to make something right again," he says. "Do you understand?"

"Yes, Father. I do."

He smiles. "Good girl."

14. AFTER

The woman is poisoning my food.

Yesterday, when I went to the bathroom, it felt like I was being stabbed with needles. And it keeps getting worse. I refused lunch today, just to be on the safe side.

I'm doubled over on the toilet when the woman knocks and enters. "Piper, what's going on in here? Be honest."

I shoot up, trying to cover myself, but the pain rips through my abdomen. Sweat moistens my brow, but I won't wipe it away. Not in front of her.

"You need to see a doctor, Piper. I'm worried about you."

I say nothing.

"It's only a short drive to the doctor's office, and you'll feel so much better once you go and get checked out."

I haven't left this place since They brought me here. This might be my only chance to get a look at my surroundings, to figure out where she's keeping me.

"Or the doctor could make a house call," she continues.

"No. I'll go." My voice is hoarse and weak from disuse.

My vow of silence broken, another battle lost.

She shuts the door, but no footsteps follow. Her breath rattles from the other side of the door as I pull up my pants and wash my hands. The soap burns my skin. I make a note to stop using it.

She's waiting in the hallway, her purse swung over one shoulder and a pinched look on her face. Downstairs, she unlocks a door off the kitchen, which takes us into a garage.

The woman instructs me to fasten my seat belt as the entire wall behind the car lifts into the ceiling. We drive toward the gate, the house swelling behind us, puffing up to show me its full power. Every surface is a different shade of blue, as if the painter couldn't make up his mind.

The neighbor's house seems empty. No girl in the window.

The woman stops in front of the gate and gets out of the car to use a black box with a lid and a keypad. I lean forward in my seat, but she positions her body to block my view, and I can't see the code she enters.

And then, suddenly, we're past the gate. The first time I've been past the gate since They brought me here.

We drive a stretch of road flanked by open fields and vineyards. Fall has tinged everything yellow and orange. I think of Mother, of Caspian, and wonder if they're looking up at the same blue sky this very minute, missing me.

"Our hearts will forever be connected," Mother told me. I hold on to her words now.

The road takes us into a small town. Lush green lawns lead to neat houses tucked behind carefully trimmed hedges. Soon enough, the houses are replaced by brick buildings with big front windows lining each side of the road. People carry bags and cups of coffee as they wander up and down the sidewalks. Trees overhang the road. We pass a three-story brick building with sage-green trim, like something straight out of *It's a Wonderful Life*.

The woman finally parks the car in front of a gray stucco building. "Dr. Anson's office," she says.

✖

A lady wearing a blue shirt and matching pants takes me through a labyrinth of hallways. I am weighed and measured, poked and prodded, and she records everything on her clipboard. When I try to read it, she presses it against her chest.

I'm left, finally, in a windowless room with peach-colored walls. Music plays overhead. A cartoon bear painted on a wall smiles at me.

The sense that I've already been here makes my head ache. But I couldn't have been.

A small TV sits on a desk, and a picture of a stethoscope bounces around the screen. What looks like a typewriter's keyboard sits in front of the TV, connected by a wire. I push one of its letter buttons, and the screen asks for a password.

The phone next to the keyboard has no dial tone, but I push a button, and a woman says, "Reception, how can I help you?" I slam it down, push the next button. That connects me to the lab. I can't dial out. But my parents don't have a phone number, anyway. I slam the receiver against the desk until the tendons in my shoulder become tight enough to snap.

The temperature of the room claws toward boiling. I peel off my sweatshirt and stare at the pamphlets in a clear plastic rack bolted to the wall. Measles, flu shots, fevers in children, menstruation.

These won't help me.

A red plastic box hanging above the trash can is labeled HAZARDOUS WASTE, and inside a tiny window used needles are stacked like kindling. I could steal a needle, stick the woman with it, get her sick.

Someone knocks on the door, and a short woman in a white coat steps inside. "Hello, Piper," she says. "I'm Dr. Anson. You can call me Debbie if you'd like."

Debbie motions for me to take a seat. Then she sits in a chair with wheels, scooting closer than I am comfortable with. I move away from her a hair, and she moves back a touch as well.

"Jeannie said you've been experiencing pain when you urinate," she says. "Does it hurt when you go to the bathroom?"

I nod.

"Is your urine cloudy?"

I nod again.

"I'd like to examine your abdomen. Please lie back on the table."

The paper crinkles as I climb up and lie back. She lifts my shirt and pushes with her hands. The pain is sharp, and I suck in a breath.

"Does that hurt?" she asks.

"Yes."

"Classic symptoms of a urinary tract infection. You can sit up. I'm going to prescribe an antibiotic. Should clear up within a week to ten days, but you'll start feeling relief in two or three days. In the meantime, you can take some ibuprofen for the pain."

She slips a pen out of her coat pocket, clicks the top, and scribbles on a white notepad. "I have a couple more questions for you, Piper. Are you sexually active?"

My mind flashes to Caspian. I shake my head, try to stop my face from burning red.

"Sometimes sexual intercourse can cause a urinary tract infection. There's no shame in being sexually active, Piper."

I want to ask if poisoning causes these symptoms, but I don't know Debbie well enough. She might be working with Them. The fluorescent lights buzz a warning.

She lifts something from her pocket. "While I've got you here, how about a quick exam?"

I shrug.

Debbie clicks on a light. "I'm going to check your ears with this scope. It won't hurt." She moves close, and I can smell her soap, clean and benign. She doesn't breathe as she gently sticks the scope in one ear, then the next. She listens to my heart and my lungs, then wraps a cuff around my arm until it cuts off my circulation.

My body doesn't belong to me anymore.

She smiles and puts away her tools. "You're healthy," she says, beaming. "Though underweight. Did the doctors at the hospital speak with you about your nutritional deficiencies?"

I shake my head. *Hospital?*

"Chronic malnutrition can cause problems with blood sugar. Jeannie said you get dizzy a lot? Your body might not be able to regulate glucose as well as it should. So make sure you're having small meals or snacks every couple of hours. You can even carry a piece of candy with you when you go out, to help when you feel faint."

She looks at me for a while, then rises from her chair and collects a few pamphlets. "Here, take these."

One is about mental health, the other about visiting the gynecologist.

"If you're comfortable, I'd like to perform a pelvic exam before you leave. I'll be wearing gloves the whole time. Would that be okay?"

I shake my head. "No."

"I understand, Piper. Sometime soon, though, you'll need to get one. Do you have any questions for me? About your health or anything else?"

"When can I go home?" I whisper. My voice is weak and child-like. "My *real* home."

She tries to smile, but it looks painful.

Her silence says everything.

Back out in the waiting room, Debbie gives the woman the prescription. "Good to see you again, Piper," she says before she leaves.

Again?

The woman hugs me, but I keep my arms straight at my sides. She is stiff as well, her gesture just a show for everyone on the Outside to see.

Once we are back inside the house, she'll be as cold as ever.

Yet here I am, away from the locked doors and windows of her home.

An idea takes shape.

"I want to see that doctor again," I declare, my voice coming back to me. Back to the daughter my parents raised.

Her eyes widen. "Debbie?"

"No. Dr. Lundhagen," I say. "At his office."

15. AFTER

I wait three days for my appointment.

I can't sleep or eat, and I lose four pounds.

16. AFTER

The woman's perfume stunk up the waiting room, but I'm finally in Dr. Lundhagen's office.

Alone.

"You seem distracted." He sits in a wooden chair with spindles across the back, hand poised over a yellow notepad. His desk is mammoth: dark wood, distinguished looking.

He tries too hard to seem important.

I shift in my seat. The antibiotics haven't fully kicked in yet, and I'm still in some discomfort. I glance around his office, at the potted plant by the closed door, the shelf lined with leather-bound books to make him seem smart.

"What would you like to talk about today?" the doctor asks.

I still have not spoken to him. I wouldn't know what to say, anyway.

He uncrosses his legs and crosses them again.

We stare each other down.

"Maybe I can start by telling you a bit about myself," he says. "I grew up in Iowa and moved here for college. I attended UCLA and have been a psychiatrist for nearly twenty years now. My wife, Sheila, and I have been married for eighteen years this May. We have two daughters, Adrien and Molly. Adrien's in middle school, and Molly is a freshman in high school."

He's waiting on me now.

I touch my hair, imagining myself swimming in the lake with my siblings.

I can play this game. I *have* to play this game. This is how I'll get out of the woman's house.

Cas always said I could do anything.

"I'm nervous," I say quietly.

I dive below the surface of the lake.

"It's normal to feel anxious when talking to a psychiatrist. I hope the longer we work together, the more comfortable you'll feel sharing things with me."

"*Sometimes you have to tell people what they want to hear,*" Father always said.

"Me too," I lie.

The warm water surrounds me in safety.

"Good." He smiles and jots something down. "Last time we met, you said you weren't eating much."

"*She* said that," I correct him.

The lake is gone.

He adjusts the watch on this wrist. "Are you eating?"

The water evaporates off my skin.

"Yes, some."

"Good, good. And getting enough rest?"

I'm ashamed of the nights I sleep all the way through, waking refreshed. I'm becoming too comfortable in that bed. I tried curling up on the floor once, but when I woke up, I was in the bed again.

"I sleep okay."

"I want to talk about your relationship with Jeannie."

I dig my hands into the arms of my chair. "We don't have a relationship." The ache in my temples returns.

He writes on his notepad. "Describe your interactions, then. Are they pleasant? What kinds of things do you talk about?"

If I relax my eyes and look just past him, he almost resembles Father. The pain ebbs.

"We talk about what we're having for dinner…if I want to watch television with her. She makes me watch this dumb show with her sometimes. She says it's a soap opera."

"Which one?"

"*The Young and the Restless*." I pause. "It's actually kind of good."

He chuckles. "I used to watch it all the time in grad school."

"You did?" I ask, trying, suddenly, not to smile.

"It's a very addictive show. What else do you talk about?"

I shake my head. "I don't want to talk to her."

"Why not? Jeannie cares for you very much."

The pressure builds in my head, my bones threatening to crack. "Please don't say her name."

Dr. Lundhagen stops writing mid-sentence and stares at me. I'm standing now, breathing heavily, though I don't remember leaving my chair.

Taking deep breaths, I sit, folding my legs under my body. I want to look calm, even if this position hurts my knees. I can't keep showing him my weakness.

He sets down his pen. "Piper, I want to explore your feelings for Jeannie during our sessions. I know you're confused and afraid, and aren't able to trust her yet, but we will work through this together. I won't push you to go too far, too fast."

A car drives past the office, and a dog leans out its back window, mouth wide open, tongue hanging out.

"No one will tell me why I'm being punished," I say, my voice growing louder. "I didn't do anything wrong. So why did They take me away from my family?"

"What do you remember from your stay in the hospital?"

No.

Enough.

I refuse to utter another syllable. Not until I can regain control.

I bite my thumbnail. If Mother were here, she'd tell me to stop.

✖

When we get to the house, the woman says we should spend some time in the sunshine. "It's a pity to waste such a gorgeous day." She puts on her gardening gloves and hat. "Want to help?"

"No."

She nods, looks away quickly, and moves to her garden.

I sit on the porch steps. Not many cars pass by this place, so when one stops outside the closed gate, I rise. A man steps out and lifts a pot of flowers out of the trunk.

Run.

My feet propel me down the drive. I scream and wave my hands. "Help!" I shout until my throat shreds itself. "Please help me!"

The woman rushes to the man. She says something to him, and he quickly gets in his car.

Just as I reach the gate, the car peels away, spitting exhaust in my face.

When its engine backfires, one sharp bang,

> *I see a man lying on the ground at the lake house,
> facedown.*

"Why did you do that?" I scream at the woman.

"Piper, please," she says. She's crying, and I want to hit her. I want to hit her until she hurts like I hurt. Until I can't feel my fists anymore.

I turn and run back inside the house, kick off my shoes. Her shelf of figurines watches me as I enter the living room. All those fake, unblinking eyes.

I pick up the doll with angel wings, the one her sister gave her.

Squeezing it, I picture Mother in the back of that police car, the look of fear on her face.

My mind flits, and I can feel Cas's lips against mine.

The doll is smashed on the floor before I even register throwing it.

The thud echoes.

It feels good.

With one sweeping motion, I knock an entire line of them to the floor.

I pick up a doll sitting in a bubbly bathtub.

My first day here, in the bathtub with the too-cold-too-hot water—she was probably laughing at me the entire time.

I throw the doll to the floor as hard as I can.

Shards of porcelain scatter. Beautiful chaos.

"Piper!" she gasps.

She's standing in the doorway.

"What have you done?" she asks, barely able to speak.

I'm holding a figurine of two parents standing over a baby's crib. The name *Amy* has been painted along the bottom.

Who's Amy?

The woman's chin quivers, and she clears her throat. "Go to your room, Piper. Now."

How does it feel? I want to ask. *To have everything that's precious to you taken away?*

But she wouldn't understand.

Monsters don't have empathy. They have sharp claws and teeth that thirst for blood.

I hurry past her to my room and slam the door shut, but it doesn't make me feel any better. I sit on my bed, my breathing shallow, my heart pumping. A hint of red seeps through one of my socks. When I pull it off, I find a shard stuck in my foot.

A few moments pass, and there's a knock on the door.

"Piper, I'd like to talk to you."

She lets herself in without being invited.

She's holding a figurine in her hands.

Guilt washes over me, even though I have nothing to be guilty about. She started this, after all. When an animal is backed into a corner, it will lash out. She should understand that better than anyone—she's backed me into a corner for far too long.

She stares at the figurine in her hands, turning it over and over.

Her eyes are red when they meet mine.

"I'm very upset," she says. "I've been collecting these for years. Each one means something to me. My mom gave this one to me after—" She stops herself.

She's holding the one with the crib.

"I should have told you how important they are." She wipes her eyes. "I wish I could help you, Piper, and make you feel at home here. I'm trying very hard to put myself in your place, to do what's best for you. I don't want to make you talk about things you're not ready to talk about. But we've got to have some boundaries and respect."

"Boundaries and respect?" I ask. "You take me from my home, from my family, and then expect me to just *forget them*? Where were the boundaries and respect then?"

She stifles a sob. "I'm sorry, Piper. I can see you still miss them."

My muscles tense. "Why am I here?"

"You know why, deep down. At least I hope you do."

"When can I go home?"

She takes a deep breath, and I suddenly wish I hadn't asked that question. "This is your home now."

"But what if I don't *want* this to be my home?"

She collects herself before reaching into a pocket on the front of her cardigan, then lifts out another figurine and sets it on the desk.

"I'm sorry," she whispers before she leaves.

I don't want to look at it. I push it across the desk with my elbow, and it lands in the trash with a thud. I ball up some tissues and toss them on top.

I am nobody's fool.

I search for my necklace, wanting its comfort, but it's not where I left it on my desk.

The drawers are empty, the floor is clear. No monsters under the bed. Nothing at all.

I use the tissues to carefully lift the figurine from the trash, set it aside, push through the garbage, but no chain. No green stone.

No connection home.

The woman sits alone in the living room, staring at a darkened TV.

"Where's my necklace?"

She blinks, looks up at me. "Your necklace?"

"My chain with the green stone. It was on my desk."

She wipes her eyes. "I was going to surprise you today." She goes into the kitchen and returns with a small white box. "I had it fixed."

"I never asked you to do that!"

She holds the box out. "I wanted to do something nice for you."

I snatch it from her. "Don't ever touch my things again," I say, and rush into my room. My hands shake as I set it on my desk, lift off the lid, and fold back a thin layer of cotton.

The stone winks at me.

17. BEFORE

It's almost lunchtime, but it isn't my grumbling stomach that makes Father and me hurry from his office.

It's Beverly Jean shouting from downstairs.

Our feet thud the stairs, taken two at a time by Father. "What's going on?" he asks.

Beverly Jean's glued to the living room window with Cas and Samuel. She launches herself into me, and I stumble back a step before planting my feet.

Cas turns. "There's a van here, and some men with guns!"

"Don't panic," Father says. "Those men are here to protect me. To protect us. The Community has received some threats. It's only a precaution, but stay inside." He goes out the front door. The men stand up straighter the moment they see him. They're dressed in black pants and T-shirts and holding assault rifles.

I'm grateful to be a woman; it means I never have to handle a gun.

"How long have they been there?" I ask as Cas moves next to me. My elbow brushes his, and I want to move away from the spark on my skin, to be loyal to Father and his trust in me. I don't think he would approve of these feelings, especially now that he's chosen Thomas as my husband.

Husband. I swallow away the fear, the doubt. Father doesn't make mistakes.

"Only a few minutes."

"They're scary, Pip," Beverly Jean says. "They look mean."

I squeeze her tight, then pull Samuel close with my other arm.

As we watch, Henry comes running up from the beach. He sees the guns, and makes a beeline straight toward them. Cas and I take off, the door slamming behind us as we sprint across the lawn. Cas scoops up Henry just as he reaches for one of the weapons. Henry's cowboy hat tumbles to the ground.

"Put me down," Henry huffs, squirming. "That's my present! Mommy promised we had presents!"

"Those are real, dangerous guns. You are never to touch them. Understand?" Father's face is red, and veins pop from his neck.

Henry pouts, and Cas and I take him back inside the house, where he promptly kicks me in the shin before running upstairs into his room.

"I'll talk to him," Samuel says.

"Are you sure?" I ask.

"Yeah, he listens to me." Samuel seems so much older than his age sometimes. He should just be a kid, but with so many of us, we all have to do our part taking care of one another. He puts his hands in his pockets and slowly walks up the staircase.

"Where are the Aunties?" I ask, my jaw tight.

Cas shrugs. "Haven't seen them since breakfast. Not that I'm complaining."

"They should have been watching him. It's not safe for the littles to play at the lake by themselves. What about Millie?" I turn in a frantic circle, guilty for having forgotten her.

"She's napping with Angela," he says, and grabs my hand. "Quit worrying." That same pesky jolt dances along my skin.

I pull away. "I'll see you later, okay? I need to go start lunch."

✖

Down at the far end of the lake, I pick my way through the brush and trees to a small clearing no one else knows about. I come out here to swim sometimes and to think. There's even a piece of driftwood I use as a bench.

I strip down. The lake isn't clean, but being in the water will soothe me. I have no worries, no responsibilities here.

When I was a kid, Mother bought me a pink swim cap and took me to lessons at a fancy pool. We would always get ice cream after and eat it in a park. Those are some of my happiest memories from before we moved here.

The wind pushes waves across the surface of the water as I wade in. It's lukewarm and murky.

I scrub my hair with a bar of Mother's lavender soap; she buys it from Paris and always remembers to bring me a block or two. Then I float on my back, my clean hair spreading out like vines. I let myself start to sink.

Something splashes, loudly, and I curl up.

It's Cas, standing on the shore.

He can see everything: my breasts, my pubic hair, the scar running across my stomach from when my appendix burst. I dive all the way under, hoping he'll leave. Cas can hardly swim, after all.

But then hands brush my arm and grip as hard as they can, heaving me to the surface. My hair plasters over my eyes like wet leaves on the forest floor in fall.

"Cas? What are you doing?" I shout.

He looks at me like he's seen a ghost. It's like he can't answer.

"Come on," I say, and swim toward the shore. My feet dig into the pebbled beach as he follows closely behind.

"I hope you're happy," I say, crossing my arms over my chest and stomach to hide my body. "You scared the ever-loving shit out of me." Water drips down my bare shoulders and back.

"I thought you were drowning," he sputters finally. "You were sinking." His eyes sweep over me, and he blushes and averts his gaze.

"You thought *I* was drowning?" I laugh. "You can barely even swim! Were you following me?"

"N-no," he stammers. "I came here to cool off."

"This is my secret spot."

"Mine too...or at least I *thought* it was."

"Don't look while I get my clothes." He sits on the ground and closes his eyes while I quickly snap my bra and pull my underwear up my dripping legs.

"Caspian and Piper! Just what in the hell do you think you're doing?" Mother's voice rings through the trees.

My skin prickles over.

Caspian stands. "I came here to be alone. I didn't know she was here."

Mother's face contorts. She raises a hand to Cas like she's going to slap him, but then she drops it. "You're practically brother and sister."

But we're not. I only have two brothers: Samuel and Henry. Why is she saying this now?

"Nothing's happened," I plead. "You have to know that."

"Put your clothes on," she says, her eyes traveling over me. "You can't run around half naked anymore, Piper. Men have urges, and you'll get yourself in trouble."

"Not with me," Cas says.

"Quiet. Go to the house, *now*, and we'll discuss this later."

Cas clenches his jaws. "We haven't done anything wrong, Piper," he whispers to me before jogging away.

She and I face each other, the lake lapping at the pebbly shore.

"Mother, I'm—"

She cuts me off. "You're lucky it was me who found you, and not your father. You are the emotional head of this family when we're gone. The younger children need you." She massages the back of her neck. "Romance is just a distraction."

"Romance? With *Cas?*" My cheeks burn hot, and I look down.

"Don't play the fool with me, Piper. I've seen the way you look at each other. If you're not careful, your father might expel Caspian."

"Expel him? Why? Where would he go?"

"Your father has chosen Thomas for you, my darling. If Caspian were to get in the way of that..." She trails off, and then gathers me into a hug. "Forget whatever feelings you may think you have. They're inconsequential compared to the battles ahead."

18. AFTER

I'm lying on the ground, and I don't know how I got here. My lips stick to my teeth, my tongue as dry as the bark peeling off the oak tree back home.

A camping light in the corner flickers and dies.

The bed is gone.

And the window seat, and the desk.

I'm not in my room.

I touch the wall. It's cold, and I think it's white. It smells like dirt after a rainstorm.

When I stand on my tiptoes, my fingers brush against the ceiling. Light creeps in around the edges. It's a door of some kind, closed over me.

"Help!" I scream, but the sound only bounces back at me. My mind spins, trying to figure out where They could have put me.

The gardening shed with that lock. Or the basement, if this house has one.

I step in a puddle of water in one corner and press myself up against the opposite wall. I kick and scratch and scream until my throat burns and I am nothing.

Finally I curl back up on the ground and stick my thumb in my mouth.

The shivers overtake me, and I try to remember Mother's voice, the lullabies she used to sing to me. I whisper her name over and over again. She's sitting with me in spirit, telling me not to worry, rocking me in her arms. I pretend we're at home, picking wildflowers in the sunshine.

Then the ceiling raises up, and Mother climbs down into the room.

"I'm here now, baby," she soothes.

She gives me a bottle of juice, and I drink it down. Then I burrow into her warm, soft body. She rocks me slowly back and forth, running the back of her hand across my forehead and cheek, humming. Her voice floats around the room, wraps itself around me, and I fall asleep in her arms.

✖

When I awake, I'm not lying on the ground. I'm in bed, covers to my chin. A glass of water sits on the table where I left it last night.

My fingers, which were raw and bloody from clawing the walls, are fine. Mother is gone.

I snap my eyes closed. I want to go back to wherever I just came from, where it's just me and Mother. Safe. Together.

But I can't.

✖

"Does this house have a basement?" I ask the woman at breakfast.

She rinses her coffee cup at the sink, quiet for a long time. "Nope, no basement. Why do you ask?"

"No reason," I answer quickly.

"I have an idea. How about we have some ice cream for breakfast?" She opens the freezer. "We've got chocolate and vanilla. A scoop of each?"

I'm not sure what her angle is, but I'll take the ice cream.

As she gets down two bowls, a memory tugs like a fishing lure snagged in my brain. It's the woman, and she's asking me if I want ice cream for breakfast, but her hair is longer. I turn my head, try to catch the moment, but it evaporates, along with my appetite.

"Are you all right?" She sets the bowl in front of me. "Look at me, Piper." Her eyebrows are knitted together with worry, her hands on my shoulders. "Where did you go just now?"

"I'm not hungry anymore," I say.

"You don't eat enough. How about some toast with butter? It'll be gentle on your stomach."

I try to recall if Mother ever fed me ice cream for breakfast and decide that must be it. I'm just confused. My memories are in some kind of spin cycle, jumbling together.

And the woman, Jeannie, doesn't get to be a part of them.

19. BEFORE

Father stands next to me on the beach, feet bare, pant legs rolled to mid-calf. He holds up the stopwatch, his thumb above the start button.

He looks at me. "Are you ready?"

We've run this drill a hundred times, maybe more. When the war comes, I may need to perform water rescues, or help the others into the lake to shield them from nuclear fallout.

"I'm ready."

He clicks the button, and I tear off down the beach, heels spraying sand behind me. I splash into the water, diving under the surface.

It's twenty freestyle strokes to the buoy.

Nineteen.

Eighteen.

Seventeen.

Breathe.

I am stronger in the lake than I am on land. My arms pierce the water. It closes around me, keeping me afloat, pushing me toward my goal:

Initiation.

I can feel it this time: approval. Father's pride reaches me from shore, propelling me farther.

I'm already around the buoy, calculating the seconds in my mind. But as I kick away, my foot grazes it, slowing me, and I go blank.

I hesitate.

Just for a moment.

My arms aren't quite lined up with my kicks. I inhale a bit of water. My focus wavers.

Stupid.

I thrash toward Father. As I climb out of the water, I keep my head lowered. I don't want to see how disappointed he must be.

"One second slower," he says as I pass him and fall onto my hands and knees. "Again."

He has me run the drill again and again until my muscles ache, until my arms and legs turn to lead, weighing me down. But each time I'm slower.

Two seconds.

Ten seconds.

Thirty seconds.

I dry heave into the sand.

"I'm sorry," I gasp.

He says nothing as he walks away.

20. AFTER

I wake in the middle of the night, sheets soaked with sweat, heart pounding.

A little girl's laughter pierces the walls of my room.

It sounds like Beverly Jean.

I bolt upright and try to get out of bed, but Daisy's curled up on my knees, trapping me; she sleeps with me most nights now. The laughter seems to be coming from close by.

Daisy wakes as I wriggle away from her, scooting out of bed. "Stay, girl." She watches me, angling her head from one side to the other. "Go back to sleep."

In the bathroom across the hall, the drawers below the sink are mostly empty, but a pink bag holds squares of blush and tubes of mascara. The light catches shiny silver tweezers, their little tips sharp and perfect for lock picking. I grip those in my palm and ease into the hallway.

The staircase has remained in the same spot for a few days now. The house is holding its breath, waiting for me to make a mistake.

Grainy nothingness obscures the bottom of the stairs.

I hurry away from it, wading through the unknown, rushing down the hallway.

I will not let Them break me.

Beverly Jean's laughter is louder now.

I inch toward the closed door at the end of the hall, light bleeding from beneath it, and press my ear up against it. She laughs again, the sound muffled. My head swims, and I brace myself against a wall, afraid I might pass out.

Deep breaths, in and out.

The doorknob turns easily in my hand, unlocked after all, and I open it a crack.

A little girl sits on a bed, a flashlight in one hand, a book on her lap. She laughs. I remember when I used to be able to laugh like that.

But she's not my Beverly Jean, and my heart dies a little bit more.

Cold prickles my scalp as a realization crystallizes—Beverly Jean or not, I'm not the only girl who's been taken. She must be a child of one of Father's followers, stolen like I was, like he warned we all would be. I almost call out for Caspian, forgetting for a moment that he's not here to help me.

I have to save this little girl, even if she's not my sister.

When I enter the room, she startles.

"I'm sorry to scare you," I tell her, hiding the tweezers behind my back. "I'm Piper."

The girl sticks her thumb in her mouth before pulling it out again.

"You don't have to be afraid. My room is down the hall."

"Mama told me about you," she says, her voice shaking.

I sit next to her. She smells like strawberries and laundry detergent.

Things were bleak enough when it was just me trapped here. Now I have someone else to think of.

"I'm going to get you out of here. I promise."

She crinkles her brow. "But I just got here."

"When?" I try not to let my voice grow shrill, but it threatens to anyway.

"When you were sleeping. I'm not supposed to meet you until the morning."

They took her last night, then. There's a pinch of pain at my temples, and I rise from the bed.

"What's your name?" I ask.

"Amy."

"Amy," I echo. The name feels strange on my tongue. "Are you okay?"

"You're pretty," she says. "I want to grow my hair as long as yours."

"Your hair is beautiful just the way it is," I answer. Amy has the hair of a child, thin and wispy.

Why are we here?

Because They put us here. The government. Forms were filled out, I was told. The woman had paperwork, records, documentation. Those things can be easily forged, but no one believed me. No one cared. The police drove me here and left me.

"Where are your parents, Amy? Are they back at the compound?"

"Mama's probably asleep."

"Mine, too," I say, though I can't be certain. Mother kept strange hours. She said her years working all hours of the day and night destroyed her body's natural rhythm. Most mornings she was up before the sun, brewing coffee, making food. When she was actually with us, that is.

"What about your dad?" I ask, afraid to upset her but needing to know.

"Daddy lives somewhere else," she answers. "Mama says he'll be home soon."

"My father is at our compound," I tell her. "They won't let me see him."

"Mine, too," she says, and continues reading her book.

My heart slips into my stomach. "Your father's at the compound, too?"

She nods. "I think so."

"Do you remember how long ago you were taken?"

"Today."

I pace the room, stepping over a half-completed puzzle and a jump rope. "Someday soon I'm going to take us away from here, back to the compound. Okay?"

She ignores my question. "Wanna see my fort?"

I sigh, feeling time slipping away from me. Amy opens the door and waves me toward the closet, pride a lopsided smile on her face, and I can't say no.

As I move toward her, the floor groans in the hallway.

A bright light turns on, oozing under the door.

And then a shadow blocks it.

They're here.

I cross the room and tumble into the closet. Holding my finger to my mouth, I count to ten in my head.

Nothing happens. I lean out and check the door.

The light is gone.

"What's wrong?" Amy asks, perplexed.

"Nothing." I rub the goose bumps from my arms. We have to be quiet. They could come back, and if they do, they won't want to see us together.

Amy crawls into the closet, too, all the way into the back corner, and suddenly a hundred twinkle lights spark to life. White garlands of them hang from the ceiling.

They are cruel to give her faux starlight.

"It's like magic, right?"

Stacks of soft satin pillows clutter the floor like a nest, and she pats the one next to her.

As I sink into the fabric, she pulls the door toward us.

I can almost smell our firepit at home, hear the littles' laughter. I can almost feel Cas's skin against mine.

"Look," Amy says, bringing me back. "I made these."

Swirls and scribbles cover the walls. Drawings. She did all of these tonight? A bunny nibbles a carrot, next to a racecar driving over a rainbow, next to a whale swimming in the waves. It is love and innocence and

and

and

I cover my mouth with a fist, trying not to cry in front of this little girl who must be even more afraid than I am.

The room shifts.

The drawings are gone.

There is the smell of urine and fear.

A woman's voice whispers, "*She's too cold.*"

Amy touches my shoulder. "My sister lives here," she says, and the room snaps back to itself.

I wipe my eyes and look at her. She smiles a conspiratorial grin, a Cheshire Cat with baby skin.

"She lives in the closet?" I ask.

"Yep, and I come to visit her. We have tea parties." Amy points to a drawing of two stick figures. One is small, one big. They hold hands, smiling out into the void. "That's me," Amy says, touching the little one. "And that's my sister."

"What's her name?"

"Jessica. Isn't that a pretty name? Like a princess."

"Very pretty," I agree. Is Jessica back at the compound?

Amy smiles and finds a pack of colored pencils tucked behind a pillow. "Wanna draw something in my fort?"

I find an empty spot above Amy's reach and sketch out a lily, trying to remember Carla's drawing. I add a few vines and leaves and give her back the pencils. Carla used the same brand, although this packaging is different.

Every day here feels like I'm drifting further away from my old life.

"That's pretty," she says. "Maybe you can teach me how to draw that sometime?"

"Mm-hmm," I mumble. My breathing has grown shallow.

They could return at any minute. Whatever sense of safety this space offered is gone.

When I burst out of the closet, Amy follows. "Don't be afraid of the monsters. They never come in here!"

The monsters.

Jeannie and Them.

I want to run down the hall. Hide under my covers. But I need to be strong for Amy—help her, like I wish someone would help me. I can't scare her.

"I better go back to sleep," I say, "and you should, too."

"Will you tuck me in?"

My hands shake as I pull the covers up under her chin. She closes her eyes. "Good night, Piper." Dozily, she smiles. And then I recognize her: She's one of the girls from the photos downstairs. In the photo her front teeth were missing, but they've grown in now.

I try to say good night, but I can't make any sound come out.

Once I'm back in the hallway, I slowly click her door shut. No sounds, other than the blood whirring in my ears.

I creep down the stairs, keeping my footsteps as light as possible. I take a photograph of Amy off the mantel. Then I take one of the other girl, slip them under my shirt, and go back to my room.

Under the light of my desk lamp, I study the photos. Amy's smiling at the camera and hugging a doll with neon-blue hair. She stands in front of a tree, and it looks a lot like the big oak at home.

The girl in the other photo sits in a kiddie pool, splashing water toward the camera. She has long, blond hair and blue eyes.

She's me.

I knew it the moment I first saw it, but didn't trust my own eyes.

Somehow, the woman has stolen photographs of us as children and framed them. She's trying to fool us into believing we belong here.

We don't.

I decide to keep the photos, and set them on top of my dresser.

If Jeannie can play mind games, so can I.

21. BEFORE

A siren blasts through the walls of our bedroom. I sit up and switch on the flashlight I keep under my pillow.

Beverly Jean whips back her covers and dives into my bed. "I'm scared, Pip!"

I gather her into a hug. "It's only a drill, Beverly Jean. But we have to hurry." She waits by the door as I peel back Millie's blanket and lift her from her crib. Millie wakes for a moment, then falls back asleep on my shoulder.

"Carla!" I hiss when she pulls her covers over her head. "Let's go!"

"This is so stupid," she says. "I'm tired."

"We're all tired," I say as we go into the hallway. The boys meet us there, rubbing their eyes.

"Shoulders back," Thomas commands as Mother exits her bedroom. We follow him outside to the benches.

Father waits for us. The men stand behind him, holding their guns across their chests. Thomas moves to stand with them, too, shoulders straight. His pride in the Community must be returning, and I feel relieved.

"You and Thomas are a perfect match."

I shiver.

"Three minutes," Father says, looking at the stopwatch in his hands. "That's unacceptable. If the government were here to take you away, you'd have been captured by now. If an atomic bomb had blasted into the sky, you'd be choking on ash."

Beverly Jean burrows her face into my side, and I try to flex my muscles to stop from shaking. Henry and Samuel cling to Caspian.

Mother yawns, unafraid. I wish I had her courage.

"I have important news to share with you," he continues. "The government knows I have special knowledge—a second sight, if you will—and is monitoring the Community. They're afraid of our beliefs, of the hope I give my followers. I've known this for some time, as have you. But now a few of our members have been taken."

I raise my hand, and Father calls on me. "Taken?" I swallow, grateful for his protection.

He nods. "Government agents posing as Community members have infiltrated our compound and taken members by force. We're very dangerous in their eyes. We reject mindless spending, crowded cities, and the widespread use of psychotropic drugs. Without these things, these distractions, the entire economy fails. The government can't risk me spreading that truth. The rich would lose their forced labor, and the Outside's twisted society would collapse."

His face darkens. "I have been informed that the government will target the Community's children next—especially *my* children. They want to steal you, brainwash you, and pump you for information in order to bring me down. They think young minds are weak and malleable. I hate to think what depraved punishments they would subject you to. Knowing this government's history of torture, anything is possible.

"And understand, my children: The president is engaging in a war of words with a hostile foreign government that has an arsenal of nuclear weapons at its disposal. The doomsday clock is running down. Nuclear fallout is a real threat now. Everything we've been preparing for is on the horizon. This is no longer a drill."

He pauses. Millie's diaper stinks, but I know better than to walk away during one of his teachings.

"More Community members will be arriving to construct a fallout shelter here at our lake compound. Thomas is here to head up the build. We must be prepared for nuclear war. You, my children, may be our world's best and possibly last hope."

Beverly Jean's chin quivers. "Are we going to die, Pip?"

I put my free arm around her and hold on tight, as much for me as for her. "Of course not. Right, Father?"

Mother straightens her hair and forces a smile. Father doesn't.

"It only takes one madman to press one button. That's why we must prepare. A failure to plan is a plan for failure. And I don't fail. I *won't* fail. We *must* survive the bombs, so we can build this world anew.

"We're also going to need to be more diligent with security," he goes on. "Joan and Barb already have their hands full, so this will be up to you older children. Starting at sundown, Piper, Caspian, Thomas, and Carla will take turns on watch." His eyes move over each of our faces. "I've had a small platform built at the top of the old roller coaster. It will serve as one lookout point. The other will be at the property's front entrance, at the only access point by road.

"Caspian and Piper, you'll take watch the first week. I'll give you more instructions later. But remember: No matter what you do or what you see, *stay inside* the perimeter fencing. It's not safe on the Outside."

"Maybe Piper should be on watch with Thomas," Mother suggests.

"Are you questioning me?" Father's voice is so soft, I can barely hear it.

"No." Mother falls silent.

My head swims.

"But when will we sleep?" Carla asks. Already her roots have begun to show, peppering her snowy white hair. Mother touches it and makes a face, and I get the feeling the bleachings will continue.

Father stands in front of her. "I'm trying to protect our family, Carla. You'll sleep when you sleep. Just do as I say. I don't ask much."

At that, Father signals the men, and they follow him inside.

Carla scowls, a show of will, and I know tears will come later when we're back in our beds. I reach past Mother and try to grab Carla's hand, but she crosses her arms.

"Father knows best," I hear myself saying without really thinking. I touch her shoulder, but she shakes me off.

"Shut up, Piper." She hurries toward the house, arms still wrapped around herself. She's practically humming with anger.

"Carla!" I call out, but Cas tells me to let her go. "I'm just trying to help her understand," I explain. "It's all for the best, she'll see!"

"Let me handle this," Mother says, hurrying after her.

As everyone else starts to trickle back toward the house, Beverly Jean takes Millie from my arms, knowing how heavy she gets.

Cas surprises me by taking my hand. "Can we talk?"

"Yes," I say, turning to Beverly Jean. "You take Millie inside, and I'll be right behind you."

I switch off my light as he leads me between two rows of corn so tall they block out the moon. The leaves have sharp edges that cut into my skin.

"Do you ever wonder if Curtis is wrong?" he asks. The whites of his eyes almost glow in the darkness. "What if there *is* no war coming? We haven't seen any tanks or soldiers or fighter jets. If there was a war coming, wouldn't there be some signs? Even here?"

I shake my head. "Father's not wrong. He's never wrong."

"Everyone's wrong sometimes, Piper. Curtis is only human."

I study his face for signs of a smile or a laugh, but the way his eyes burn into mine tells me this is how he really feels.

"You're being serious," I say, after a beat. "You really don't trust Father to protect us?"

"I never said that." He licks his lips and leans closer. "But I think he's wrong about this. If it's really as dangerous as he says, how safe can it be to put us on patrol? Wouldn't we be the first to get killed? It doesn't seem right, forcing Carla into that position. Or you."

"We're protecting ourselves!"

My voice comes out like a shriek, and Cas puts his hands on my shoulders. "I'm sorry, Piper," he says in a hushed tone. "I'm not trying to upset you. Keep your voice down."

"Then you shouldn't question Father. That's what the Outside wants. Can't you see that? They want to make us doubt each other. We're weak then."

Don't be like Thomas, I almost say. *Don't let your faith waver. Please.*

"When I was younger, I was in school for a while," he says slowly. "Our teachers talked about questioning things. About thinking freely. I've been remembering that a lot lately. Things don't...don't *feel* right here, Piper."

"I *am* thinking freely," I tell him. "And *I* feel fine. I'm sorry you were stuck in the Outside for so long, but you're here now, Cas. With me. We're safe here. Can't you see that?"

"I know," he says. "And I'm glad to be here—with you. But does having a single thought separate from Curtis's make you disloyal? He's a freethinker, right? That's why he set up the Community. If he hated freethinking, we wouldn't be standing here."

I blink hard, too many thoughts jumbling in my head. The corn blocks the breeze, and I'm sweating through my nightgown. "Can we get out of here? I can't breathe."

I don't wait for an answer—I run back into the yard, grateful for the cooling wind on my skin.

22. AFTER

The woman knocks at my door earlier than normal the next morning.

"We need to talk," she says.

Yanking the covers up around my throat, I lie still and slow my breathing, as if I can will myself to disappear. I don't hear Amy. Maybe it was all a dream.

But the woman picks up the photo of Amy from the dresser and sets it back down. "Amy told me you came into her room last night."

I dig my fingernails into my covers, picturing the dull knife under my mattress. It would probably take me two seconds to pull it out.

"She came home early last night, from her grandparents' house. That's where she's been staying. You were already asleep, or I would have introduced you. She's my daughter, Piper."

Daughter?

"She was going to stay away a few more weeks, but she got too homesick."

She paces the room, taut and jumpy.

"You need to stay in your own bedroom at night, Piper. I know you were curious, but it's not appropriate or safe to go wandering around the house at late hours. Understand?"

Safe for who? I want to ask.

I nod instead.

"I'm very glad you agree." She swallows. "My husband, Rich, he's still at his parents' house. Well, we're separated at the moment, but that doesn't matter. He'll come to the house when you're ready to meet him. You just let me know, okay? There's no rush."

"Why would I want to meet him?"

She fidgets.

"What about the girl?" I ask.

"The girl? Amy?"

"No. In the neighbor's house."

The woman stutters and plays with her hair. "Oh, her? No. She's just a neighbor. No one for you to worry about. I'll introduce you to Amy properly now."

I nod and reach for Daisy, but she isn't on my bed.

The woman calls down the hallway, and soon Amy appears outside my door. I notice she's waiting for permission to enter.

"Come in," I say, and she flies into the room, a whir of color and kinetic energy.

"Hi, Piper!" She jumps onto my bed, wraps her arms around me. I'm a mummy tangled up in sheets and kid hugs.

I close my eyes and hug her back. It feels good.

"I'm so glad you live here now." She keeps her hold on me, in that way children aren't embarrassed to love and be close. "We can play every day! How about grocery store?"

"How do you play that?"

She grabs my hand. "Come on. I'll show you." She drags me into the kitchen downstairs and pushes a chair against the counter, then climbs up and grabs for cans of soup and vegetables.

"Put these on the table," she tells me, and I follow orders.

She climbs down and arranges them in rows.

"Mom, we need a basket!"

The woman, who's been hanging back, gets down a large, plastic bowl. "Will this work?"

Amy scrunches up her nose. "I guess." She gives me the bowl. "You be my customer. Shop and then you have to pay for it. Okay?"

"What should I use for money?" I ask.

"How about Monopoly money?" The woman goes into the living room and returns with a box. She digs out some colorful pieces of paper and gives them to me. "I'll let you girls play. I'll be cleaning the bathrooms if you need me."

Daisy comes trotting into the kitchen, the tags on her collar clinking. I place a can of green beans and a can of tuna in my bowl before scratching Daisy's back and hips.

"I'm ready to check out."

Amy drags each can over the table, making beeping sounds, and places them back in my bowl. "That'll be one thousand dollars."

"Geez, that's spendy." I make a big deal out of counting the money, which makes her giggle.

"I love you," she says.

I don't know how to answer that. My eyes burn. She sounds so much like Beverly Jean.

"Mom says you're staying here now, not with the bad people anymore."

The bad people?

"They're good people," I correct her.

"I know," she says. "That's just what she told me. She likes it when I agree with her. Her face gets kind of sad if I don't."

"Has she said anything to you about working for the government?" I ask, unsure if Amy even understands what the government is or does. But I'm desperate for answers.

She stares at the play money in her hands. "I don't know," she says after a while.

"You can tell me, Amy. I promise. Whatever you tell me stays just between us. I won't tell her you told me."

"I'm not allowed to talk about it."

"Not even to me?"

I must sound harsh, because her mouth bends into a frown and she won't look at me. I force a smile onto my face. "Your turn to buy something!"

She picks out some food, but I can tell her heart's not in the game.

Neither is mine.

✖

My heart's not in another session with Dr. Lundhagen, either, but I have to go.

Getting out regularly is the only way I'll be able to escape.

The potted plant in his office has been moved from its spot next to the door. Now it sits next to my chair.

He clears his throat. "How are you today, Piper?"

Amy is all I can think about.

How many others have been stolen from the Community?

I stare out the window, at the cars that pass by, until I realize that he's waiting for me to speak. "What would happen if you told Jeannie what we talked about?" I ask.

"Everything we discuss is confidential. The only instance where I would have to break that confidentiality is if I felt you were in immediate danger of hurting yourself or someone else. Otherwise, I will keep everything you say to me inside this room. Jeannie will never know what we discuss."

I consider him for a moment. "Okay. There's another girl living with us. I met her last night."

He raises an eyebrow. "Oh? What happened?"

"She thinks Jeannie is her mom. Jeannie told me she's her daughter."

"Okay."

"Okay? Is that all you have to say?"

He stares at me for a while, trying to work out something. "Amy *is* her daughter. She's been living with grandparents."

I say nothing.

"I've known Amy since she was a baby."

My skin flushes, and I grip the chair's armrests.

"What are you thinking right now?" he asks.

"You want me to be honest?"

He nods. "Always."

"I think you're lying."

"What am I lying about?"

"Everything that's been happening to me. Why I was taken from my family. Who Amy is. Who Jeannie is. I think you're part of it, trying to gain my trust in order to brainwash me. Father said this would happen, and now it is."

"I can understand how you would feel that way. Now it's my turn to be honest with you." His face relaxes as he sets down his pen. "I assure you that I'm not lying about Amy. Child Protective

Services deemed your living situation as unhealthy and dangerous. That's why you were placed in protective custody. No one is trying to brainwash you. I want you to think for yourself."

"I *am* thinking for myself."

"Did your parents let you make decisions as you were growing up? Did they let you have opinions?"

"Of course they did."

"Opinions you formed on your own? Or opinions they taught you to have?"

I shake my head, suddenly feeling like I can't focus my eyes. "You're trying to trick me."

"I'm not, Piper. I'm trying to understand why you distrust everyone but your parents."

"Because," I say, though I know that's a weak answer.

"Can you expand on that?"

"Everything they told me was true. They said people would try to take me, and it happened! That's all the proof I need!" I pound on the arms of my chair, trying to make him understand.

He studies me before speaking again. "What kind of people did they say would take you?"

"Government operatives."

"Like spies?"

"Yeah. Yes. I guess so." Father was never specific.

He flips through his notebook. "A woman named Caroline and a man named Jason from Child Protective Services were assigned to your case and removed you from the house. They aren't government operatives or spies. They're social workers. So your parents were wrong in this instance. Is it possible they were wrong about other things?"

I squeeze my hands into fists. "Spies, social workers, it's the same thing. They're from the government." I swallow. "You're trying to make me doubt my parents."

"What would happen if you doubted them?"

I close my eyes and take deep breaths, but my heart won't slow down. "If I doubt them, I might die. I might get my brothers and sisters killed. Don't you understand that?"

He leans forward. "That must be scary, to think that thoughts can cause actions. But thoughts aren't actions. Does that make sense?"

I don't answer.

"Try to imagine a pink elephant sitting between us. Can you picture it?"

I stare at the dirty gray carpet, and a translucent pink elephant appears without me even trying to see it.

"Let's both concentrate on that elephant as hard as we can, and see if we can't make it a reality."

"This is bogus," I say, rolling my eyes.

"How so? You said a minute ago that thoughts can get a person killed. Why can't they make pink elephants appear out of thin air?"

"They just can't, that's why."

"So only negative emotions cause things to happen in real life?"

"Exactly."

"Why is doubt a negative emotion?"

I sink down into my chair a little. "Because it shows that you don't trust a person. That you don't love them."

"Doubt can be very healthy and helpful, Piper. Doubt makes you question situations and people. It's what keeps you alive."

"How so?" I ask, almost spitting. "Doubt is the opposite of faith, and faith is what saves."

"Well, for example, I'm a terrible swimmer. Let's say my wife wants to go snorkeling in very deep water. Doubt makes me stop and think about safety precautions and whether it's something I'll even be comfortable with. It doesn't mean I don't love my wife or trust her."

"If you say so."

"If you doubt something your parents tell you, that's normal. Children question their parents every day. And sometimes parents can be wrong. Knowing that doesn't mean you've betrayed them or don't love them."

I got so upset with Cas and Thomas when they doubted, and now this doctor is trying to get me to do the same thing.

Well, I won't.

"Could I go to the bathroom?" I ask suddenly. I can't listen to this anymore.

"Of course you can, Piper. You don't need my permission. Bathroom's at the end of the hall."

Once I close his office door behind me, my temples pound. I roll my head on my neck, tired of these headaches, but I won't ask for painkillers. They're full of toxins. They make you weak.

The door to the women's bathroom glides open, and I lock it behind me. A rectangular window is set high on the wall above the toilet and sink.

I place one foot on the toilet seat, then the other. My sneakers are a size too big, just like all the clothes the woman gave me, but I don't complain. Father hated complainers.

My fingers graze the window's bottom. I move onto the sink, balancing on my toes. My body wobbles and shakes, my muscles twitching as they try to keep me upright.

I can almost taste the air on my tongue, feel the pavement under my feet as I run from this place, these people. I could run until I found my way home. Tell them where Amy is.

But I am getting ahead of myself.

The window is no more than two feet wide and maybe half a foot tall. I can't squeeze through it. It's meant to let in sunlight, not hope.

Someone knocks on the door, a quick succession of raps.

As I turn around, my foot slides on a wet patch on the sink.

My ankle hits the floor sideways, something pops, and pain shoots up my left leg. Shoving my fist into my mouth, I stifle a scream.

The floor's coldness soaks through my jeans and T-shirt, and I curl up in a ball, my ankle pulsing, my head spinning.

I am nobody's fool.

Or maybe I am. I can't tell anymore.

23. BEFORE

Father says the only way to be brave is to do what scares us.

The roller coaster slopes upward about a hundred feet, the top lost in shadows, the bottom buried in black dirt.

I clip the walkie-talkie to the front of my purple corduroy pants, put the flashlight in my back pocket, and grip the side railing, where wooden planks are nailed down every few feet to make a rudimentary ladder. White paint chips from the wood and drops into the murk below as I climb. I imagine the former amusement park workers scrambling up the ride when it broke down to rescue terrified riders.

I've climbed this coaster dozens of times before, but for the first time, I'm afraid I might fall.

The coaster sways. Next to me, the metal track rises toward the first drop. I crane my neck toward a weather-beaten sign: LAST WARNING. DO NOT STAND UP.

I asked Father what the sign meant, once. He said it's a reminder to keep your ears and eyes open.

To always be vigilant.

At the top of the coaster I sit on the small platform Father ordered built, letting my legs dangle over the edge. I rest my chin on the railing. The breeze ruffles the tops of the trees, and their leaves catch the moon's glint, winking at me.

From my bird's-eye view, our house becomes miniaturized. Smoke rises from the chimney, and I can picture Mother stoking the fire as she makes chamomile tea. When she's here, we drink it every night to improve digestion, help with sleeplessness, and ease the cramps that come every month. It's a small miracle I'm grateful for.

My eyes droop closed. I force myself to sit up straight and slide off my backpack—inside is a thermos of black coffee. I try not to drink any if I can help it, but this is my third night out here. I haven't slept more than a few hours in days, and I need a boost.

More than that, I need to show Father that I'm ready for my initiation, ready to keep the Community safe. I think of Millie asleep in her crib, her mouth slightly open, arms stretched out at her sides, her giraffe on her belly. If anything ever happens to her, I'll never forgive myself.

Father has barely spoken to me since I failed my timed swim.

I sit up even straighter and scan the grounds. Every so often, people will try sneaking inside to see the old amusement park rides. I never worried about it before—they aren't interested in the house—but now Father says that they could be government operatives, that we can't make any assumptions.

It's been a year since anyone has tried infiltrating the property. Which means it's bound to happen sooner rather than later. The law of averages, as Father says.

My walkie-talkie crackles, and my fingers fumble as I slip it from my pants.

"You there, Piper? Over."

It's Cas, on watch at the front gate. Hourly checks are mandatory.

"I'm here."

115

Cradling the walkie-talkie in my palm, I stare at it, willing Cas to speak again. It can be scary out here all alone in the dark. But he's been weird ever since we talked in the corn row.

Our teachers talked about questioning things. About thinking freely.

"Okay. I'll check back in an hour." As I try to think of something to say, he signs off and the crackling between us goes dead.

I hook the walkie-talkie back on my pants and scan our property again. Someone left the porch light on for us. The moon paints a shimmering yellow stripe on the lake.

I roll my head until my neck cracks, sending satisfying jolts down my spine. Father says we're all spiritual beings, no matter the age of our physical bodies. He says that's why we're out here: We're wise and capable, and we have to contribute. Still, I can't imagine Carla sitting all alone like this.

A deer steps out of the woods and wanders to our blooming hosta plants. She ignores the plants' thick green leaves in favor of the stems bursting with pale purple flowers.

I slurp more coffee. It's bitter and dries out my mouth. It also goes right through me, and I pull down my pants and squat off the front of the platform. The first night I tried to pee out here, I went all over myself.

My walkie-talkie crackles again. I yank up my pants as Cas says, "It's been an hour. Over."

I button my pants and grab my radio. "I'm here."

"You see anything?"

"A deer is eating Mother's hostas. That's all. How's it look up there?"

"Nothing to report here. Talk to you in an hour. Over and out."

I consider telling him a bad joke, something to lighten up the mood, to make him the old Caspian again, the one who doesn't look at me like he pities me, who won't talk to me, who glowers at Father behind his back. Sometimes I forget that he spent most of his life in the Outside. I would speak to Thomas about it, but Thomas is being distant, too.

You and Thomas are a perfect match.

Maybe if I think it enough, it will start to feel true.

I start my scan again as I drink my second lid-full of coffee: first our house, then the beach, then the rides. I can barely see the bumper cars; they've mostly been swallowed up by vegetation. I turn around again. The deer's still nibbling her midnight snack.

"Hey. It's me. Over." Cas's voice startles me, and I drop my thermos. Hot coffee scalds my legs, and I scramble to my feet, cursing and flopping around.

I grab my radio. "You just made me spill my coffee. Over." I shimmy out of my cords and lay them over the platform's railing. The weather's been warm, so at least I won't be cold. The breeze glides against my bare skin, and something about talking to Cas half naked sends a spark between my legs.

"Stop it, Piper," I whisper to myself. "Get a grip."

Cas. "Are you okay?"

"I'm fine. Took my pants off."

Silence.

"I'd pay to see that."

"Caspian!" I laugh into my radio. His laugh comes through, deep but also airy, and he sounds like himself again.

"Sorry. I'm just bored," he says.

"Me too."

Father says no task is boring. That boredom comes from a place of ego and vanity.

I hold the radio close to my mouth. "Maybe we shouldn't say that."

"Say what?"

"That we're bored. It makes us sound ungrateful."

"We're just talking."

"But what if Father's listening? Or the Aunties?"

"Why would he listen?"

"To make sure we're doing our job."

"You're half naked and I just woke up from a nap. I'm pretty sure we've already failed whatever test he's making us take."

I wrap my arms around my bare legs, all the while wishing Cas were next to me. "Don't say that, Cas."

"I'll leave you alone, then."

"We can still talk, if you want to."

"I don't feel like talking anymore. But I'll check in later. Over and out."

A gust of wind tears through the trees, and I imagine it's what the ocean must sound like. Endless and powerful and filled with grace.

The deer stands alert, ears pricked.

And then she trots into the brush and is gone. I wonder what freedom like that feels like, running wherever you want to, whenever the urge strikes. She wanted to eat, and she ate. She wanted to explore the woods, and she did it. How many times have I acted without thinking, without calculating every possible action and reaction? Sometimes I'm so many steps ahead of where I am that the present moment doesn't feel real.

Resisting the urge to call Cas, I pour another lid of coffee and gulp it down. Sleep is what I need. Sleep, so I can get rid of these traitorous thoughts. Sleep, so I can regain Father's trust.

My eyes burn as I stare into the woods, waiting for the deer to return.

She never does.

24. AFTER

I've stopped bathing.

My nails collect the dirt.

My skin wears sweat like armor.

The woman says I need to stay clean, especially now that I've fractured my ankle. Amy pinches her nose and tells me I stink. But it's the one thing I can control. I will not make this easy for anyone.

"Jeannie says you aren't cleaning yourself," Dr. Lundhagen says at our next appointment. He steeples his pointer fingers and holds them against his lips.

"You talked about me? I thought these sessions were just between us."

"They are, Piper. She just voiced a concern to me."

"It's *my* body, isn't it? Or does she own that, too?"

He watches me for a moment.

"I'd like us to talk about your mother." The doctor clears his throat. "I think it would be healthy for you to talk about her, about any memories you have from before."

"*Before?*" I snap. The memories cascade, bubble and churn, falling over one another. I remember the day They pulled me from my home. I remember the night Caspian and I kissed for the first time. The night of my initiation, when everything changed.

He holds up a hand. "I don't mean to upset you, Piper," he says. "How about we talk about childhood memories instead. What's your earliest memory?"

My childhood.

There were always my parents, always the Community. I will guard my memories like organs, as vital and real as my heart or lungs or bones.

"How about a favorite memory? What comes to mind first?"

"Swimming," I answer, forgetting to censor myself.

"Oh? Tell me about that."

After a minute, I do. I want to remember something happy. "I was pretty young, I think. Mother took me to a swim class, and then we had ice cream at the park. She was so happy that day, just laughing and being silly. She even popped me in the nose with her ice-cream cone."

When I was little, Mother would read me *Pippi Longstocking* or *The Wizard of Oz* every night before bed, before she and Father moved away to the compound. She'd braid my hair, then hers. My eyes burn, and I dig my nails into my palms.

"That sounds lovely, Piper. Were you with Angela or Jeannie?"

The room turns gray, color draining from the walls like blood from an opened vein.

"You know my mother's name?"

He nods.

"What else do you know about them?"

"Their names are Curtis and Angela Blackwell, ages forty-one and forty."

"What else?"

He flips back a few pages in his notebook. "Curtis was born in Corona, California. His father was a minister in a small church. His mother was a homemaker. Angela was born in Minneapolis, Minnesota. Her parents owned a cereal manufacturing business."

Father and Mother have never discussed their parents with me. They didn't believe in the Community.

"Are my grandparents still alive?"

He shakes his head. "Curtis's father passed away from cancer two years ago; his mother took her own life when he was a young boy. Angela's parents have been gone about ten years. Her father died from cancer, her mother from heart disease."

I look down at the carpet. "I never knew any of that."

"Curtis and Angela kept a lot from you, Piper."

"They did what they thought was best," I say, keeping my voice even. I won't allow myself to fall into another one of his traps.

"Do you think they did their best?"

"Of course," I answer automatically.

"Do you remember a time when they perhaps didn't do their best?"

Father put us on a fast once, and I fainted. I hit my knee on a rock, and blood gushed from the cut. He was so proud of me for making such a sacrifice, but at the time, it felt like a punishment I didn't deserve.

"My parents are wonderful people."

"Even wonderful people make mistakes."

"Have you ever made a mistake with your kids?"

He chuckles. "Too many to count."

"Well, that's you. My parents are different. They're better."

"They're only human. No human is perfect. We all make mistakes, even them."

"I mean, sure, there were small things. But the big things, no. They didn't make big mistakes."

"Name a small thing they did wrong. Indulge me."

I play with a hole fraying in the knee of my jeans. "Okay, so this one time, Father put us on a fast. We didn't get much food, and I have these dizzy spells if I don't eat enough. I get what he was doing—trying to get us used to hunger in case that time ever came. Maybe…maybe he should have eased up some."

"He was being unfair."

"Maybe. A little. He's not a bad person. He just made a mistake, like you said."

✖

After our appointment ends, I collect my crutches and hobble into the hallway, shutting his door a little harder than I mean to. I lean against the wall. The muscles in my neck seize up, sending rockets of pain to my temples.

The truth, the truth that I will never tell any doctor, is that my childhood memories are grainy, and white, and fuzzy around the edges, and if I think about them too much…

…they disappear altogether.

What's happening to me?

When I get back to the woman's house, I refuse dinner and go into my room. It's taken on a sickly sweet smell now. I try opening the window again to air it out, but it still won't budge, as stuck as I am.

As I turn away from the latch, movement in the neighbor's house stops me.

It's the girl, framed in the same second-floor window.

Only this time she waves.

Just a lift of the arm, harmless and simple.

I raise my arm in return.

She's so far away, but it almost looks like she's smiling.

Her hand moves across the glass, and then she pulls down the shade.

She's written something on her window in bright red letters.

P-I-P-E-R.

✖

The woman's slurping a bowl of cereal when I limp past her, my foot in its walking boot.

"Where are you going?" she asks, and drops the spoon.

The front door opens. I don't look back.

Rounding the house, I hobble to the fence, putting as little weight as possible on my walking boot.

The girl is gone, but my name is still written on her window. It wasn't a dream.

My skin burns from the inside. I want to peel it away, to become someone else.

I turn in circles, looking for what, I don't know.

But then—there. There's a door on the ground, butted up against the house. One I don't remember seeing before.

Curiosity piqued, I approach it. Two handles. No lock, not like the shed.

It calls to me.

Look inside.

I grip one of the handles and pull.

It reveals a set of stairs leading into blackness.

The woman told me this house didn't have a basement.

She lied.

I open the other door, and a bit more light tumbles down the hole.

Father used to say that ghosts and devils only lived in the minds of the weak.

My legs shake as I descend. I place my hands on the stone walls next to me, afraid they'll collapse and bury me alive.

But they don't, and I make it to a dirt floor. The room smells of rot. It's dank, the air thick, and I can't breathe.

The same as my dream.

The doors fall shut, and I am entombed in darkness.

25. BEFORE

It starts with a missing pair of Mother's shoes.

Her fancy hairbrushes gone from the bathroom sink.

Then a drawer is emptied out.

When the toothbrushes disappear, we know.

They are leaving us again.

The little ones cling to Mother's legs, crying and begging her to stay. "I wish I could," she coos, covering Samuel's and Henry's faces with kisses. Beverly Jean openly weeps, and Cas hugs her. Millie strains to get out of my arms. Mother takes her, and she nuzzles into her neck. Carla skulks off by herself, looking at Mother every so often. Thomas wasn't at breakfast this morning, but Father and Mother don't seem concerned. He has the shelter-building to oversee, after all. Man's work.

Father motions for me. He stands near the limousine while the driver loads their bags. "When I return, we'll discuss your initiation. Until then, be diligent. Report anything strange to me, understood? No matter how small or innocent something may seem, I need to know about it."

I nod, and he disappears into the limo.

My initiation! My feet barely touch the ground now. I want to tell Cas, but somehow I don't think he'd want to hear about it.

And I *know* he won't want to hear about my impending marriage to Thomas. I don't even want to tell him. Not yet.

Mother tries to get away from the littles, and finally Cas has to peel Henry off her leg. She gives Millie to me, blows us one last kiss, and ducks into the limo.

We stand together, watching as the limo backs down the drive.

"She f-forgot to hug me," Beverly Jean cries, breaking the silence. She can't catch her breath and doubles over. I give Millie to Cas and drop down next to her.

"Deep breaths in and out," I coach, and soon her breathing slows. I kiss her forehead, cradle her in my arms like when she was a baby. "Mother loves you very much. I'm sorry she was so frazzled. She and Father have such busy schedules. She didn't mean to forget you, I promise. We'll write her a letter tonight, and after that we can play paper dolls if you want."

Everything should go back to normal now. Lessons, chores, games, and sports. Cas with his gardening, me taking care of Millie and the little ones. The Aunties bossing us around.

Except that nothing will go back to normal, because of the men Father left behind.

Even now, another truckload of them barrels up the drive, towing an enclosed trailer. When the transport stops, four men step out, all of them dressed in black, one with a pistol holstered to his chest.

"They're here to work on the shelter, nothing else," Auntie Joan hisses. "Don't pay them any attention. Now get moving. The breakfast dishes aren't going to wash themselves."

Beverly Jean wipes her nose on the back of her hand and does as she's told, as always. Carla glares at the men as they open the trailer and set to work pitching tents in the yard.

"How long do you think they'll be here for?" I whisper to Cas.

"No idea, but I hope it's not long. I don't have a good feeling about this."

As we walk side by side to the house, Thomas comes up the driveway, moving at a brisk clip, his hands shoved in his pockets.

"Where have you been?" Cas asks. "You missed breakfast."

Thomas brushes past us. "Don't worry about it," he says. "I had things to take care of." His eyes are bloodshot, and his cheeks are sunken in. I'm looking at a stranger, and I grab Cas's hand.

"Thomas, come on," Cas urges. "You can talk to us."

"No, I can't. Those men are watching us now," Thomas snaps. "That's why they're here."

"Who are they?" I ask.

"Men from the Community," he says. "Curtis's top soldiers. Now be quiet and pretend like everything's normal."

A clank rings out, and I turn around. It's the men, pounding tent stakes into the ground. Auntie Joan waits at the house door, tapping her foot on the step, and Thomas hushes us.

Father's directive to report anything unusual or disloyal blares in my head, but it's *Thomas*.

As we wash dishes, I find myself staring through the window at him as he works with the men, trying to puzzle him out. I think of all our Sunday night talks, and all the times he gave me extra food so I wouldn't feel sick. I could never betray him, but by keeping everything to myself—his lies about the compound, his contempt for these men, his waning faith in Father—I'm betraying Father.

And Father wants me to *marry* him.

As I watch the lake water lap the shore, and the men unroll large pieces of canvas, I am overcome with the realization that things are changing.

"Get drying," Auntie Barb says, tapping my shoulder.

"Sorry," I mutter, and keep working.

✖

That night, after we write the letter to Mother, I tuck my sisters into bed. I've just blown out the candle when whimpers drift from Carla's side of the room. I climb out and go over to her bed.

"Carla," I whisper. "What's wrong?"

She's a lump, hidden in covers. The top of her head pokes out, revealing just her eyes, but she won't speak.

"Come on, you can tell me."

"Lean closer," she whispers. Once my face is right up next to hers, she tells me what's wrong. "It was all over my underwear when I went to the bathroom."

"Oh, Carla," I say, and force her into a hug. "It'll be fine. Let's go into the bathroom.

She lets me hold her hand as we slip down the hallway to the bathroom we share with the boys. Carla takes off her pajama bottoms and underwear, and they're bright red. I pour some water into the sink from the jug we keep filled. "This will prevent a stain," I tell her, and proceed to rinsing and scrubbing her clothes.

"The Aunties will be mad at me."

"Forget about them. I'll do the laundry, and they'll never even know." I hang the underwear over the side of the sink. Then I wet a rag with water. "Wash yourself, and then I'll show you how to use a tampon."

"What's a tampon?"

"It's a small piece of cotton you put inside yourself to soak up all the blood. We don't have many, but maybe Thomas can get us more soon."

Her eyes open wide. "I can't stick something *up there*!"

I try not to smile, knowing it would mortify her. "Carla, it doesn't hurt, and it's so much cleaner than using cloth pads. Here, let me demonstrate." I open a tampon and pretend to insert it.

She grimaces. "I'm not looking forward to this."

"Well, get used to it. It's every month now."

She sighs. "Just one more thing we have to deal with that the boys don't. It's so unfair."

"Carla," I ask gently, "why didn't you tell me right away?"

"I don't know. Those men showed up, and I just got scared."

"I'm scared, too," I admit.

She looks at me. "You are?"

"I am."

She bites her bottom lip. "Do you really think there's going to be a war?"

Her face is earnest now, the usual scowl gone, and I'm reminded of when she was little like Millie. She'd follow me everywhere, to the bathroom, to watch TV, to go outside. She was my shadow, and then the others were born, and my attention went to them. It feels good to be able to focus on her again.

"I know that we're safe here. Even if there is a nuclear war, there's no way we'd be affected. Big cities maybe, but not us. So you don't need to worry, okay? Father's just being overly cautious.

That's what dads do. They worry, just like Mike from *The Brady Bunch*."

She nods, but I'm not sure she believes me.

I'm not sure I believe myself.

"Now, how about you try a tampon?"

She rolls her eyes.

26. AFTER

"Piper."

Someone grips my shoulder. Shakes it.

"Piper."

My eyes are glued shut. My hips ache from the hard, cold ground.

When I open my eyes, Mother stares down at me. Light from above encircles her.

"Oh my God," she says in a whir. She pulls me to a seated position. "Are you all right?"

"Mother? Where am I?"

"You're in the root cellar. What happened?"

"I wanted to see what was down here. That woman said she didn't have a basement."

Mother touches my cheek, but then her blue eyes turn brown. Her hair shrivels, darkens.

It's the woman.

I scramble backward on my hands and feet. "Where am I?"

"This is the root cellar. I keep my canning stuff down here." She uses a small black rectangle to light up the space; glass jars filled with vegetables line shelves. It doesn't look like the white room. "The doors blew shut. Happens sometimes. I found you lying on the ground. Did you faint?"

My eyes sting, and I take deep breaths. I blink, but it's still her.

Mother is gone.

"Come on," she insists. "We need to get you inside. Maybe to the doctor's office."

"No! No more doctors."

"Then at least come inside and let me fix you some soup. You're cold as ice."

✖

She makes me lie down on the couch and covers me with a blanket. Pots bang in the kitchen, and a few minutes later she brings me a bowl of steaming soup.

"It's chicken noodle."

I slurp the broth, and it warms my throat and belly. I begin to relax into the cushions as I eat. I hadn't realized how hungry I was, and soon the bowl is empty.

"I'm glad you've got an appetite." She refills the bowl. Father would warn me that she may have put something in it, but if she were trying to kill me, I think she would've done it by now. I take the second bowl.

Amy drifts into the room and climbs onto the opposite end of the couch. She slips her legs under the blanket. "You don't look at all how I remember you," she says.

My back tenses. "Have we met before, Amy? Before we got to this house?"

"Yep."

"Where were we? At the compound?"

She shrugs. "I can't remember. Can we watch a movie?"

I lean toward her and grab her small shoulders. "Amy, if we've met before, you have to tell me when and where. This is important, okay? Try to remember!"

133

"You're scaring me," she says, and I release her.

I lean back into the couch, defeated. "I'm sorry. Let's just watch a movie."

She pushes a bunch of buttons, and red fills the screen. "It's called Netflix," she says. "It's TV with cartoons and stuff." She chooses a cartoon I've never seen, about a fish and his son who get separated. The only cartoons we watched at home were *101 Dalmatians* and *Sleeping Beauty*. This one looks strangely lifelike.

At the end of the movie, Amy catches me wiping my eyes and frowns.

"It's just dust in my eye," I say.

27. AFTER

The next afternoon I have an "emergency" appointment with Dr. Lundhagen.

He smiles as I shimmy out of my jean jacket and lay it across my lap. "How are you feeling today?"

"Same as always."

"And what does 'the same' mean? How do you always feel?"

I bristle. "I feel fine."

He writes in his notebook. "Jeannie said you had an episode yesterday. She found you passed out in the cellar. Is that right?"

"I was just disoriented. From the darkness. It was no big deal."

"She said you thought she was Angela?"

"Like I said, it was really dark. And I was tired."

"Do you confuse Jeannie and Angela often?"

"I miss Mother," I say. "What's so wrong with that?"

"Have you been having any other confusing thoughts? Maybe thoughts of harming yourself?"

This question pushes me back in my chair. "Harming myself?"

"It's perfectly normal in your situation and nothing to be ashamed of."

My situation.

I take a deep breath. "Of course not," I tell him. And it's the truth.

They have done this to me. Why should I make things easier on them? If They want me dead, They'll have to bloody their own hands.

"Good, good," he says. "I've been thinking, though, that medication might be appropriate at this time."

"Medication?"

Jeannie has tried giving me headache medicine and sleeping pills, but I won't take them. I don't want my edges dulled.

"An antidepressant. I would start you at a small dose, and we can adjust the dosage if need be."

"I don't want to be on any medication."

"I'm worried, Piper, about your state of mind. You've been through so much, too much, and you're not progressing as I'd have hoped."

Progressing, he calls it.

"You want me to become a zombie, to accept the lies They feed me. I don't want to be on pills. Maybe if I wasn't *stolen from my family*, I wouldn't be so sad. I wouldn't need to be fixed."

"I understand," he says. "It can be scary to start a medication." He touches his top lip with his pointer finger. "But there's no shame in taking a medication. If you had diabetes, you'd take insulin, right?"

"No," I say. "Western medicine is filled with poisons."

"Is that what Curtis Blackwell taught you?"

"Yes."

"He couldn't be more wrong, Piper. Insulin saves millions of lives every year. And for people with anxiety and depression, antidepressants can also be life saving. I would start you on an SSRI, which is a selective serotonin reuptake inhibitor. Serotonin is a chemical in the brain that helps carry signals between brain cells.

Sometimes our brains reabsorb too much of the serotonin, which messes with those signals. An SSRI makes more serotonin available. Your thoughts become clearer. Does that make sense?"

"It sounds like propaganda made up by the pharmaceutical companies to sell more drugs to people who don't need them."

"How's this. We'll start at just ten milligrams a day. That's a tiny dose, Piper. It might help you feel better, more clearheaded. Combined with our continued sessions together, I think it will do you a world of good."

A good girl would agree. She would swallow the pills along with the lies.

"I want you to know that there's no shame in taking an anti-depressant, or any other kind of medication. It's no different than taking antibiotics for an ear infection. This is sound medical advice, Piper. I went to medical school. Curtis didn't."

He plucks a notepad from his desk and scribbles on it. Apparently I get no say in what I put into my body.

Not that They've ever given me a choice.

As he writes, I notice the potted plant is gone. I can't breathe for a second. "Where'd the plant go?"

"It was dying," he says. "I don't have much of a green thumb, I'm afraid."

"But it *was* here, right?"

"Yes, I had it for about two years. I bought it right after my mother died. Why?"

I pause, unsure if I should admit this. "Sometimes I have trouble keeping track of days, of time." He waits, not interjecting or offering hollow reassurances like Jeannie does. "I don't trust my own judgment anymore."

"Have you always felt that way? Or just lately?"

I chew the cuticle around my thumb. "It comes and goes. And not…not just lately."

"It comes and goes? How so?"

"Like when I couldn't find my favorite pink swim cap a few years ago. Mother gave me a new one, and she was so excited that it was just like the old one. But it wasn't. My favorite was all pink. The one she gave me had daisies on it."

"Did you correct her?"

"She was too happy. I didn't want to hurt her feelings."

"But you could sense that something wasn't right."

"Sort of."

"Did you feel that way often with your family?"

I hesitate. "Sometimes."

"Can you think of another example?"

In one of my earliest memories, Mother, Father, and I were driving in a car. Mother sang along to the radio. Father drove. I think we stayed at a hotel or with relatives. I remember Mother cutting my hair short and dying it brown. I hated it and wouldn't stop crying.

"Whenever I reminded my parents of this horrible haircut they gave me when I was little, they told me it wasn't true. That it never happened. That I probably saw it on a TV show. But I can remember the way the hair dye smelled. It seemed so real."

Dr. Lundhagen sets down his pen. "Where are you right now?"

"In your office."

"What's your name?"

"Piper Blackwell."

"What color is my shirt?"

I smile. "Baby blue."

"So you see what I'm doing. You're not unreliable, Piper. It's okay to trust what's right in front of you."

"But what about my memories?"

"Memory is a tricky thing," he says. "The human mind is notorious for its faulty memory. Ask ten witnesses to a crime what happened, and you'll receive ten different accounts. I like to tell my patients that memory isn't very reliable when it comes to the little details. Sometimes our brains even patch together several different memories. But the *feeling* a memory gives you, that's what you can count on. *That's* what's true. If you remember receiving that haircut, the smell, the feeling of disliking it, then trust that it happened."

I take a deep breath and lean back into the chair. It's like there's static in my brain.

"What are you thinking about?" Dr. Lundhagen crosses his legs, and one of his pant legs rides up to reveal pink argyle socks.

"You're wearing pink socks," I say.

He looks down and smiles. "It appears I am."

"Don't you think that's weird, being a man and all? Isn't pink a feminine color?"

"What do you think?"

"Father and Mother always brought dark clothes for the boys. Black, blue, brown. They said boys should never wear bright colors."

"Why do you think that is?"

"I thought you were the shrink? Aren't you supposed to have all the answers?"

He shakes his head. "You know that's not how this works, Piper. I'm here to help you find the answers, not give them. I know that's probably very different from the way Curtis and Angela raised you. I'm here to help you learn to think for yourself."

I let my gaze move about his office. A framed photo of a cat sits on the top of his cluttered bookshelf. "Is that your cat?"

"Ralphie." He takes down the photo and hands it to me. "My daughters picked him out when they were in grade school. There was a whole litter of kittens, all climbing over one another for attention. Ralphie stayed off in the corner by himself, nervous. Molly pointed to him and said, 'That's our cat!' He passed away a couple of years ago, but we still keep photos of him all over the house."

Ralphie stares out from the photo with green eyes the color of seaweed and fur as dark as Caspian's hair.

"I had a kitten once," I say.

"Tell me about it."

"Well, she was only mine for a day. I found her alone in the woods near our house. She was starving, and Caspian and I tried to feed her, but she wouldn't take anything. It was too late."

"Too late how?"

I look at the doctor. "She died in my arms."

"I'm sorry, Piper," he says, his voice soft. "That must've been very hard."

"It was just a kitten, right?" I feel tears in my eyes. "Besides, Father didn't allow pets. He said they're a distraction. It was stupid of me."

"Curtis didn't like animals, and yet you tried to save one anyway. Why do you think you went against his wishes?"

"Because she was so small and alone. I couldn't stand the thought of just leaving her in the woods, wondering where her mother was. Wondering what she'd done wrong." My throat feels thick, and the more I try not to cry, the more it hurts. "I had to protect her."

"You had empathy for the kitten?"

"I did."

"And you chose your empathy over Curtis's opinion that pets are a waste of time."

Over Father's opinion.

"Yeah. I guess I did."

"How did that make you feel?"

"Disappointed? Because he was right. If I'd left well enough alone, I never would have felt so sad when she died."

"How do you think you might have felt if you had left her out in the woods to die alone?"

The answer comes to me easily, but I'm still surprised. "I would never have forgiven myself."

"So would you say trying to save the kitten was worth the heartache? Was thinking for yourself and using your empathy worth it?"

"Maybe. I don't know. I guess it was." I bite a hangnail on my thumb. "Were you heartbroken when Ralphie died?"

He nods. "We all were. My wife pulled out every photo we had of Ralphie, and the four of us sat around the dining room table, telling stories about him late into the night."

"But was loving him worth the pain of losing him?"

"Absolutely. We gave Ralphie a wonderful life filled with lots of love, and he gave us unconditional love back. Well, sometimes it was conditional. Cats are funny that way."

I wipe at my eyes. "Sorry, I shouldn't be crying. I'm such a goon."

"Says who?"

"Father."

"What does Piper say?"

I let the tears fall freely as I think of the kitten's soft, warm head, her pink nose, her shrunken little body. "I would say it's okay to cry when you're sad. That there's no shame in that. Is that right?"

"Do you think it's right?"

"I do."

Dr. Lundhagen twists in his chair and sets his notebook on his desk. Then he leans toward me. "I'm really proud of you, Piper. It might not feel like it, but you just took a huge step today."

"A huge step toward what?" I ask, tensing.

"Toward getting to know who you are and what you want apart from anyone else's influence. That's not easy for *anyone*. We all want to please our parents, our friends, our teachers. It's easy to adopt someone else's belief system as your own without even realizing it. You're building your own belief system now. How does it feel?"

Father's warnings about chemicals and nuclear war slip under the door, dissolving along the floor like mist. I take a deep breath. "Scary," I say. "But also…also kind of"—the word hits me, a total shock—"freeing. Is that how it's supposed to feel?"

"What do you think?"

I smile. "I think you're driving me a little nuts, but maybe I get what you're trying to tell me. My feelings are mine, and they're okay. Is that what you want me to learn?"

He returns the smile. "Exactly."

28. BEFORE

It's been weeks since our tutor came to the house. The books Father wrote for us to study gather dust. We haven't watched anything, haven't made dessert, haven't caught frogs.

We've been helping Thomas and the men build the fallout shelter.

The men work all day, breaking only for lunch. They're around Father's age, all of them lean and muscled.

So far they've dug a large hole in the ground, about twenty feet by twenty feet, and at least ten feet down. They hacked apart half our garden. I wanted to scream at them to stop, but I know Father ordered them to do it. I have to trust in his reasons, even if I can't see his plan all the way yet.

Most nights the men sleep in their tents, but sometimes they're gone from dusk to dawn. No one knows where they go or why when they disappear into the woods.

We know better than to ask.

Cas, Carla, and I spend our mornings carrying cement blocks from a pallet to the hole. Thomas and the men lower them down one by one as they build the shelter's walls. Thomas says a cement truck is scheduled for the day after tomorrow, and that we need to hurry.

The little ones play like always, but they watch us with worried glances. Beverly Jean's nightmares have flared up again, the one where the house is on fire and no one can get out in time. It's been so long since they plagued her. Most nights, she climbs into bed with me.

"Lunch!" Auntie Joan yells out the kitchen window.

I wipe my face with my shirt, and it comes away smudged with sweat and dirt. I want to sneak off for a quick dip in the lake, but my eyes drift to Cas, and I'm embarrassed all over again.

Inside, Auntie Joan and Auntie Barb have made two plates of bologna sandwiches. The men take most of them. After I hand out what remains to the little ones, there's not enough left for me, Cas, and Thomas.

"I'll make a few more," I offer, but Auntie Barb grabs my wrist as I open the icebox.

"Food's tight right now," she says, her grip like iron. "I'm under strict orders to ration it out."

I jerk my arm away; red marks bloom on my wrist. "But those men took two apiece."

"They're working for the good of us all." She wipes a bit of mustard from the corner of her mouth. "A couple of crates of fruit arrived last night from the main compound. You can eat that. But you leave that garden alone!"

Thomas stares at Auntie Barb, balls his hands into fists, and shoves past her out the back door.

Cas and I follow. My stomach feels hollow, hunger cauterizing it, and I sit on the bottom step and drop my head between my legs.

"Dizzy?" Cas asks.

144

I nod. It's because I haven't eaten for a few hours. Lately, that's been happening more often.

Beverly Jean sits next to me. "Here, Pip. Eat mine." She's only taken a couple of small bites of her sandwich.

I push it away.

"That's yours. You need it. I'll be fine."

Thomas jogs over. "I found an apple that's not too bruised."

He's being generous, because the apple is far from pristine, but it makes Beverly Jean feel better. I eat it all, the rotten bits, too, telling myself there will be more for supper. Then I drink down a huge glass of water and start to feel better.

One of the men throws a piece of crust onto the ground, and it takes every bit of self-control I have not to bark at him that he's wasteful, that there are hungry children here, that nothing should be thrown out. Thomas must have the same idea. He takes off, trampling Mother's daisies—but instead of chewing the man out, he picks up the crust, blows it off, and brings it to me.

"Hurry, eat this before they see you."

You and Thomas are a perfect match.

I shove the bread in my mouth and chew, grateful. It helps a little.

"Break's over!" Thomas shouts at the men.

We resume our positions, but my strength is already fading. That little bit of food won't last me all afternoon, so I move slowly to conserve energy.

"Are you okay?" Cas whispers. He and Thomas watch me.

I nod, afraid the men will notice.

"Pick up the pace," one of the men tells me. I try to heave a block into his arms, but I lose my footing. The block tumbles into the dirt, and he jumps away before it lands on his foot.

"She needs more food!" I hear Thomas saying. I keep my head down, trying to make the ground stop spinning; Caspian helps me sit, and I lean against him.

"We're rationing, Thomas," the man says. "What do you want me to do about it?"

"We can all give her some of our share."

"No. You can take it up with Curtis," the man says.

"Curtis put me in charge, and I say she gets more food."

"In charge of *construction*, not rationing. What's with you today, Tommy? You on the rag or something?" The men laugh. "Listen. Curtis said no one gets any special treatment on this project."

Thomas drops down next to me. "Sorry, Piper," he murmurs. "I'll give you more of my share tonight."

"So will I," Cas says.

The men keep working as we sit there, and I know Thomas and Cas will get in trouble if they don't stand up and help. But I can't seem to let go of them.

One of the men cracks his neck. "We really *could* use some more food. Did the trust fund run out or something?" he asks the others.

"Quiet," someone says, nodding our way. The man puts on his hat and gets back to work.

"Rest until you're feeling better," Thomas tells me. "I'll explain to Curtis if I need to."

"Thank you, Thomas," I say as he gets up and wipes the dirt off his pants.

"Piper. Let's sneak into the woods tonight, just you and me," Caspian whispers into my ear. "If you're feeling better, I mean. I've

146

got a surprise for you, and I think you're really gonna like it. It'll cheer us up." He swallows. "What do you say?"

My heart skips, and I remember Mother's warning.

But it's been so long since we've had any fun around here.

"I'm in," I say, hoping I'm not making a huge mistake.

A part of me doesn't care if I am.

29. BEFORE

My skin flushes every time I think of being alone with Caspian in the dark.

Lights-out was hours ago, but I lay in bed fully dressed, unable to close my eyes. Cas said he'd come get me when it was safe to show me my surprise.

Whimpering trails in from the hallway. At first I think it's Carla with more period troubles, but she's snoring in her bed. When I open the door, Henry lays curled up on the floor, tears streaking down his small face.

"What's wrong, Henry?" I whisper, gathering him into me.

"I wet my bed."

"It'll be fine, buddy. I'll get you all cleaned up." We tip-toe to the hall bathroom, stepping around spots we know will squeak and wake the Aunties. They don't tolerate bedwetting. I help him change into new underwear and pajamas, change his bedding, and tuck him back in. Cas's and Thomas's beds are empty. Thomas took watch alone tonight—he refused to let Carla help.

"Sleep well," I say, and kiss his forehead. "I love you, Henry."

He looks up at me. "Am I in trouble?"

"For what? Wetting the bed?"

"Yeah." His soft voice quivers, and I lean down and hold him against me. "You are not in any trouble, little buddy. It's okay. I'll keep you safe. Always."

I hold him for a while, rubbing his back, until he starts to snore. Then I carefully lay him down and pull up his covers. I kiss his hair, and breathe in deeply. He smells like soap and little boy.

I gather the soiled sheet and sneak outside to the back of the house where we keep our wash shed. I fill a wash tub with water from the pump and add a small amount of soap, enough to get the sheets clean but not so much the Aunties will notice the level in the box has gone down. I put the sheets into the water and swirl them around until it bubbles. Then I scrub them against the ridges of the washboard, up and down. The rhythm calms me. I should use hot water, but I'm too tired to boil any.

As I'm hanging them on the line, the rustling of footsteps makes me drop a clothespin.

"What's going on?" Cas asks, appearing out of the trees' shadows.

"You scared me!" I whisper, wrapping my arms around myself. "Henry wet the bed. I got him all fixed up."

"I have that surprise for you, remember? Do you still want to see it?"

I glance at the dark windows, waiting for Auntie Barb or Auntie Joan to come up the basement steps and catch us out of bed. We have a curfew, though they haven't been too strict about enforcing it lately.

"Maybe we should skip it for tonight. Henry might need us."

Cas's face falls. "Okay, I understand. Maybe another time."

He moves toward the side of the house, and something propels me toward him. I grab his hand, my silent consent. His smile rivals the moon.

We move quickly around the house, away from the men's tents, and head deep into the woods toward the bumper cars.

There, a large white sheet hangs between two saplings. Our parents' old movie projector sits on an overturned cardboard box in front of it, powered by a portable generator. The perimeter fence is visible just beyond the projector, but I try not to look at it—the Outside is beyond, full of toxins.

"Since we're not allowed to go into town to see a movie, I brought the theater to you."

"Seriously, Cas? This is too much." I don't ask why he *wants* to go to town.

"I feel bad for what happened that day at the lake—the way Angela yelled at you, like you'd done something wrong. You didn't." He pushes his rumpled hair off his forehead. "And I'm sorry I've been kind of weird lately. I get so mad at my brother, at Curtis, at everyone. But I shouldn't take it out on you. You don't deserve that."

I smile.

"So, do you want to watch it? I got popcorn." He produces a plastic container full of popcorn from his bag, a luxury I haven't seen since I was a little girl.

I shove some of it into my mouth, grateful for food. "How'd you get this?" The buttery crunch melts on my tongue.

"I have my ways."

I shoot him a look. "Please tell me you didn't steal this from the Aunties' cupboard."

"Don't worry about it, Piper. Just please try to have some fun." He pulls two hourglass bottles of Coke out of his bag, too, and gives one to me.

"What are we watching?" I twist open my soda.

"I know you really like horror movies."

"And you don't," I remind him. "I made you watch *Psycho*, and you kept your eyes closed through most of it. Remember?"

"Tonight's not about me," he says. "We're watching *Night of the Living Dead*. It's the only other movie I could find that's really scary." He climbs into the lime-green bumper car directly in front of the makeshift screen, and I climb in next to him. Our shoulders touch, and everything inside me screams to leave, to run away, to do what Father and Mother would expect.

But I don't want to.

I stare at my lap. "You didn't have to do all this."

"Of course I did."

"I love it, Cas. Thank you."

He takes a deep breath. "I think about you a lot, Piper. I worry about you."

My heart ticks, and I'm afraid to move. He reaches for my hand; his is warm and strong. "I'm not happy unless I'm with you," he says, in a rush. "I walk around this place, and everything is black and white. Until I see you. It's like I can't see in color without you. You're the only good, true thing in this whole damn place. Nothing matters but you, Piper. You and Thomas and the others. Not the Aunts. Not even Angela and Curtis."

I bite my bottom lip, trying not to cry.

"Was I wrong to say all of that?" he asks quietly.

"I don't know. Father probably wouldn't like this."

"Good thing he's not around much."

Cas leans toward me, angles my chin, and our lips meet. His are warm and soft, a little salty from the popcorn. I keep my eyes open, but his close. His lashes fan out on his cheeks like spider's legs, delicate and frightening at the same time.

Then I close my eyes, and he parts my lips with his tongue.

Electric.

With my vision gone, our kiss intensifies, heightened by the only sense I have that matters, that will ever matter again after this moment. My skin prickles in goose bumps, my heartbeat so loud I'm sure he can hear it.

"You're my first," I whisper, and rest my forehead against his.

"First what?"

"Kiss."

"Mine, too." He wraps his arm around my shoulders and pulls me close, flicking on the projector.

Currents dance off my body.

Crickets play their summer symphony, and lightning bugs wink on and off around us. He kisses me again, hungrier this time, greedy.

This kiss feels worlds different from the first one. Maybe that's the thing about second kisses—they're intentional. A first kiss can be a fluke. But this, this is something real. I feel it in the darts of electricity that shoot everywhere, but also in how safe I feel with his lips against mine. Like I'm home, more home than I've ever been before. I move onto his lap and mourn all the days and nights we've spent together not doing this, not touching, not knowing.

I think I've always wanted Caspian this way. I just couldn't admit it to myself.

Now that I know, I can never go back.

Caspian runs his hands up my arms and takes the band off my ponytail. My hair falls about my shoulders, and he combs his fingers through it, curling a strand around a finger and touching it to his lips. He slips a hand under the bottom of my T-shirt and tickles my stomach, right where my scar runs.

The guilt runs a single finger down my spine.

"Maybe we shouldn't do this," I whisper.

"Why not? You don't want to?"

"Father says it's a distraction. It makes us weak, Cas. We can't be weak."

"Touching you makes me feel stronger than I've ever felt." He takes my hand and kisses my inner wrist. The heat of his lips on my skin quiets all the doubts; it answers a question I didn't know I'd been asking.

"Me too," I say, my voice shaking. I lean down to kiss him, but he pulls back slightly.

"I'm in love with you, Piper," he says, locking eyes with mine. "I think I've loved you from the first time I saw you."

Tears sting my eyes, and I bite my bottom lip. It's all too much—and yet somehow not enough.

I want to be seen.

"I'm in love with you, too, Caspian."

And then it's happening, his skin against my skin, all the fear and pain from the past few weeks melting away. "Is this okay?" he asks, breathless.

"Yes. It's more than okay."

His body is warm and hard as he kisses my neck, my breasts, all of me. "You're beautiful," he says, and tonight I believe him.

Tonight I am free.

✖

We lie together for a while, his chest rising and falling with each breath. I can hardly believe what just happened between us and am glad for the dark; I wouldn't have had the guts in the daylight. Shame prowls around the bumper car like a hungry tiger, and I snuggle in closer to him, to his safety.

"Aren't the stars extra beautiful tonight?" I ask. Their light peeks through the leafy canopy above us. "When I was little, I used to think the stars were broken."

Cas laughs. "Why would you think that?"

"Because they kept blinking. I thought they were light bulbs about to burn out."

He takes a deep breath and strokes my hair. "How do you feel? Are you okay?"

I smile to myself. "I feel fine. Better than fine."

"Sometimes I think we should run away together," he says. "Start a new life somewhere else. Someplace better than here."

"We can't leave the Community, Cas. It's not safe out there."

"There's more to life than this place. I've seen it."

"If we left it would destroy Father and Mother and the little ones. I can't imagine what it would do to Beverly Jean."

"Children grow up and leave home," he says. "That's how life works."

"That's not how *our* life works. Besides, Father says I'm ready to be initiated."

"He did?" he asks, alarmed. "When?"

"Right before he and Mother left."

"Why didn't you tell me?"

I shrug. "I felt bad that it was only me, and not you with me." I don't dare mention Father's plan for Thomas and me to marry.

"But is that what *you* want? Have you thought about your future?"

"It's all I think about, Caspian. I want to be initiated into the Community and help make the world a better place. With you by my side. Can you think of a future more important than that?"

He ignores my question. "If we left, we could look for colleges. I bet you'd be a great teacher—you're so patient with the little ones."

"Teacher? Like our tutors?"

"Sort of, only you'd teach at a real school. You'd have your own classroom, and the students would show up every day. They'd sit in desks and do homework and take tests. You could take them on field trips to a zoo or a museum."

It's hard to imagine having anything that's mine, let alone a whole room where I can teach children. I've seen schools in TV shows, but I don't fully understand them. I want to ask Caspian where we'd sleep inside the school, but I don't want to sound stupid.

"Pretend you could do anything you wanted, for a whole day. What would you do?" he asks.

"I would go swimming and eat ice cream and kiss you."

He kisses me. "We could do all that every day if we left. We could do anything. *Everything*."

"Quit saying that. We can't leave, and you know it."

He sighs. "I know."

I want to tell him about Father's plan for me and Thomas, but I'm afraid.

Afraid of what Father would do if he found out I told. Afraid that I'm tainted now, unfit to join the Community. Afraid of Cas's reaction.

Afraid of ruining this night.

We watch the end of the movie wrapped up together. Black-and-white zombies break into a farmhouse and kill everyone inside. I think of the fallout shelter, and Father's warnings about nuclear war. It feels like we're in the farmhouse, and the Outside is full of the dead.

30. AFTER

All those nights spent up on the roller coaster, watching every leaf, every corner, every dark shadow, has prepared me for this. I miss nothing. I am vigilant.

They can't take away Father's lessons.

It's been days since the girl wrote my name on her window. I watch for her every night. I'm a ghost in a reality of my own making: Nothing exists but the window and the possibility that she might appear again.

When morning comes, I fade away.

It's dark. The house is silent; everyone else is asleep. Silent except for Daisy, who's snoring on my bed.

But I wait. And I watch.

Eventually, my eyes grow dry from not blinking, and I go into the bathroom for drops.

When I return to my perch, something moves in the girl's window, a human shape, and I'm down the stairs and outside before I consider how dangerous it might be.

The gate is locked, so I creep along the fence, pretending I am made of air, soundless, weightless.

The knot in the wood is right where I left it, rough and decayed. When I put my eye up to it, there's no one on the other side.

I push against the board with my hands, and it flexes. The bottom of the fence has started to rot, black with dirt and mold. I kick the bottom with my good foot, and the wood snaps off.

Easy.

A few more kicks and I've created a space big enough to wriggle through. Digging my forearms into the dirt, I half crawl, half slide through the fence. I wipe myself off and rise up to survey my surroundings.

The grass is mostly dead. Leaves float atop a fancy swimming pool, curled up and aimless. A lawn chair has been overturned. A drinking glass lies broken on the ground, next to a paperback with wet pages.

The deck's sliding door is ajar, and I move toward it, keeping my steps light. A cat meows from somewhere inside the house.

"Piper?" A voice comes from right behind me. "Is that you?"

Slowly, I turn.

It's the girl.

She has dark hair, large brown eyes, and brown skin. Dressed in a yellow velvet dress, she takes a drag off a cigarette. The end glows red in the dark.

"Are you okay?" she asks. "It's kind of late to be over here."

"Are you the girl from the window?" I ask, barely able to get the words out. My head spins.

"I am." She sticks out her hand. "I'm Holliday."

Hesitantly, I shake her hand. Mine is sweaty, and I'm sure I smell. I still haven't been cleaning myself. "Piper. But I guess you already knew that." I can't keep some suspicion out of my voice. I need her help, but can I trust her?

"Yeah. You're the only other girl my age in the neighborhood, so I wanted to meet you. But you never leave your house, so I wrote your name in my window. Sorry if that was kind of creepy." She points at my walking boot. "What happened?"

"I broke my ankle."

"How?"

"Trying to escape my psychiatrist's office."

"Oh, for real?" She smiles, drops her cigarette, and stomps it with one of her black ankle boots. Then she smooths her hair, which is braided all over. "Why'd you break into my yard at this hour? Not that I'm complaining. I couldn't sleep anyway."

I chew my thumbnail, but Mother's voice blares in my head, and I stop. "I don't know. You're the one who invited me."

"True." She gives me a half smile. "Well, I'm glad you finally came over. How do you like living with Jeannie? Is she going to let you go to school soon?"

"How do you know her name?" I can hear my heart beating in my ears, and I try to take some deep breaths.

"We've been neighbors for a long time. Since I was little."

I can't shake the familiarity of her eyes, her voice. "Have we met before? I feel like we have."

"We were sorta friends a long time ago. When we were really little."

"How old were we?" I ask, trying to comb through my mental file of people I've known, places I've been. She isn't there.

"Young, like first grade. A long time ago. Do you remember me at all?"

"No. Did I…did I come to this house?"

Holliday nods and picks up the overturned lawn chair. "Wanna smoke with me?"

"Wait. You said I…" I want to ask the question again, but the words die on my tongue. Instead I say, "I don't smoke."

I want to ask her if I can sneak through her house, leave by the front door, disappear onto the road. But without a plan and money, running won't get me far.

And I don't know yet if it's even safe to ask her to help me.

"That's wise," she says. "I should quit." She lights up another. "My parents would kill me if they caught me. But honestly, it calms my nerves—or I like to pretend it does. I signed up for too many AP classes this semester and haven't been sleeping so well."

"You and me both."

"A couple of insomniacs, eh? I think we can build a friendship on that." She smiles, but then she cranes her neck to look around me. "Shit. Jeannie's at the fence." Holliday quickly puts out her cigarette. "I gotta go." She hurries inside, shuts the patio door, and closes the curtains.

"Wait!" I shout, but it's too late.

She's gone.

The woman stands on the other side of my makeshift hole; only her legs are visible. "Piper?" she calls out. "Are you over there?"

I wriggle back under the fence.

"Piper?" she gasps. And then she loses it. "It's the middle of the night! What are you doing breaking into the neighbor's yard?" She has never raised her voice before. "What were you thinking? You scared me half to death!"

This is rich, coming from her.

"I was only in the next yard," I offer.

"You know," she says, looking at me, "I've tried to be patient. I've tried to be understanding and listen to the doctors. But now you're putting yourself at risk. What were you planning to do? Run away? To where?"

I shrug. She doesn't mention Holliday.

"Answer me, please!"

"I needed a minute to myself."

A vein pulses in her neck. This is the first time she's let her mask of niceness slip. She ages as she sweats. Lines and wrinkles settle in.

A gust of wind hits us, and she tightens her robe.

"Please go inside. Now."

I've seen that look before, from Father. I do as I'm told.

Inside, the woman flicks on the lights. Her face turns pale again, and her voice lowers to its usual monotone. "Are you hungry? I can make you a midnight snack. How about some strawberry toast? My jam won a blue ribbon, you know."

A *fucking* snack?

"No." I turn and rush to my room, to the only safe place I have, that isn't safe at all.

The door shuts.

I'm bathed in sweat. This could be anyone's room. If I died tomorrow, there would be no sign that I was here.

I have to leave a record, something to prove I existed.

Rifling through the desk, I pull out pens and markers and a pencil that looks like a pen. I click on the top to make more lead come out.

I miss the sharpener at home, and the way my newly sharpened pencils smelled.

The motion of cranking the handle.

The feel of something dull becoming sharp and useful.

I grab a pen and draw my home on the wall: the garden, the lake, the woods. The pen eats into the paint, slicing through layers as I bring the house to life, a love letter to my family.

When it's finished, I move into the closet, push apart the clothes, and write my name on the back wall.

> *My name is Piper Rose Blackwell. My mother's name is Angela. My father's name is Curtis. We live at an old amusement park somewhere in Northern California. I am being held here against my will. Someone help me. Please.*

When I fire the pen across the room, it smacks the wall and lands on the floor.

No one will ever read my note.

No one will ever see my drawing.

"The pen is mightier than the sword," Father would tell me. *"But only if your opponent can read."*

I sit cross-legged on the floor and write my name on the wall. I write again and again. Somehow, the world will know I was here.

> *Piper Blackwell.*
> *Piper Blackwell.*
> *Piper Blackwell.*

I write until my hand cramps, until the pen falls from my useless fingers, until my name becomes a mash of lines and squiggles that have no meaning at all.

31. BEFORE

A stolen smile.

The brush of Caspian's elbow against mine.

Everything has become heightened since our night under the broken stars. I don't even mind working on the fallout shelter. It means we get to stay close all day, every day.

He hands me a brick, and his finger dances across mine.

Invisible sparks rain down.

But then Father's face flashes before my eyes, the sight of Mother's hand raised to slap Caspian, and the guilt makes my skin itch from the inside. I touch my lips, sure everyone can tell what I've done. But no one pays me any attention, except for Cas.

"Hurry up, you two," one of the men says, the one who dropped the sandwich crust. He always keeps one eye on Thomas, though I can't understand why. Thomas is supposed to be in charge.

Carla hauls over a jug of water and some paper cups, and we each have a drink. The little ones are inside with the Aunties.

"Break's over," the man says, throwing his cup on the grass.

"But I'm tired," Carla whines.

"We're all tired," he snaps. "But that's life. We've all got to do our part, understand?"

Thomas puffs out his chest. "Don't speak to her that way."

The bigger guy, the one with the side pistol, steps closer to Thomas. "Enough. We're all trying to get this thing built without any trouble."

"Sorry," Carla mumbles, and Thomas's anger melts away. He pulls her into a hug, shielding her from them.

The front door slams, and Auntie Joan comes running down the lawn. "They're coming!" she huffs, flailing her arms. When she gets to us, she puts her hands on her knees, wheezing.

"Who's coming?" I ask, frightened.

"Your parents. They're only ten minutes out." She takes deep breaths, and I pour her some water. She actually says thank you, which is a nice surprise.

"Did you know they were coming?" Caspian asks.

Auntie Joan shoots him a look. "Of course not! And we let the children play all morning in their pajamas." She snaps her fingers at me. "Come on, help me get them dressed."

Father won't care if the littles aren't dressed, but it will upset Mother. We race inside, and Carla and I wrangle them into their burgundy outfits. I try running a brush through Millie's hair, but it's too fine and full of knots. Everyone's blond hair has started to grow out, but there isn't any time for bleaching today.

"They're coming? Really?" Beverly Jean ties on her sash and smooths her hair with water.

I try to smile. "They really are."

It's not like them to show up unannounced, and my hands shake as I fix Millie's sash.

By the time we get outside, the limousine is already parked in the drive. Auntie Barb and Auntie Joan wear tense smiles. Father and the men converge on the shelter, admiring the completed interior walls and the staircase we started yesterday.

Mother steps onto the lawn, dressed in a blush-rose sun dress and gold heels. Henry, Samuel, Beverly Jean, and Millie race toward her, same as always. I hope she doesn't notice their hair, or the wrinkles in their outfits.

"My darlings!" she says as they topple onto her lap. She sits on the ground, letting her dress get dirty. I love that about her.

"What do you think's going on?" Caspian whispers into my ear. His breath is warm on my skin, and I forget how to speak for a minute.

"I-I don't know," I stammer.

Thomas sits at the picnic table, apart from everyone, a scowl on his face. His eyes are fixed on Father.

Cas nudges me with his shoulder. "Let's go swimming later. At our secret spot."

Heat floods my neck and face. "Someone will see us," I say under my breath. "Father's back."

"I can't stop thinking about you."

"I know. I can't stop thinking about you either." I grow brazen and brush my pinky finger against his.

Dangerous.

"Piper."

It's Father, standing in front of us, materialized out of thin air. I jerk away from Caspian.

"It's time," he says.

"Time for what?"

"For your initiation into the Community."

Thomas leaves the table and storms off toward the beach.

"Are you ready?" Father asks.

We've been so busy building the shelter, and then my night with Cas. I haven't given initiation much thought lately, although I should have been.

But I won't let Father down.

"I am," I say, and Father gives me one of his rare smiles. It's like a secret only I know.

32. BEFORE

Today is not a day for dreaming.

It's not a day to kiss a boy in the sunshine, or to touch his skin.

It's not a day to pile secrets on top of secrets.

Still, I find myself taking Cas's outstretched hand, running alongside him as we slip away to our secret spot by the lake. I know it's foolish. I know it's a risk. But the house is bustling with activity in preparation for my initiation, and the chaos works to our advantage.

"What did Thomas say happens exactly during initiation?" I ask, trying to catch my breath. He's been having hushed conversations with Father and the men all day, and I haven't had a chance to speak with him.

Cas stands on the shore, trying to skip rocks. So far all he's landing are clunkers. "He never really told me," he says. "I guess only members can talk about it, and since I'm not a member, I don't qualify as good enough for him. He's such an asshole lately."

Cas and Thomas have always been close. When they first came to live with us, they moved together as one, light and shadow. They were thin then, and Mother admitted later that their parents couldn't feed them very often.

"He's definitely been moodier than usual." I sit on my piece of driftwood, my stomach a ball of worry. I skipped lunch after the first bite of salad threatened to come right back up.

The Aunties are preparing a big meal for later tonight. Mother's been busy with the littles but says she has something special for me to wear.

Cas drops the leftover rocks in his hand and sits next to me, and I lean against him, our bodies like magnets. I lay my head on his shoulder, and somehow the realness of him, flesh and bone, brings me down to earth. "I'm afraid," I say.

He's quiet for a while. "I am, too. A little."

"You're supposed to be the brave one. Tell me a bunch of clichés to make me feel better."

He laughs. "I'm sure it'll be fine. It's just kind of strange, is all. Why does it have to be so mysterious?"

"I just want to get it over with, and then I can finally do some good in this world. I'm sick of feeling like a child."

"You're not a child." He kisses my temple, and then I wrap my arms around his neck and pull him into me. I curl my hands into his thick hair and dance my fingers along the back of his neck. It's hard and warm.

I lean away. "We should go," I say. "They're expecting us back with the extra chairs from the shed."

Cas stares at my mouth. "Let's sneak out tonight, after everyone's gone to sleep."

"After my initiation? Do you really think that's a good idea?"

He nuzzles my neck. "Probably not. But I need to see you. Alone."

"Maybe," I tell him. "Let's get back."

We hurry through the woods to the small shed, grab a few folding chairs, and head back up to the lawn.

Father sits cross-legged on the picnic table with his eyes closed. He looks so peaceful. Behind him, Mother, the Aunties, and the littles sit on the benches, which have been arranged in a circle. A single folding chair waits in the circle's center.

Father opens his eyes and looks at Caspian. "It's been a long time since you've had a cleansing," he says.

Caspian swallows. The air thickens. "That's true, Sir."

Father scoots off the table. "Before we can perform Piper's initiation, you must do a cleansing."

I can't recall the last time Father performed a cleansing. In a cleansing, you confess out in the open and let the wind carry your shame away.

But why does Cas have to be cleansed for *my* initiation?

Does Father know our secret? It's possible. There's so little Father doesn't know.

A chill creeps down my neck.

Slowly, Caspian takes his spot in the center of the circle. He rubs his palms on his jeans and takes a deep breath. Cleansings can take hours, and they can be exhausting. Father says we're spiritual beings on a journey, and that time is a loop, so we confess to things we've done *and* to things we might do later.

Maybe it's I who should be sitting in Caspian's spot. But I take my seat between Mother and Thomas.

"You may begin when you're ready," Father says. He walks around us, no shoes, hands behind his back. I can't imagine how hard it is for him to listen to our transgressions.

Cas hangs his head and folds his hands. His shoulders slouch as he breathes in and out deeply.

The air is sluggish and damp. Sweat rolls down my nose and onto my top lip.

"It's up to you, Caspian," Father says in a hushed tone. "Unburden yourself. Trust us. We are your family."

Cas's spine is curled over, and from this angle, it looks broken.

"We want to help you," Father continues. "You're clearly in pain, and you need to be honest with us. Rid your body of the toxicity of deceit. I can smell it on you."

Cas sniffles, and then his voice snakes along the ground, low and quiet. "I still miss my parents."

No one speaks. Thomas tenses beside me. Father continues pacing, head down. I can't decide if Caspian is brave or stupid to admit such a thing. Maybe both.

"Go on," Father urges.

He wipes his eyes. "I want to know why they don't come for me. I wish they were here."

"You don't love us, then?" Father asks.

Cas is quiet. "Of course I do," he whispers.

"How can you have it both ways?" Father asks. "Your parents were hurting the Community. Is that what you want?"

"No, never," Cas says quickly.

Mother pulls my hand from my mouth. I hadn't realized I was chewing my nails.

"What else are you hiding, Caspian?" Father asks.

"Nothing."

Father narrows his eyes as he stares at the back of Cas's head. "Why don't I believe you?"

Thomas balls his hands into fists.

"Do any of you have any thoughts?" Father asks.

No one answers.

The longer we sit, the more difficult it is for me to catch my breath. The heat radiates off Mother's body, off Thomas's body next to mine. I can smell Millie's diaper, pungent and sour. I try breathing through my mouth, but my throat is already too dry. I cough into my elbow.

"Piper. Do you have something to share about what Caspian just said?"

Father steps inside the circle and stares down at me. All I can see is the line of his mouth.

I am so close to initiation. Too close. I can't lose it now.

I nod slowly.

"Go on, then," he urges me.

"You're not being fair to the rest of us." My voice comes out raspy, and I clear my throat, lick my lips. I can feel Caspian looking at me, but I dare not look his way.

"What else?" Father steps out of the circle again and stands directly behind me.

"Your parents are a danger to the rest of us. They're Outsiders. They're addicts."

Father puts his hands on my shoulders, a small gesture of affection, and relief floods through my entire body.

Sometimes doing the right thing feels wrong. That's what separates us from the Outside.

"I worry you care about them more than our safety," I continue. "I think if you had to choose, you'd choose them."

Father moves away, the connection lost. Mother squeezes my hand as if she is proud of me. But I don't feel pride. I feel something else, something darker, and now I want to take it all back. But some things can't be undone.

"They see through you, Caspian," Father says. "Please, put them out of their misery. Tell them what you've done. Admit to them why you're sitting in the circle. Then we can all go about our day."

Caspian tries not to cry, sucking in big mouthfuls of air. Thomas cracks his knuckles.

"You owe your brothers and sisters the truth," Father says. "You owe us all the truth."

Carla joins in, begging Caspian to answer. Beverly Jean whines for him to speak. Mother yells so loudly my ears ring, and Millie repeats Mother's admonishments. The Aunties stomp their feet, raising tiny plumes of dust.

Faces and shadows and screaming and Cas's crumpled body, and Father moving around us like hands on a clock.

My stomach turns acidic, and I clamp my eyes shut.

Caspian's voice breaks through the chaos. "I've had thoughts of running away to find my parents."

"What else?" Father asks.

I open my eyes. A lock of hair hangs in Cas's face, and he looks around the group, eyes darting, searching for something. When he stops on my face, he doesn't look away.

"I've doubted you, Curtis. I've called you a liar." Cas seems impossibly small, nothing like the boy who kissed me under the stars.

But he doesn't say anything about us. About me.

I don't deserve him.

Father raises his arm and brings the back of his hand across Cas's cheek in one fluid motion. Cas cradles his face as Beverly Jean begins to cry. Carla closes her eyes, and Henry whimpers.

Thomas stands, jaws clenched, anger turning his face into stone. But when he meets my eyes, the anger melts away, and his gaze holds a sadness so deep I'm forced to look away.

Father kneels before Cas. "Thank you, son." He takes Cas's face in his hands. "You've been very brave to admit something so shameful. I'm proud of you. We all are." He gently touches the welt on Cas's cheek.

As soon as Father moves away, Thomas rushes to Caspian, and Cas collapses into his brother's embrace.

They are as small as the day they came here, a single suitcase between them.

I try to say something, but I can't make any sound come out.

Mother holds out a hand to me, and I take it. Together, we walk toward the house.

I don't look back.

33. AFTER

When I dream now, I dream of the small room. Of dirty white walls and no air and the smell of wet animal.

Sometimes Mother is there. Most times, she isn't.

When I wake up, the room expands around me.

Walls rearrange themselves.

Windows bloom.

A hint of sunlight peeks in around the shades, and I pull the covers tighter around myself. It's only six thirty. Jeannie won't knock on my door for another half hour.

She brings me my pill and a glass of water every morning. Get me good and drugged up before my feet even touch the floor.

I climb out of bed and try the lock on the window. It still won't budge. She must have fastened it shut from the outside. She painted over the names I wrote on the wall, too; the room stinks of chemicals and lies.

"Good morning."

She stands in my doorway, a glass of water in one hand, pills in the other. She sets them on the table and waits. Daisy waits next to her, a leash attached to her collar.

"I need to see you take them."

Crossing the room, I try not to look at her. To pretend she doesn't exist. I place the pill in my mouth, maneuver it under my tongue, and take a drink.

Satisfied, she leaves, taking Daisy with her. I spit the pill into my hand, then slide it under my mattress.

After that I sleep for hours. It's hard to keep track of time.

✘

Voices trail into my room. Jeannie's and someone else's. A familiar voice.

Scrambling from bed still half asleep, I careen into my doorframe.

Jeannie is speaking to Holliday downstairs in the living room. Today Holliday is wearing a long red cardigan over a flannel shirt that's tucked into tight, high-waisted jeans. I've never seen jeans like that. Mine have always been loose.

"Piper, you're awake," Jeannie says. "This is Holliday. She lives next door."

Holliday steps toward me, arm outstretched, and winks. "Nice to meet you, Piper."

I say nothing. I don't shake her hand. I haven't brushed my teeth in days, and I'm sure my breath stinks.

Jeannie clears her throat nervously. "Holliday is around your age. I thought you might like to spend some time with her. I'll leave you two girls alone to chat." She disappears down the hallway.

Holliday plops onto the couch and stretches. "Sorry about that. Pretending I hadn't already met you. Just seemed easier not to say anything."

I cross my arms. "Why are you here?" I swallow, then add, "Not that it's a bad thing."

"I thought we could hang out. It was hard to convince Jeannie at first, but I wore her down. That woman is crazy protective of you."

"You want to hang out with *me*? Why?"

She squints. "A girl who busts through a fence with a broken ankle is my kind of friend."

"Okay," I say cautiously. "What should we do?"

"You could show me your room?"

"It's not much to look at."

She smiles. "Why don't you let me be the judge of that?"

I lead her upstairs, down the hallway that's becoming familiar, and into my bedroom. She surveys it and sits on my bed. "You're right, this place is kind of barren. It's so dark in here. You're not a vampire, are you? I mean, you don't vanish in mirrors, right?"

"I don't think so." I try to smile, but exhaustion creeps back into my bones.

"Who's your favorite musician? We could hang their poster on your wall, or something."

"I don't really listen to music."

Her eyes widen. "What? I need to make you some playlists ASAP." She pulls what looks like a small TV screen from her bag. "I'm making myself a note. Wait, do you have Spotify? You do, right?"

"What's that?" I ask, pointing to the thing in her hand.

She looks at it, surprised. "This? It's my phone."

"Cell phones can cause electromagnetic radiation," I tell her, and back away.

"I don't know about all that, but I can't live without mine. How about a selfie? They're fun. We can use, like, an animal filter." She stands next to me and holds the phone in front of us.

"What's a selfie?" I ask, covering my face.

"Just a picture, but I won't take one if it bugs you." She puts the phone away and spots the lake house on the wall. Jeannie hasn't painted over it yet. Holliday carefully runs her finger along the roofline, the roller coaster rising behind it. "You drew this?"

"Yeah, but I'm not very good. I get so bored here."

"You're an artist?"

"Not really."

I almost tell her about Carla, how she's the real artist in my family, but I don't know Holliday. I don't know why she's really here.

But…Dr. Lundhagen said I should trust my feelings, and Holliday feels like she could be a friend if I let her in a little.

Besides, I need her.

"That's where I used to live," I say, playing with a hangnail on my thumb.

She touches the drawing. "Here? Where is it?"

I sit on the desk chair. "At a lake. My family lives at this really old amusement park. Most of it had been torn down, though." I blush, remembering my night with Cas at the bumper cars.

"What are you thinking about?" she asks, smiling. "Your face just turned about ten shades of red."

"Just this boy," I say. My face grows hot when she whistles.

"A boy! What's his name? What does he look like?"

I describe him, the boy with hair like the night and eyes like the ocean.

"He sounds super hot," she says. "Where is he now?"

The high of sharing this secret with her wears off as reality sets in. "I'm not sure. I haven't talked to him in a while."

"That sucks. Did you break up?"

"Something like that," I say, unable to forget my cruelty at Cas's cleansing. I wouldn't blame him if he never forgave me.

"Sorry, Piper. If you ever want to be set up, just ask. My boyfriend, Dev, has a single friend. We could all go out sometime."

I want to ask her what she means, being set up. Instead I stare at the floor.

She stands and points to my chest. "That's a gorgeous necklace. Where'd you get it?"

I instinctively cover it with my hand. "It's a family heirloom from my mother. I...I miss her."

She looks away before putting her bag over her shoulder.

"Well, I should probably get home. I have a test tomorrow. I almost slipped a disc lugging all these books home. Can we hang out for real sometime?"

"Sure. If you really want to."

Holliday hugs me, and right before she pulls away, I hug her back. "See you around, Piper. Don't be a stranger. I'll talk to my mom, see if we can have a sleepover soon."

After she's gone, I wonder if she was ever here at all.

As I crawl back into bed, something twists inside my chest, as if the fibers keeping me together are ripping apart. I know I should be strong. Swallow down my feelings.

Have faith.

But I can't. Not this time.

I cry for what I've lost and what I can't remember. For Amy. For my loneliness. For the silence from my parents. For Millie's big blue eyes. Even for Carla's surly attitude.

I let myself cry until my face swells and I run out of tears.

Then I rip out the window shades.

No more darkness. This is where I am now. Not at the lake house, not with Father and Mother. I need to make the best of this new life for however long I'm stuck here.

I catch a whiff of myself and decide to bathe later.

The fading sun streams in through the windows as I pace the room, illuminating the white walls, my drawing of the lake house.

There's a smudge on the door that I never noticed before. Up close it has no meaning, so I back up all the way to the desk and stare at it. Letters bleed through the paint, trying to escape. I think I see a J, maybe an S.

My eyes relax and focus until a complete word reveals itself to me: *Jessie.*

My heartbeat pulverizes my chest.

They kept someone else in this room.

34. BEFORE

Mother combs my hair in long, even strokes. The comb catches a knot, and she yanks it through, snapping my head back a fraction.

"There," she says, setting the comb down on my dresser. "You're almost ready." She unzips a garment bag lying on my bed and removes a long, white, shapeless gown. "Undress and get into this."

I take off my short-sleeved sweater and bell-bottoms and step into the dress. The fabric is stiff and itchy, but I don't complain. Mother tells me to turn around. The zipper's metal teeth lock into place. The house is too quiet; the Aunties took the others into the woods for a picnic.

"When's everyone getting back?" I ask.

Mother hushes me. "None of that matters, Piper. This is the most important moment of your life. Focus on that." She retrieves a box from the bed and takes out a necklace. "My mother gave this to me when I was your age, and now I'm giving it to you." A green stone dangles from a delicate chain, and when I touch it, it cools my hands. "It's amazonite—it stands for courage and truth. You're going to need those things now more than ever." I spin around and pull back my hair, and Mother clasps the necklace. The green glows against my white dress.

"I love it," I whisper. "It's like a tiny ocean is trapped inside."

"I knew you'd recognize its magic." She gathers me to her and strokes my hair. "I am so proud of you, Piper."

Mother takes me out the front door and down to the lake. Torches line the beach, each one sending up black puffs of smoke. A table has been set up on the sand, covered in a gauzy white cloth that blows lazily with the breeze. It holds three lit candles, all white, and a tea set with one cup. A framed photo of Father sits on a chair next to the table.

Mother pours me a cup of tea. The sun settles below the horizon, bathing her face in pinks and oranges.

"Drink," she says, and I swallow some. It's bitter, and I wince. "All of it, please," she instructs, and I do as I'm told, pushing my tongue up against the roof of my mouth to keep it from coming back up. She takes the cup and sets it back on the table.

"What's going to happen?" I ask.

She smiles and takes my hands. Hers are ice-cold. "Have faith, my darling daughter. I am so proud of you for taking this step. It's not easy joining the Community. Many people want to, but Curtis, your father, only chooses the very best. People who are strong, and kind, and selfless. People like you."

The smell from the candles grows stronger, an overpowering scent of vanilla mixed with seaweed, and I have to breathe through my mouth.

"I must leave now," she says. "All will become clear soon. I'll see you after, for the celebration."

She slips away from me, and I watch as she goes inside the house. Then I pick up the photo of Father, too quickly, and I grow dizzy.

Lowering myself onto the chair, I take deep breaths. I wish Cas were here with me.

The trees jump, and I blink my eyes, trying to make them stand still. The brownness of the sand under my feet smells like toast, though I know that can't be right. Colors don't have smells. But this one does, and when I reach down to touch the sand, my hand smears a trail of peach.

I sweep my hand to the left, and then to the right, leaving behind flesh-colored rainbows. A chuckle bubbles its way up my throat, and then I can't stop laughing.

My voice sounds far away, like a beautiful echo, and I am more me, more alive than I've ever felt in my entire life.

The photograph of Father twitches in my hands, and I hold it close. The blue of his eyes is neon, practically blinding.

I think of all he told me, about the outside world, the president threatening nuclear war. I think of what it would be like to be bombed, our skin melting away as if it were wax.

As if we were nothing.

Tears roll down my face as I curl up on the sand, feeling the weight of human suffering move through me. I have a chance now, a chance to do some real good in this world. To save humanity from itself. I wonder if this is what Father feels like all the time. How can he bear it?

The sand is cool, and I run my fingers through it. How many millions of years did it take to make each grain? I could be lying on top of a once-giant mountain, slowly chipped away by rain and wind and joy and pain.

I am the sand and the mountain and the rain.

Minutes or hours pass, it's hard to tell. I lie on my back, counting the shadows on the clouds. They flutter and combine. My lips tingle with the memory of Caspian's kiss, and I want this for him, to be initiated with me. I can't do any of this alone.

When I sit up, a white haze crawls along the water's surface, reaching out long, ghostly fingers. It undulates and rises as it moves toward me, a dance I don't understand, but I'm not afraid. The fingers reach the sand, and then they wrap around me, trapping me inside a cloud. Suddenly, Father materializes at the end of the mist. He's all in white, glowing from within.

He walks on the water.

"Father," I say, but I can't get out anything else.

He reaches out his hand and pulls me to my feet, and then he's cradling me against him while I cry. He doesn't speak out loud, but he's talking to me, to my mind, telling me everything will be okay, and I know it's true. I've always known.

He sits me down on the chair and kneels before me. "Do you know who I am?"

I can't speak. My mouth won't work.

"I'm your father, Piper. But I'm also more than that. I'm a messenger, sent here to save you. To save all of mankind."

"Are you *God*?" I manage to whisper. Tears spill down my cheeks, and I turn away.

He takes my face in his. "God is an invention of man," he says. "I'm something more than that. You're ready now, to know the truth about me and about this world. It can be frightening. I frighten a lot of people. But that's my burden to bear. Not yours. You're ready to join me now, to join my group, as we work to heal the planet. Are you ready?"

A bluish mist flows from his mouth as he speaks. I reach out to touch it.

"Sit with me," he says, "and put your toes in the sand. Connect to the earth. Feel the currents of time and space run through you. *Feel* your power."

We sit next to each other, facing the water. A crack of lightning punches the sky. My body hums, and I am reborn.

35. AFTER

Who's Jessie?

I throw aside clothes.

Wrench out dresser drawers.

Rip the curtains from their rods trying to find signs of Jessie.

There are none. They've either been hidden or destroyed.

I overturn the garbage can and claw through papers and used tissues. There it is; the figurine Jeannie gave me. A mother holds a baby with angel's wings. It says *Jessie* across the bottom.

My head throbs, and I sink to the floor. That name beats along with my heart.

Jessie, Jessie, Jessie.

My mind won't slow down. I can't begin to calculate how much radiation I've been exposed to since I got here. It's scrambling my thoughts, messing with my perception, attacking my cells.

But I know Jessie was here.

✖

Jeannie is drinking coffee in the kitchen while reading the newspaper. "I hope you and Holliday had a nice time. She mentioned you two might like to have a sleepover sometime."

I sit across from her. "I've been wondering about something."

"What's that?" She sets down the paper, gives me her full attention.

"Who lived here before you?"

She thinks for a moment. "An older couple sold the house to us. They lived here twenty-odd years."

I scrape a nail across the top of my thigh.

A prick of pain.

Courage.

"Did they have children?"

Jeannie freezes, the coffee cup at her lips. She sets down the cup and blinks. "I think so? But I can't really remember. It's been a long time since we moved in. Why do you ask?"

"There's a name painted over on my door."

She goes to the sink and loads her dirty coffee cup and plate into the dishwasher. Then she puts soap in the washer and twists the knob. It hums. "Oh? What name is that?"

Blood rushes into my ears. "I couldn't make it out," I lie.

"Then I wouldn't worry about it. I have to pick up Amy from school. You can come with me if you want."

"No," I say quietly.

As soon as she leaves to get Amy, I push open the front door.

She forgot to lock it.

Everything looks gray and a little distorted. The shed is fat and misshapen. The trees are skeleton hands.

I don't trust what's right in front of me.

The shed is still locked, and none of the combinations I try work. I spin the dial recklessly from left to right, my breath shallow. My hands shake so goddamn bad I can barely hold on.

"Fuck!" I kick the shed and sink to the ground. Daisy gallops across the lawn and sits facing me, slowly scooting closer and closer until she's almost in my lap. I hug her, letting her warm, soft fur dull my fear.

It usually takes Jeannie about thirty minutes to get Amy from school, and I've wasted ten out here on a lock that won't cooperate.

The section of fence that belonged to Holliday's house has been covered with wrought iron bars, same as Jeannie's fence. The hole I kicked out is an inaccessible taunt. Now I know why she didn't bother to lock the front door; she knew there was no way out.

I have to find out about Jessie, and I know where to search. The woman's bedroom.

When I go inside, her door at the end of the hall is locked, like I knew it would be. I grab the knife from under my mattress and jiggle the lock until it clicks open with a satisfying *pop*.

It's an ordinary bedroom with a large bed, a couple of lamps set on bedside tables, and a dresser.

Somehow I expected more and am disappointed.

I move deeper into the room that smells like sweat, sleep, and her perfume. Daisy waits at the bedroom door, afraid to come inside.

If I've learned anything, it's that everyone has at least one secret. Some secrets they even hide from themselves.

Those are the hardest to find.

The closet doors open to racks of clothing smashed into one another. Rows of shoes sit below them. I flick through the outfits, all beige and baby blue and benign.

At the back of the closet are plastic bins. I drag one of them onto the bed. It yields nothing of interest, just some old jeans that smell musty. I don't bother refolding them.

The next bin is full of worn-out tennis shoes. They have dirty soles and frayed laces. Why is she keeping this junk?

My fingers graze the last bin, and a tingle flows through me. I peel off the lid. Little-girl dresses and shirts and shoes are heaped on one side. They'd probably fit Amy.

Buried underneath are several VHS tapes and round, silver discs. Each has been labeled: *Hawaii 2011*, *Christmas 2008*, and *Jeannie's Master's Graduation 2015*.

It's the last one that makes my chest seize up: *Jessica's Swim Meet*.

My mind swirls with possibility. Is Jessica another stolen girl? I stare at the tape in my hand.

Jessie could be a nickname for Jessica.

At the very bottom is a gold frame. The picture inside shows Jeannie holding a girl in her arms. The little girl looks like me. She holds a blue ribbon toward the camera. They're both smiling.

My eyes burn, and I shove the bin back in the closet.

I won't let her break me.

Then I close the bedroom door behind me, the tape burning my hand. I don't lock the door. I want her to know I've been here.

"Hello, there."

A man stands at the bottom of the stairs. I hide the tape and knife behind my back and freeze as Daisy trots down the hall to get petted.

He wears the boots I saw in the kitchen. He has the same cornflower-blue eyes as my mother and me...I know him, almost.

Finally he smiles. "I hope I didn't startle you. I'm Rich, Jeannie's husband."

I had almost forgotten about her husband.

Funny the things our minds choose to forget.

I can breathe again, but I don't approach. The pulse ticks in his neck, and I grip the knife harder.

"I thought you'd be with Jeannie," he says. "I just came to fix the furnace. She said it's on the fritz again." He checks his watch. "How about some ice cream? I picked up a tub of mint chocolate chip. Jeannie wouldn't want you to ruin your dinner, but I won't tell if you won't."

He stares at me with hopeful eyes. I don't want to rouse suspicion, so I agree. "Okay. But I'm cold. I need a sweater."

I hurry to my bedroom and hide the tape, slipping it between my bed and the wall. I hope it's still here when I need it.

I keep the knife, slipping it into the waist of my pants.

In the kitchen, the man, Rich, has scooped two heaping bowls of ice cream. He hands one to me.

"I thought you were getting a sweater?" he asks, his eyebrows drawn together.

My face grows hot. "I forgot," I mumble.

He opens his mouth to say something but stops himself. "Mint chocolate chip is my favorite," he says instead. "What's your favorite?"

"Cherry chip," I answer without thinking. Mother and I used to eat it after swimming. I smile at the memory of that day we went to the park when she tapped my nose with her cone. We laughed so much.

"That's an excellent flavor. Should we eat on the porch? It's too nice to stay inside."

As he opens the front door, I'm more aware than ever of my status as prisoner. If I ran, would he chase me? I wouldn't make it far with my bum ankle. He would catch me, and I don't want to think about what could happen next.

He goes outside and sits in one of the wicker chairs. I step out behind him and scan the fence. The gate is closed. So I sink into the other chair, a hundred feet from freedom, and eat my ice cream. Daisy lopes through the front yard, up onto the porch, and lies at my feet. I curl my toes into her warm fur.

"How are you doing?" he asks.

The ice cream hurts my teeth as I chew, either from the cold or cavities. I'm sure I have a few by now.

"Fine."

"What do you like to do for fun around here?"

"You don't have to make small talk or pretend to care."

He is quiet for a while. "I do care," he says.

"Are you going to live here now?"

"Only if you're comfortable with that, Piper. There's no rush for me to move back home."

Home.

I wonder where Father and Mother are, what they're doing, whether they're thinking of me. I used to be certain they were, but I'm not so sure anymore.

"Do what you want," I say. "No one cares what I think, anyway."

"That's not true."

"Isn't it? I'm forced to live here, locked inside all day like a criminal, like *I've* done something wrong."

He stares at the bowl in his lap. He hasn't eaten much of his ice cream; it's soup now.

"I'm sorry, Piper. This must be really scary and confusing for you."

His concern seems genuine, and I'm not sure what to make of it. It's easier with Jeannie; with her, I know what to expect. Cold and distant.

I don't know what to do with his warmth.

The gate opens and Jeannie's car comes up the drive. As soon as it stops, the back door opens, and Amy sprints across the lawn. "Daddy!" she yells. Rich scoops her into a hug, laughing into her hair. Their closeness makes my chest hurt, until I remember none of this is real, that she's also a hostage.

"What are you doing here, Rich?" Jeannie asks. She eyes me nervously.

"I thought she'd be with you. I came to fix the furnace."

"Maybe you should go," she says.

When he sets Amy down, she starts crying. "Please don't make him go away again," she blubbers.

Rich ruffles her hair. "It'll be okay, sweetheart."

Jeannie turns to me. "Why don't you take Amy inside to play, let me talk to Rich for a second?"

Amy wipes her nose and slumps toward me. "We can play Candy Land," she says, though she doesn't sound very excited about it.

As I open the front door, I turn back. They're watching me.

Inside, I peel back the curtain on the front window. "How do you play this game?" Jeannie's arms are crossed. Rich reaches out to touch her face, but she leans back.

Amy stares at me in disbelief. "You've never played *Candy Land*?"

"Nope, never."

She sets up the game on the kitchen table, carefully making a pile of white cards.

"I'll teach you. Queen Frostine is my favorite. Isn't she beautiful?"

She traces her chubby finger along a winding path made of colored squares to a character with long, silver hair standing in a corner, frozen forever.

"My daddy looks different," she says abruptly.

"Different how?"

"I don't know. His face isn't the same as I remember."

Father's warning about government operatives blares in my head. If Amy's real father is still with the Community, then Rich must be one of Them.

The front door swings open, and Jeannie and Rich come inside.

"We're playing Candy Land!" Amy exclaims.

"Can I play, too?" Rich sits next to her, but he's looking at me. He wants to say something, I can tell, but he doesn't.

Jeannie takes out pots and pans, puts them back, slams into our silence. She keeps watching us, fluttering around the kitchen. "Piper," she says after Amy wins the game. "Would you mind if Rich had dinner with us tonight?"

"That'd be fine," I say, and he smiles again.

"Good. I want to make sure you're comfortable." She gets a package of chicken from the refrigerator and sets it next to the sink.

"Since when?" I ask.

Her eyes are wet. "Since always."

Amy hits the board with the yellow gingerbread game piece. *Tap. Tap. Tap.*

Something rings. Jeannie pushes a button on her cell phone and it stops.

"Let's play again!" Amy says.

"We care very much," Jeannie continues.

Tap. Tap. Tap.

"I don't have to stay," Rich offers.

I lurch away from the table. Jeannie reaches for me, but I easily slip past her and upstairs to my room.

Alone.

Just me and the ghost of Jessie.

✘

Later, Jeannie knocks on my door. "Meeting Rich like that was probably a big shock. I sure haven't been handling things very well. I'm sorry."

I say nothing.

"He's a good man, Piper." She beckons for me to follow. "Come on, I have a surprise for you. Something I've been working on for a while now."

She leads me to a plain door next to the staircase. "This goes to the tower room," she explains, opening it. Steep steps rise in front of us. She goes first, and I trail after her. The stairs squeak and groan.

At the top of the stairs, she moves aside.

The colors vibrate and dance.

The walls have been painted blue, and it reminds me of the sky and lake at home. Framed paintings of lakeshores hang on every wall. My favorite shows an island floating above the water. The trees' roots dangle into the calm waters below, and children climb them like ladders. I almost reach out to touch it until I remember I'm not alone.

"I don't want you to forget where you've been," she says. "It's a part of you. I won't make you choose us over them. But I want you to try to be happy here. To make this your home now."

193

In front of the window there's a purple chaise lounge chair with a yellow blanket thrown over the back. The setting sun blazes through the window's stained glass, casting prisms of color around the room.

When I look at her, she blurs again, changing into Mother for a moment before snapping back.

I turn away, push my hands into my stomach.

"I thought you might like to come up here sometimes, to be by yourself," she says. "You mentioned the other day that you need more time alone."

I run my fingers across the chair. The fabric is so soft.

I don't know who's standing behind me anymore.

"I hope you like it," she says.

Footfalls, and then the door at the bottom of the stairs clicks shut. Once I'm certain she's gone, I sink into the chair, close my eyes, and fall asleep.

36. BEFORE

Something wet and cold slides across my forehead. My head feels bent at an odd angle, and when I try to move it, my neck aches.

"Stay still." It's Thomas. I open my eyes, and he's seated over me, holding something to my forehead. "It's a cool cloth. Just relax."

I'm in my bed, door shut. No one else is in the room with us. "Where are the girls?" I whisper. My throat is on fire.

"They're with Caspian and the boys. They're fine." He puts the rag into a bucket, squeezes, and reapplies it. The cooling sensation makes me float out of my bed. I grip the mattress, and Thomas puts his hands on my arms.

"You're still in bed," he says. I quickly look around the room, and everything stays in place: the other beds, the dresser. "I know you feel strange, but you're safe. Nothing bad will happen to you, not anymore."

Bad? Nothing bad has happened to me. What does he mean?

"Thomas," I manage. "We're supposed to be married."

He stiffens. "Please don't try to talk, Piper."

"Where's Father?" I croak.

Thomas dabs my face. "He's gone back to the compound." He leans toward the nightstand and returns with a glass of water.

"Drink this. It'll help you feel better." He puts a straw between my lips, and I suck in mouthfuls of water.

"I saw him," I sputter, letting some water fall onto my neck. "He came to me. My initiation. It was so beautiful."

Thomas sets down the glass and re-wets the rag. "Don't worry about that now."

"Did it happen to you, too? When you were initiated?"

His jaws clench. "Yes."

I close my eyes. It wasn't a dream, then. It was real.

But that also means everything Father has told us is real, too. We could all die any minute.

My eyes flash open, and I reach for Thomas. "We're not safe here," I say. "The shelter. We should go."

"It's okay, Piper." He leans in close to my face. "Everything is fine. There's no war, no bombs. Nothing bad is going to happen."

"But how do you know?" I ask, barely able to make the words come out.

Thomas's doubts crowd into the room. And I wish I had told Father about them.

"Because I do," he says heavily. "Just trust me."

37. AFTER

I sit on the floor in the dark, fiddling with the stone on my necklace.

The chain pinches the hair on my neck, and I rise from the floor, take it off, and place it back in its box.

I feel like I'm losing my connection to home.

That I don't deserve this necklace.

Maybe I never did.

The others fell asleep hours ago, so I fish out the VHS tape and sneak into the tower room. I'm quieter now that my walking boot came off a few days ago. I asked Jeannie if I could have a TV up there, and she finally hooked everything up this morning. I pretended I wanted to watch one of her VHS movies she keeps boxed up, something called *Clueless*.

This day took forever to get through.

I push the tape into the VCR, and gray static fills the screen. A solid blue bar slices across the bottom before slowly climbing the screen.

A scene pops to life. A pool, kids in swim caps. The picture is wobbly. Whoever holds the camera doesn't point it at anything specific. Ambient noises and splashing.

"Go, Jessie!"

It's Jeannie's voice.

The picture shakes, passing over a boy who sticks his tongue out, and then it zooms in on a little girl. So this is Jessie. The girl who lived in my room. She clings to the side of the pool. She's smiling, I think. The tape is grainy, so it's hard to see her face clearly.

But there's no mistaking her pink swim cap.

It's the same color as my old cap. I scoot closer to the screen.

Someone blows a whistle, and Jessie shoots down the pool. Arms and legs thrash, and Jeannie cheers her on. The camera shakes.

She loses the race, but Jeannie keeps cheering. "Yay, Jessie! You did so great!"

Jessie climbs out of the pool. Water drips off her black suit. She is all smiles as she pulls off her swim cap.

The scene cuts off. More static.

Another scene cuts in.

Jeannie and Jessie eating ice-cream cones in a park.

Jeannie puffs out her cheeks at the camera. Then she taps her cone against Jessie's nose. A man laughs. It's Rich's laugh. He must be holding the camera.

Pain rips through my temples, and I hold my head in my hands.

This isn't right.

I remember that day clearly. Mother and I laughing and eating ice cream in the park. It was just us; Father didn't videotape it for posterity.

This isn't right!

I curl up on the floor. Those people must've gotten into my head somehow, altered my memories. What else could explain what's happening?

I don't know how long I lie there, but suddenly my stomach turns traitor. I scramble from the floor and heave open the window, grateful it hasn't been locked shut. Fresh air hits my face as I throw up on the hydrangea bushes below.

I wipe my mouth and take deep breaths.

I have to get out of this house.

As I stumble through the garage and into the yard, my lungs expel a breath I didn't realize I'd been holding. I try to inhale, but my chest is full of concrete. It's almost winter now, the air colder, less forgiving. I stagger toward the fence, trying to breathe in. My vision narrows to pinpricks, and my ears are stuffed with cotton. I claw at my neck, fingers searching for my chain that isn't there.

Laughter pours over from Holliday's side of the fence. I scan the yard for something to climb. All I find is a patio table. I drag it across the yard.

Jeannie wouldn't want me outside at night.

Father wouldn't want me to associate with people from the Outside.

But they're not me. And they're not here.

My lungs fill with air, greedy for oxygen.

For freedom from all these expectations everyone keeps putting on me.

I hoist myself onto the table. It wobbles, but I don't slip, and I can peer over the fence. Holliday sits near a fire with two boys.

"Could I get some help?" I ask.

They all turn and look up at me. "Piper?" Holliday asks. "Oh my God! What are you doing? Is everything all right?"

The stars above her brighten from slate to vivid jewel tones, and I can hear the wind rushing, and suddenly I realize I'm not dying.

And Holliday might be my new favorite person.

"I just need to get away," I say, my brain still trying to make sense of what I saw on the video. "Can someone help me over?"

The taller boy with the brown skin drags a ladder to the fence and climbs up. "I'm Dev," he says, his voice rich and deep. He holds out a hand, such a simple gesture.

I remember taking Father's hand at the beach.

Nothing has turned out like it was supposed to.

But I take the boy's hand, and he helps me over the fence and onto the ladder. It's higher than I thought, and I wobble. I glance down, and I imagine Cas standing at the bottom, telling me everything will be okay.

And I climb down.

"So," Holliday says once I'm on the ground. "Everyone, this is Piper, the girl I've been telling you about."

"I'm Jakob," the other boy says. He has a mop of wavy blond hair and wears tight jeans with white high-tops. He reminds me too much of Henry.

"Jakob Easton, who's set two school records in swimming," Holliday quickly adds. "He thinks it makes him special."

Jakob pushes his sleeves up to his elbows. "I'd be special without them, and you know it." He turns to me. "She's jealous because the only record she's ever set is number of cigarettes smoked before age eighteen."

Holliday scoffs. "Whatever. And this is Dev, my boyfriend, who you just met."

His height reminds me of Father, and I can't help but smile. He wears holey jeans and a denim jacket that's black on one side and blue on the other. "Dharamdev Bansal, at your service." He does an exaggerated bow and kisses my hand. When he stands, he pushes his shaggy black hair away from his face.

"Corny," Jakob says flatly, rolling his eyes.

"We're all just hanging out," Holliday tells me. "My parents are gone for the night."

I want to ask why she hasn't stopped by to see me again, but I don't. Instead I just stand there like an idiot.

"You should chill with us for a while," she says.

"Sure," I say slowly. "That'd be aces. Yeah. Right on."

The boys exchange a look I don't understand.

"Come on, I'll make everyone a drink," Jakob says. We follow him inside, into a large dining room. Bottles and cups and a bucket of ice take up one end of the table. "What's your poison?" he asks me.

"I don't drink," I admit. "It's bad for your body."

"You for real?" He looks at me like I've got arms growing out of my face.

"I need to stay healthy and sharp. When the end of days comes, I have to be prepared."

The three of them look at one another, and then Jakob mixes something in a red plastic cup. "Peach schnapps and orange juice. I'm pretty sure the world's not going to end tonight."

I take it from him but don't drink any.

"And for the king and queen of debauchery, a shot of whiskey each." Jakob pours brown liquid into two glasses. Holliday and Dev toss them back and immediately start coughing.

"I need a light," Holliday announces, once she's regained her composure. We follow her back outside.

Lawn furniture is grouped around a firepit, flames crackling and popping. I ease onto one of the chairs as Holliday opens a pack of cigarettes.

"Menthols," she says when she catches me looking at them. "They cool your throat. Way better than the Camels I used to steal from my cousin."

She lights one and tries to hand it to me, but I shake my head. "Cigarettes are harmful to your lungs and heart. You're basically poisoning your own body."

I feel bad for her that she doesn't understand this. That none of them do. I wish Father were here to help them.

No one says anything for a while. We just watch the fire. Jakob whispers something into Holliday's ear, but I pretend I don't notice. I hold my breath until her cigarette smoke dissolves into the air.

Dev suddenly puts his head between his knees and takes deep breaths.

"Please tell me you're not going to throw up," Jakob mutters.

"No. Dude. I'm fine." But Dev's face goes gray.

"Shit," Holliday says. "He's gonna be sick." She turns to me. "I'm gonna take him inside. You mind hanging out with Jakob for a bit?"

"Okay," I answer, though Father would never approve of me being alone with a boy I don't know.

Holliday gives Jakob a pointed stare. "Be nice," she warns.

He holds up his hands in mock surrender. "I will be the perfect gentleman."

I stare at the drink in my hands, still full, and set it on the ground. I miss the crackling fires we had at the beach. Roasting marshmallows with the little ones. Braiding Beverly Jean's hair. Watching Cas watching me.

Jakob messes with his phone, and then music starts to play. A guy speaks in time to an up-tempo beat about people giving him fake love. His voice is a little sad. "Who's this?" I ask.

"Drake. You heard of him before?"

"No, but it's a far-out song."

Fake love, real love. I had real love once.

I close my eyes. Swallow down the sadness.

I can't keep drowning in it.

"Yeah, Drake's great," Jakob says, after a long silence. "So when did you get back? I mean, when did you move in next door?"

"A couple of months ago, I think. It's hard to remember."

He sneaks a look at me. "How do you like living with Rich and Jeannie?"

Why does everyone know their names?

"No one cares what I think about anything," I say. "Why should you be any different?"

He shrugs and leans back in his chair. "Sorry. Just trying to make conversation."

My head hurts, and I rub my temples. "How can you stand the EMF poisoning?"

"What are you talking about?"

"Poisoning from cell phone signals. Don't your parents know to keep you protected?"

"No one worries about that," he says slowly, his voice trailing off. "There's no scientific proof or anything—"

I turn toward him. "There's proof. Only the government keeps it under lock and key. They want us to be sick and weak. We're easier to control that way."

He glances at me. "Uh, okay. Sorry I brought it up."

203

We stare at the flames, our floundering conversation all dried up. My memory flits to swimming with Mother, to getting ice cream after. Then Jessie and Jeannie invade the memory, stealing it.

"Should we head inside, check on Dev and Holliday?" Jakob asks. He doesn't wait for an answer before getting up.

Dev is lying facedown on a sofa in the living room. It's dark, save for light tumbling in from an adjoining bathroom. Holliday kneels next to him, cleaning up a pile of vomit. The room reeks, and I open a window. A digital clock blinks midnight.

Jakob runs his hands through his hair. "I advised him against that shot of Aftershock. Makes him spew every damn time."

"He obviously didn't listen. Call the press, I know." Holliday sits back on her heels. "I'm sorry, Piper. This probably isn't very fun for you."

"It's okay," I say, though I don't mean it.

"So," Holliday says to Jakob, "do you think you can handle him for a while?"

Jakob smacks Dev on the back. "I think I can manage."

Dev groans, then slurs, "I'm *never drinking again*."

"You said that after the battle of the bands when you drank an orchard's worth of cider. No one believes you," Jakob says.

Dev's hazy eyes find me, watch me. "I saw you on TV. God, I can't believe it's really *you*."

"Shut up, Dev! Shh!" Holliday grabs my hand and yanks me from the room. Dev is saying something else, but Jakob closes the door.

Outside, she lights up another cigarette. "We really should have a proper sleepover. Those boys are fun, but our hangouts usually end with someone barfing in a toilet. Trashy."

The red tip of the cigarette glows brighter as she inhales.

The house is still dark.

"Why did Dev say he saw me on TV?" I ask, my voice wobbling. Did he see the video I just watched?

"He says a lot of weird shit when he's drunk. Just ignore him."

She won't look at me.

Father says liars always avoid eye contact.

"How come you never came back over?" I ask in a rush. "I thought you wanted to be friends or something."

"I've tried coming over lots of times."

My ears burn.

If They are preventing her from seeing me, she might not be the only one. Has Father tried to come for me? Could it be possible?

I grab her shoulders. "Have you seen anyone else come to the house? A man with light brown hair—a woman with long blond hair?"

She sputters. "Piper, no, I haven't. Are you okay?"

I release her. "No. Not really."

A light flips on at Jeannie's house. They're probably watching me.

"Listen, I need your help," I say, spitting out the words. "Do you have a car I could borrow, or some money?"

She narrows her eyes. "What d'you need that stuff for?"

I lower my voice. "To get away from them." I nod toward the house. "They won't let me leave."

"Of course not. Your leg is hurt. Moms worry. It's totally normal."

"She's *not* my mom. Don't you see?"

She stares straight ahead. "You're kinda freaking me out, Piper."

"What about your phone?" I ask, my voice rising. "We can call someone, tell them where I am."

"Call someone? Like, the police? 'Cause they've been by a bunch of times. Piper," she says, putting her hands on my shoulders, "everything's okay."

They got to her.

They *fucking* got to her, too.

She's one of Them.

I shove her off me and barrel past her to the sliding glass doors. Dev and Jakob are there, and Dev doesn't seem sick anymore.

"Everything okay?" Jakob asks.

I run back into the yard, to the ladder, and drag it away from the fence.

"Stay away from me," I warn, hauling it to a section that doesn't butt up against Jeannie's yard. I need to run. Now.

No more hesitation.

"We can't let her go," Holliday whispers.

"I think you should leave that," Dev says, wrangling the ladder away from me. It isn't much of a struggle as I try to pull it back, the tears quick and hot in my eyes.

"Please," I cry, sagging to the ground. "Please."

When I wake up, I'm in my bed.

Covers to my chin.

Sunlight seeping in through the windows.

I don't remember leaving Holliday's yard.

Pushing back the covers, I sit up and stretch. Amy's laughter and the sound of cartoons trail upstairs from the living room.

I need space to breathe, to think, but my head hurts too much. Every time I try to remember that day with Mother at the pool, eating ice cream, it splices together with visions of Jeannie and Jessie.

I don't know who I am anymore. Maybe I'm finally becoming the zombie They want me to be.

Father on the night of my initiation was ethereal and invincible. I feel like he should know I'm here. He should be able to transcend time and space to save me.

But he doesn't.

✖

After breakfast, Jeannie doesn't say anything when I go outside and wander around the yard. I walk down the driveway, consider running again. But I have no money, no warm clothes.

It's like I'm real and not real at the same time.

I turn around, head toward the trees. I want to sink into the dirt and disappear.

A shape moves near the birdbath. A man, I think. Maybe he's here to kill me on Their orders, finally. I close my eyes, resigned to the end.

I am tired of fighting.

"Piper," a voice says.

It's Caspian.

38. BEFORE

My skull is on fire.

Light burns through my window, and I roll onto my stomach. Thomas is gone, replaced by Caspian.

"Piper," he says. "Do you need more water?" He smells like sweat and pine cones, and it makes me gag.

I push a pillow over the back of my head and moan. "Too bright," I manage to squeak.

A rustling in the background. I sense less light. Cas lifts one side of the pillow. "Are you okay? Thomas asked me to take care of you. He had to leave."

"I'm fine," I say. "Just a little out of it."

He touches my hand, and the sensation of his skin on mine almost hurts. "He said you might be on something."

I try to remember what happened on the beach. Father coming to me through a mist....I can't remember what he said. Something about being a messenger. "The initiation, Cas. It was amazing and strange and scary...and beautiful. It's hard to explain."

Cas forces me to drink more water. "I'm sure it is."

"I just wish you had been there with me."

He kisses my cheek, a whisper of a kiss that doesn't hurt. "Don't try to talk, okay? You need to rest."

"Cas," I say in a rush. "I'm sorry, so sorry about what happened at your cleansing. I should have said something to Father."

"Don't worry about that now."

Crashing sounds come from outside. The men must be stacking more cement blocks. Someone shouts.

Auntie Joan bursts into the room. "Stay inside!" she yells, and then she disappears. Doors slam.

"What's happening?" I ask.

Cas hurries to the window and pushes back the curtain. "Shit."

"What's happening?" I repeat.

There's a thud in another room, and Cas says, "I'll be right back. Stay here."

I turn onto my side as a wave of nausea rolls through my abdomen. I gulp the rest of the water until the feeling goes away. There are low voices talking outside the door; it's probably Cas and Thomas.

Spiritual awakenings clearly have physical effects. I wish Thomas would come in, so we could compare notes.

Suddenly, Millie's wails pierce the room, and then Beverly Jean starts to scream.

"They're taking us!" she shrieks. "They're taking us away, just like Father said! Pip! Pip!"

I try to get up, but I fall to my knees, tangled in the bedclothes. My head swirls. A woman shouts, a voice I don't recognize, and I crawl to the door, open it, and squirm into the hallway, my legs lifeless.

Beverly Jean stands with her back to me, facing a woman with short gray hair. "I know this is frightening," the woman says. "Please, let me explain what's going to happen!"

I reach for Beverly Jean, but the woman pulls her away from me, looking horrified. "Have you been hurt?" she asks me loudly. "Do you need medical assistance?"

Her voice wobbles; my vision blurs. Beverly Jean is sobbing.

Cas kneels next to me. "I think she's been drugged," he tells the woman quietly.

A man rushes up the stairs, another stranger. There's more shouting outside. "Come on, dear," he says quickly, pulling me up. "Let us help you downstairs."

Another man in a uniform tells them that all the upstairs rooms are clear.

Clear of what?

The first man and Cas practically carry me down; I collapse, and they put me on the couch. A second woman cradles Millie, who is trying to get away. Carla stands near the front door, arms crossed, watching it all; the first woman is standing beside her. Samuel and Henry jump on me as soon as I'm seated, and I try to grip them as tightly as I can. Their faces are distorted, eyes larger than they should be. I kiss their heads, which are hot and sweaty.

"Are we going away?" Samuel asks me, putting his arms around Henry.

The first woman speaks. "Everyone, please take big, deep breaths. You can trust us."

"Where's Father?" is all I can manage to say.

The man whispers something to Caspian. "Everything is going to be fine," he announces hurriedly. "We're from Child Protective Services. You're not in any trouble, and you haven't done anything wrong. We won't hurt you. But we all have to leave right now."

The government. How did they find us?

He keeps talking, but his words bump into each other until they are nonsense. Millie bites the woman on the arm, her eyes huge as she reaches for me. "Led 'er go," I slur.

Father would want me to protect them.

Caspian puts a hand on my forehead. "She's passing out!"

There are popping sounds from outside, like fireworks, and Carla shrieks and dashes behind the couch.

"Everybody down!" someone shouts, and Cas throws his body on top of mine. I can't breathe.

There's a shattering crash. Air hits my face, cooling it—the window has broken, somehow. My eyes burn as I survey the yard. Two of Father's men lay facedown on the grass, sprawled in puddles of red. A man in a blue uniform points a gun at someone, but there's so much smoke, and everything's spinning.

Another one of Father's men has his hands tied behind his back. He sees me. "Say nothing!" he shouts, the words pelting me like rocks.

There are so many police cars in the driveway, people in uniforms, dogs on chains. Father's limousine is pocked with holes. The doors are open at the back of a large white truck, and a uniformed man sits in it, a bloody smear on his face. Where did all these people come from?

Someone struggles in the back of the nearest squad car.

Blond hair. Blue eyes. It's Mother.

She pounds on the window when she sees me, screaming behind the glass. "The world can be an evil place," she shrieks, her voice hysterical. "I'm the only one you can trust. Me and your father. Never forget that!"

I'm being moved, supported. A back seat, a slamming door. A radio is switched off, and the car bumps along.

They're taking me away.

39. AFTER

Cas and I twist ourselves together, mouth against mouth, skin against skin, sanity in the making. I finally feel like myself for the first time since I was taken.

"Piper," he whispers through our kiss. He touches my cheeks, wipes away my tears.

"I'm so glad you're here." I close my eyes and lay my head on his shoulder. "God, Cas, I don't understand anything anymore."

He rubs my back, slowly, his strong arms keeping me from falling over.

"Is it really you?" he asks.

I touch the dimple in his cheek. "It's really me."

He brings my hand to his mouth and kisses my inner wrist. "I thought I'd lost you forever."

"What happened, Caspian? Where'd you go?"

He touches my hair. "I've been with my parents. My real parents."

"It was Thomas, wasn't it?" I whisper. "He went to the government and told them where to find us. That's why They took everyone away. He was the only one missing when the police came."

Cas looks down. "Yes."

"Did you know? Did you know what he was planning to do?"

"I didn't, Piper. He'd been saying all kinds of strange stuff about the compound. But I had no idea he'd go to the police."

My head grows fuzzy, and I sink onto the ground. "How'd you find me?"

Cas sinks with me, holding me. "Turns out Curtis was right about the Internet. You can use it to track down anyone."

"Where are the others? Where's Millie? Does she have her giraffe? The people who took us, where'd they take her? She's got to be sick without us, Cas. And Beverly Jean? Oh, God, she's got to be so scared." My stomach cramps up, and I feel like I'm about to be sick.

"Piper, it's okay. The littles are safe, I promise. They're in foster care." He swallows. "I'm sorry it took me so long to find you."

"Where are Mother and Father?"

"They're gone."

"What do you mean, *gone*?" I imagine a bomb falling on the lake house, incinerating them in an instant like burning paper.

He tucks a strand of hair behind my ear. "No one's seen Curtis for months."

"What about Auntie Barb and Auntie Joan?"

Cas's face blanches. "They're gone, too."

I grab his arms, afraid I'm about to pass out. Daisy starts barking from inside the house.

"I need to get out of here, Cas. I need to go home."

"We can leave right now, Piper. I've got a car. You can trust me."

"No!" I stand and pull him up. "No. Come back later. After the people inside are asleep."

"All right," he says. "I'll come back. At midnight. I'll wait just beyond that gate. You can meet me then."

I kiss him one last time. "You better go before they see you. Daisy won't stop barking until I go inside."

"I'll wait forever if I have to," he says.

40. AFTER

Jeannie left a plate of chicken for me on the table, my pills next to it on a napkin. I slip them into my pocket just as she enters the kitchen. She looks different. Worn out.

"I made you a plate," she says. "You need to eat more."

"Can I eat in my room?"

She doesn't say anything about Caspian. Maybe she didn't see him.

"I suppose so," she says, shuffling by in sweats and slippers. She goes into her room and shuts the door.

I collect the food and retreat to my bedroom. My body screams at me to run, to hide, to never look back. Instead I push the pills under my mattress with all the others and sit on the edge of my bed.

The chicken tastes good, and I ravage it. I need my strength.

Tonight, I'm going home.

My ankle is healed. I'm clean. Caspian is here. Nothing will stop me.

I sit on the bed for hours, a loaded spring, ready to explode. Daisy comes in around nine, like always, and falls asleep on my bed.

I should have known something bad was about to happen back home. Thomas told me—not with his words, but with what he *didn't* say. In the way he walked around like he hated the world. Something was building inside of him, something dark, and I ignored it.

When the clock says eleven, I pack a bag. I don't take much, just a change of clothes and my toothbrush. If I could, I would burn the rest.

Maybe by tomorrow morning I'll be with Mother and Father again. They know I would fight to get home, no matter what. They could be hiding there, waiting for me.

A dot of blood drips onto my jeans. I've bitten my nail down to the quick. I wipe it off on a tissue.

When midnight arrives, I kiss Daisy, walk out of the bedroom, and dash into Amy's room.

She's asleep in her bed. I turn on a lamp and gently shake her arm. "Piper?" she says, her voice full of sleep. "What's going on?"

"I'm getting you out of here—*us* out of here. Tonight. Where's your bag? We've got to move quickly."

She rubs her eyes and sits up. "Why are we leaving?"

I dig through the closet. A pink backpack sits on a shelf, and I pull it down carefully.

"Because it's not safe here."

Amy starts to cry. "I don't want to leave."

I kneel beside her. "Ssshh, don't cry. I'll help you find your real parents. Help me pack." Even as I say the words, something doesn't quite add up. But I don't have time to think about it.

She shakes her head. "I'm not leaving my mama."

"Don't you see they've brainwashed you?" I want to shake some sense into her. But she is so young and so small. No wonder she is confused. That's why I have to think rationally for the both of us.

I pack the bag with pants and underwear from her dresser. "Do you want to bring any toys along?"

216

She holds out a stuffed puppy. It's pink and white, and one of its ears is falling off. I jam it in the bag. Her lip quivers and snot oozes from her nose as I pack random crap.

"Come on," I say, holding out my hand.

She stands and shakes her head. "I don't wanna go!" she cries.

"Goddammit, Amy! If we don't go now, I'm not sure we'll ever get away!" I grab her hand and pull her to the door. Finally, she relents, and we creep down the stairs, her two steps for every one of mine. She won't stop whimpering, and I am certain that every noise she makes will wake Jeannie.

At the bottom of the stairs, I walk into something, a large object that wasn't there before. A wall must've moved again. Something crashes to the floor and shatters.

Amy cries out, and I clamp my hand over her mouth. "Quiet!" I whisper.

When the sound of Jeannie's bedroom door unlocking echoes down the hallway, I pick Amy up, and we race through the garage and into the front yard.

Father couldn't save me.

But I will save her.

It'll be good for her, I can hear Father say. *She'll learn who really loves her.*

I set her down on the driveway, never letting go of her hand. "Come on, Amy!" I shout. "Run! We have to go!"

She drags her feet and falls to her knees, and I drop my bag. She's crying uncontrollably now, a pile of arms and legs on the asphalt.

The front door opens, and Jeannie's silhouette appears in the doorway.

"Piper!" she screams, stumbling into the yard. "What are you doing?"

I am faced with two choices: run, or stay and protect Amy.

Blood slithers in rivulets down Amy's tattered knee. "Mama!" she cries. She looks at me like I'm a monster.

I back away as Jeannie crouches before Amy. She gathers her up, kissing the top of her head, soothing her with hushes.

Rich bounds out the front door. I turn and run as fast as I can, leaving my bag behind.

"Piper!" Rich shouts.

The thud of his feet hitting the driveway slams into me, growing louder every second.

But Cas comes into focus on the other side of the gate. He's here for me, like he promised.

Like I knew he would be.

"Cas!" I scream.

He's parked right next to the gate and scrambles onto the car's roof. I leap onto a grouping of boulders next to the gate, but I'm still a foot or so below the top of the fence. Wrapping my hands around two metal pickets, I push up against the fence with my feet. My muscles burn as I climb. Once I reach the top, I begin to hoist myself up.

"Piper, please stop!" Rich grips my good ankle, and I slip backward a touch. I kick as hard as I can—when my foot connects with his face, he loses his grip and stumbles backward. "Goddammit!" he shouts.

"Cas!" I scramble back up the fence. Cas reaches for me over the top, grips my forearms, and pulls me onto the car's roof.

Jeannie is calling out for me.

"Hurry!" I shriek.

We slide off the car, our feet hitting the road. I can almost feel Jeannie's breath on the back of my neck, almost feel her hands gripping the hem of my T-shirt as she drags me back. We dive inside and slam the doors shut.

He flicks down the visor, and a set of keys falls into his hands. He looks at me. "I rented a motel room," he says. "We can sleep there, okay?"

The engine pops and flickers to life.

"That's fine," I say, out of breath. "Let's just get out of here while we still can!"

41. AFTER

Cas punches the gas, but the car can only chug. The engine whines, and the smell of exhaust permeates the interior.

I keep looking back, but we're the only car on the road.

No Jeannie. No Rich. No flashing lights of police cruisers.

But I know it's only a matter of time. "Hurry, Cas!"

The motel is off a highway about twenty miles from the house. An office is in one building, but doors are sprayed like bullet holes along another.

Cas's key unlocks room 105.

He gestures for me to go inside. There's a king-size bed. Carpeting the color of pea soup. A dusty TV. A dresser with mismatched drawer handles. "I know it's nothing special," he says. "But it's all I could afford. I paid in cash, so we should be safe."

I pull the green curtains across the window with a soft *swoosh*. As soon as the light from the parking lot dies away, I rush to him, bury my face in his chest, wrap my arms around his back, breathe in his scent. He's still Cas, but his clothes smell of a different laundry detergent. He holds me close and kisses the top of my head again and again.

"Are you cold?" he asks. "I can turn up the heat."

"I'm fine." I lean back a touch. "What happened, Cas? I need to know everything about the day They took us away."

"How much has Jeannie told you?"

"She tells me some things, but they're lies. Mostly I try not to listen."

He gazes at me, like he's looking for something. "Do you really want to know what happened? Even if it might hurt?"

I suck in a breath and exhale. "I'm not sure anymore. Of anything."

I let him guide me to the bed, and I curl up on one side. "Don't just stand there. Lie next to me." For a moment, I sound almost like my old self.

The bed springs squeak as he fits himself behind me and nuzzles the back of my neck. I lace my fingers through his and hold his hand against my chest, my heart fluttering away like one of the sparrows back home.

"Are you really here?" I whisper.

His warm, soft lips kiss an answer on my neck.

"I thought I'd never see you again," I say. "Don't leave."

"I never will."

I release his hand and roll over. Brush the hair from his forehead. Such a small gesture, but one I thought I'd lost forever, a memory of what I'd never get back. A tear slips off the side of his nose, and I wipe it away. "I love you," I whisper.

"I love you, too," he says, pressing his lips to mine. His kiss tastes salty, and we melt into each other, the connection keeping me safe from everything that happened before and everything that might happen in the future.

Caspian is my own perfect world, one I never want to leave.

"What happened to my parents?" I ask after a while, when even Cas's kisses can't push the fear away.

He runs his fingers down my cheek, over my jaw, and down my neck. He's hesitating, and I shiver. "You said you weren't sure if you wanted to know."

"I *need* to know."

"Curtis…Curtis and his best men left right after your initiation," he says. "Angela is in prison, Piper. She's awaiting trial for child abuse and a bunch of other charges. The Aunties, too."

My body tenses.

Father is gone. Father, who said he would never leave me.

Father, the strongest person I know. A messenger, an otherworldly being, lost to the mist.

I shoot off the bed and into the bathroom, crouch over the toilet, and vomit.

Cas follows with a bottle of water.

"Thanks," I say, and take a drink. "Sorry you had to see that. And smell it."

"You can use my toothbrush," he offers.

I collect myself, brush thoroughly, and then climb back into bed with him. He runs his fingers up and down my arm. "That tickles," I say, my voice growing sleepy.

He touches my hair. "What's it been like, living with Jeannie?"

"It's hard to explain."

He kisses me. "Try."

"At first, she kept me locked inside the house all the time. She's eased up some now." I look at the ceiling, stained brown in spots. "Cas, I keep having these memories, like I know her. But I know

222

they're not true, can't be true.…I don't know." I close my eyes for a moment. "What about you? Where are you living now?"

"With my parents, remember?" He tucks a strand of hair behind my ear. "They have an apartment by my high school."

"You…go to school?" My heart freezes. I want to ask about his parents, but I can't. This is too much.

"Yeah. But it's great, Piper. I'm behind in my studies, but I have help, and the kids are nice, too."

I roll onto my back.

"What's wrong?" he asks, propping himself up on his elbow.

"I feel like you're leaving me behind. Like I don't fit into your new life." I swallow. "Like you *enjoy* living on the Outside."

He leans down and kisses me. "You *are* my life, Piper."

"Maybe for now. But you'll meet someone else. Someone…someone more like you are now."

Caspian sits up. "I want to show you something." He rolls up his sleeve and holds up his inner wrist. My name is inked into his skin in a rolling script. "I got this a month ago. You're permanent."

I try to say something, but my stupid throat closes and all I can do is kiss him until I'm dizzy and we make a pile of clothes on the floor.

After, we wrap our arms around each other, and I watch Cas fall asleep. His eyes sink closed, his breathing slows.

Minutes tick by on the alarm clock, and I am no closer to sleep.

I carefully slip out of his arms, pull on my T-shirt and underwear, and sit at the table by the window. Everyone just expects me to move on, as if my family are lost stuffed animals I can replace with new ones.

People aren't interchangeable.

The sun rises, and Cas's soft snores cease. He stretches and sits up. The blanket falls from his bare shoulders, and I blush. "Did you sleep at all?" he asks.

"No."

"Maybe you should try to lie down for a while. You need rest."

"I can rest when I'm dead. I need to see the house now."

We both put on sweatshirts, dark and hooded, that Cas brought with him. I pull my hair over my face, so I don't look so much like myself. He says people are probably looking for us.

Then we return the key to the office, and Cas drives us to a diner nearby. "You have to at least eat something first," he says. "It's a two-hour drive."

"All this time I've been two hours from home. Might as well have been a million miles."

I pick a booth next to a fish mural painted on the wall. A woman in a blue dress and white apron greets us with a "Howdy! What can I get you?" She takes a pencil out from behind her ear.

Cas opens the large, plastic menu. "I'll have waffles, bacon, and orange juice."

She jots it down. "And you, dear?" she asks me.

"Blueberry pancakes."

I smile at the memories of Mother's blueberry pancakes. She made her own syrup, too, collected in buckets from the maple trees around our house.

Other customers trickle in. Silverware clanks, and conversations ebb and flow. Our food comes, and it's good. Cas watches me.

I set down my fork. "Would you stop looking at me like that?"

The sun illuminates his eyes, bluer than I've ever seen them. "I'm sorry. I just can't believe I'm actually here with you. That you're still *you*."

"But I'm not me, Cas. Not anymore. That's the part no one seems to get."

He doesn't know he's speaking to a ghost.

"You're still you, Piper. And I'm still me. Nothing will ever convince me otherwise." We reach for each other across the table.

"Let's please just go to the house," I say.

Cas sets money on the table and holds the door open for me. A bell tinkles as we go outside.

When we get to the car, he unlocks the passenger door, and it creaks as he opens it for me.

"You said that the littles are in foster care. What is that, exactly?" I ask, sliding into my seat. He shuts my door without answering. When he gets in on his side, I repeat my question.

"It's homes where children without parents go to live. People volunteer to be surrogate parents."

"But we have parents."

He doesn't answer.

42. AFTER

The silver maple trees that line our old driveway appear, the same and yet somehow different. The mid-morning sun colors their leaves a brilliant yellow.

I release a breath I didn't realize I'd been holding in.

I've been holding it since They first took me away. Pumped me full of drugs. Took my memories.

But today I am home. I am safe. I am me once again.

Until I remember the day They took me. The smell of copper and gunpowder, the popping noises.

The men lying facedown on our lawn.

I chew my nails.

Cas parks near the end of the drive and turns the key. The car dies with a whimper.

"Is your engine held together with rubber bands?" I tease.

He smiles. I haven't made anyone smile like that in a long time. "I have to fix it every other week. But I love having a car."

We stare out the windshield at the remains of our former lives. What's left of the old roller coaster, the trees, the garden.

I'm reminded of the first time Father brought us here, a memory I didn't know I had. I clung to Mother's side, afraid of the broken-down rides and graffiti.

"This will do just fine." He had strutted around the ruins like a conqueror. *"We'll be very safe and secure here."*

Then he went to work, building a dream life for us.

This place seems deflated as we wander down the drive. There are no people, and yet it is still so full of life—much more so than Jeannie and Rich's sterile house. I don't fit there, but I don't fit here, either.

We stand on the overgrown lawn, staring at the house.

I'm afraid, and Cas knows it. He takes my hand and kisses my fingers. I gently run my finger over his tattoo, the skin warm and slightly raised.

"You truly haven't heard from anyone?" I ask.

He shakes his head and squeezes my hand. "I've really missed you, Piper. I dream about you almost every night. My therapist says that's normal."

"You have a therapist, too?" He didn't answer my question, but I don't push him. Not yet.

"For months. It was super weird at first. Do you like yours?"

I smile. "I might. He wears the world's ugliest sweaters...but I think I kind of trust him. Father would probably be very upset if he heard me say that."

Cas lightly kisses my neck. "You ready to go inside?"

I close my eyes for a moment and remember our night at the bumper cars. We'd kissed each other in the hallway outside our bedrooms, knowing we could be caught but not caring. That life seems so far away now.

"Ready as I can be."

The front of the house is just as we left it, but for the yellow police tape slashing the front door. I rip it away and toss it on the grass. The door sits open, and when we go inside, I lose my breath.

The dining room table is gone, and the chairs are tipped over, broken.

"Piper," Cas says, but I ignore him and move deeper into the house. Mother's mason jars are smashed on the ground. The kitchen-cabinet doors hang from their hinges. All our dishes are broken.

I suck in a sob and continue upstairs to my bedroom. The door is closed, and Cas touches my shoulder. "Are you sure you want to see?"

"Yes."

I push open the door to my room. My sanctuary.

Everything is wrong.

All the furniture is gone. The beds, the desk, the braided rug Mother and I made together. Pieces of the wall have been cut away. The window is busted, and bits of glass lie helplessly on the floor. None of the girls' toys remain: Millie's giraffe, Carla's sketchbook, Beverly Jean's paper dolls. All gone.

"Our stuff," I say, my voice quivering.

"The police took it."

"Why?"

He touches the window. "Evidence for Angela's and the Aunties' trials. And for Curtis's, if they ever catch him."

The boys' bedroom is empty, too. Henry's cowboy hat, vanished. Sam's Super Nintendo. It's like we never existed.

Father's office beckons. The *Last Supper* is gone, along with his papers and typewriter.

I wonder if I am his Judas. I knew something was wrong with Thomas, but I didn't tell Father. Maybe if I'd said something, we'd still all be together.

But then you'd be married, a voice whispers. *You didn't want that. You knew it wouldn't have been right.*

"Please, take me away from here," I breathe.

"There's more you need to see, Piper."

"What if I don't want to?"

Caspian laces his fingers through mine and leads me toward the front door. "You have to."

I try not to look at our couch, the cushions damp and moldy and covered with broken glass. I try not to remember watching TV with Thomas, Sunday breakfasts, happiness when Mother and Father came to visit us.

I wish I could forget.

We are silent as we cross the driveway and move into the woods, down the same path where Father had his vision of me joining the Community and working alongside him. I'd been so happy then.

Cas says nothing as we pass the bumper cars, and I squeeze his hand tighter until we reach a section of fence that's been removed. The woods shiver in front of us, held back by nothing.

The Outside has been let in.

I can almost feel the darkness seeping through my skin, the pollution, the EMF.

Caspian wraps his arms around me. "It's okay. I promise."

Holding my breath, we walk through the fence into the Outside. The air is cooler the deeper we go into the forest. We pick our way over rocks and rotting trees, the smell of loam pungent and unrelenting.

Up ahead, a massive clown's head reveals itself, half swallowed by dirt and hidden in overgrowth, the remains of an old ride. I stop.

"Where are we going?" I've seen enough, and I want to go back.

Back to when I understood how life was supposed to work.

"To the main compound," Cas answers.

"But that's hours and hours from here."

Cas shakes his head. "No, it's not. I'll show you."

I take a step back. "But Father and Mother had to travel so far to see us. It's why they couldn't come often."

"I know this isn't what you want to hear, but it's true. The compound's right here."

"I don't believe you!"

"You need to see it for yourself."

I follow behind him this time, afraid. Caspian wouldn't lie about something like this. But neither would Father.

As the trees thin out and the sunshine brightens the ground, I keep my head down.

"We're here," he says, and I step into a clearing.

43. BEFORE

Tree branches filter past the window. My eyes try to catch each one, like the blades of a ceiling fan, but they're too fast.

I lie back down on the car seat.

"I want my father," I whisper, woozy.

"Do you know where he might be?" The Child Protective Services woman in the front passenger seat twists toward me.

I shake my head; the upholstery scratches my face. I close my eyes, try to block everything out.

My stomach cramps suddenly, and I struggle to sit up. "I'm gonna be sick," I gasp.

The car lurches to a stop.

A door opens, hands haul me out.

I fall to my knees and vomit in the wild grasses along a road I've never been on before.

The war has begun.

44. AFTER

The sound here is wrong.

Like if I screamed, the air would swallow it away.

Four long, wooden buildings stretch toward me, whitewashed with tin roofs. "These are the barracks where the members slept," Cas tells me. "Men in the first two, women and children in the last two."

He takes my hand as we walk between the middle two buildings. No grass grows here. Gravel crunches under our shoes. Some kind of metal cage is attached to the side of one building, open on the top, filled with rotting food. Curtains flap in windows left open, and the smell of old sweat rolls out of them.

Cas stops at a wooden door and nudges it open with his shoulder. He pushes something on his cell phone—he has a cell phone?—and it lights up. "Flashlight," he explains.

The floorboards squeak as we step inside. A shape scuttles along the floor near our feet. "I'll show you where my mom slept," he says.

"Father expelled your parents," I remind him. "They weren't here."

Cas shakes his head. "That's what he said, but he lied, Piper. They were here the whole time." I grab onto his hand as he shines his light over unmade beds, tables, dilapidated dressers. Motes of dust hover in the stale air. Framed photos of Father hang from the otherwise bare walls.

Cas stops in front of one of the beds. "This one was hers. The police found a photo of me and Thomas as kids under her pillow. She said she thought about us every day, and how we were so much better off at Curtis's private compound. Members went on fasts to cleanse their bodies and spirits, so she was used to not eating, but she never knew that *we* didn't have enough food."

He shines his light on the next bed. "Here's Angela's bed."

I stare at him. "She wasn't with Father?"

"Curtis had his own house, separate from the others. Sometimes Angela stayed with him, sometimes other women did. It depended, I guess."

His words slam into me, and I stumble back a step. "He had other wives?"

"Legally, Angela was his only wife. But I think he had sex with a lot of female members."

I walk to Mother's bed. It smells faintly of the same lotion she kept at the house, and I sit, afraid I might pass out. I can't imagine Mother living in such a sad, simple place. "Where are all her fancy clothes? Her shoes?"

Cas shrugs. "Maybe she kept them at Curtis's house?"

"She always talked about her businesses. Was that a lie, too?"

Caspian sits next to me. "Yeah. I'm sorry, Piper. Angela's parents left her a lot of money when they died, but she gave it all to Curtis. Most members gave him all their money, including my parents. My aunt had to loan them money to rent our apartment."

I ease off the bed. All these years, I imagined Mother flying around the world and sitting behind a big desk somewhere with big ideas. I imagined Father on a ranch with rolling hills, his people working together for a greater purpose. A fly buzzes my face, and I wave it away.

"Let's get out of here," I say, needing to escape the heat of this building, the sting of the truth on the back of my neck.

He shines his light in front of me, and I dash outside. We walk the length of the barracks and arrive in an open area. In the center stands a large wooden tower, whitewashed like everything else. Painted on its front in big, black letters are the words:

> The Community is truth.
> The Community is loyalty.
> The Community will keep you safe.

At this size, its meaning overwhelms me. All that I've lost. All that I could have been.

"This was the guard tower," Cas says. "Members took shifts, kind of like Curtis made us do at the roller coaster." He watches me, but I won't look at him.

To our right is a large stage with several tables set out before it. "This is where Curtis delivered his sermons. The lawyers told me his father was a preacher. It's where he learned, I guess."

"Lawyers?" I can barely hear myself.

He climbs up and walks back and forth, looking out over the empty tables. "For Angela's trial. And the Aunties'. No one can find Curtis yet, but they're still charging him."

"But Mother didn't do anything wrong," I say.

Cas jumps off the stage and sits next to me. "Piper, she did *a lot* of things wrong. She helped Curtis brainwash people. Brainwash *us*. She kept all of us caged in at the lake house. She drugged you." He stares at me, his blue eyes burning. "And she and Curtis stole children. That's why Thomas went to the police. He overheard the Aunties talking about them taking another child from the Outside. He couldn't let that happen."

My head snaps up. "No. Cas, no, please. How can you say these things?" My words waver. "They love us. Whatever they did, it was because they love us. Love *me*. I'm their daughter."

"Maybe. But that doesn't make what they did right."

I fold my hands in my lap and stare at them.

Everything starts to spin.

I think of my fuzzy childhood memories, of that VHS tape of Jeannie and Jessie, and an awful thought comes to me.

"Caspian...was I stolen, too?" My voice comes out so quiet I sound like Beverly Jean.

Blood courses into my ears, and I can barely hear when Cas says, "Yes."

No.

I refuse to believe this.

"Let's keep going." I jump up.

There has to be a reason for all of this, for everything that's happened. Father knows why all of this was done. I just need to trust in him.

Truth.

Loyalty.

Safety.

A fenced-in garden sprawls out behind the stage. Fruits and vegetables stick up in neat rows, all rotting in the ground. A small shed holds rakes and hoes, just like the ones we used on our garden at the lake house. On the other side of the field a barn leans to one side.

Cas takes me to another small building. It has no windows. A single door leads inside, and he uses his cell phone again to light the way. "This is where the members held meetings, worked on projects, whatever else they did. They had a few old generators for electricity, same as us. And solar power."

"Why aren't there any windows?" I ask.

"This was going to be a fallout shelter until Curtis had them build it at the lake house."

Strange masks hang from nails on the wall. I take one down. It's heavy, with big round goggles and a piece of plastic over the mouth.

"That's a gas mask." Caspian takes it from me and puts it on for a second. "You use it in case of radiation or poison gas attacks. It filters the air or something."

"How do you know all this?"

"About the compound? My parents told me. About everything else? I've been reading a lot. Researching stuff for myself."

I place the mask back on its hook. When Father returns, I want this place to be the way he left it. The way he would want it. "I want to see Father's house now."

Caspian takes my hand, but I barely feel it.

Father's essence grows stronger once we leave the building. His house is a couple of hundred feet away. Small and simple, but different from the other structures, more comfortable. It has black shutters on the windows and a tiled roof. A few bushes and succulents grow out front. A narrow brick path leads to the stoop, where the door has been left ajar, and we go inside.

A large, open room has a kitchen on one side, a couch and a few chairs on the other. A door at the back leads into a bedroom. Its large bed has a white comforter, neatly made. One of Mother's hats hangs from a coat rack in the corner, and I smile. I knew she stayed here with Father. Caspian's mom must be lying.

The closet is mostly empty except for some of Father's linen pants and shirts.

"I think the police took all of his personal stuff," Cas says behind me. "This is like one big crime scene."

I ignore him and slide a large cardboard box out of the closet. I fold back the flaps and pull out a moth-eaten crocheted blanket.

It's one of my blankets. The last one I made, with the yellow and green yarn Mother gave me.

I set it on the bed and pull out the next one.

And the next one.

All those blankets I made for shelters, rotting in a box. Spread out on Father's bed, they're a map of my past.

A map that led to nowhere.

"He never took them to a shelter," I say without emotion.

"Curtis rarely left the compound. Others weren't allowed to leave at all." Cas's words come out all warbled.

I gather the blankets and shove them back into the box, not caring that they're no longer folded. I look around the room for something to break. I pick a hairbrush off his nightstand and hurl it at the window. The glass shatters.

Cas touches my shoulder. "Are you okay?"

I shake him off and fall onto my knees. The room sways, and I squeeze my eyes shut. Maybe this is all a dream, and when I wake up, everything will be as it should be.

As Father promised it would be.

I take a deep breath and look around the room. "He was a liar, wasn't he, Cas?"

"Yes."

"Why did he do this? What was his *reason* for lying to me?"

Cas sits next to me and pulls me into a hug, and I cling to him. "There is no reason, at least no good reason. My mom says Curtis just likes to control people."

I squeeze my eyes shut as hard as I can, but I can't hold back the tears that come without permission, soaking into Cas's T-shirt. I cry until my belly aches and I am hollow.

My whole world is gone, and I'm mad at the sun for still shining.

I'm mad at Cas for starting a new life without me.

I'm mad at myself for letting down my brothers and sisters, for not protecting them like I said I would.

But most of all, I'm mad at Mother and Father.

I move back and wipe my nose on the back of my hand. "I want to see her."

"Who?" he asks.

I take a deep breath. "Mother."

45. AFTER

We wait by Cas's car, the compound and lake house tucked into the trees behind us as the sun goes down. When Jeannie's car appears on the horizon, Cas stands up straight.

"Don't worry, Piper. We'll just explain what happened. I'm sure they'll understand," he says. "They're gonna hate me, not you."

I don't say anything. I don't think they're capable of understanding.

But I didn't think Father and Mother were capable of what I just saw.

Nothing is certain.

Tires crunch gravel, doors slam, and Jeannie and Rich rush out.

Jeannie pulls me against her so tight I couldn't wiggle away if I wanted to. She strokes the back of my head, crying. "Don't you ever run away like that again." Her voice is thick, like she's trying to speak through a wad of cotton. "Do you have any idea how worried I've been?"

"How worried we've both been," Rich says, standing behind her. His eyes are damp. "God, the police have been looking for you."

"I'm sorry," I say, the first time I've uttered those words to her, to them. Something breaks open inside my chest.

"I'm sorry, too. So very sorry," Jeannie says softly. She releases me and steps back, then wipes her face and looks at Cas. "You must be Caspian Hunt." Her voice is monotone. Rich says nothing.

I turn toward Cas. "Yes, this is Cas. Please don't blame him for anything. I just needed to come here one last time—I asked him to take me and he did. I didn't think you'd understand."

Caspian steps forward and holds out his arm. "It's nice to meet you both," he says.

Jeannie hesitates, but then she shakes his hand.

"What in the hell were you thinking, taking her away like that?" Rich shouts. "And in the middle of the night?"

Cas flinches. "I'm sorry," he says. "I thought it would help her if she could see this place again. We weren't running away or—or planning to stay here."

"He's right," I say. "I wasn't thinking straight. But we're both okay. And I promise it won't happen again."

Jeannie looks around, takes a deep breath, and lets it out. "So this is where you lived."

Rich closes his eyes and pinches the bridge of his nose. He looks like he's in pain.

I nod. "The compound is through the woods. Caspian only brought me here so I could see it for myself."

"See what? The compound?" Jeannie asks.

"I didn't know it was here. I'd never been." My voice wavers. "Father and Mother always told me it was far away. That it took them hours and hours to get to us."

Rich walks in a slow circle, looking up at the trees, the sky. "Unbelievable," he mutters.

"Jeannie, I need to ask you to do something for me," I say. "Even if you don't want to."

She puts her hands on my shoulders. "What is it you need?"

I take a deep breath. "I want to see my mother."

Jeannie's eyes widen. "Angela? At the prison?"

"Yes. As soon as I can. And I want Cas to take me."

"Absolutely not," Rich snaps. "That woman does *not* get to see you, and you're not going anywhere else with *him*."

Jeannie's quiet for a while. "This was her whole life, Rich," she says, turning toward him. "We can't just pretend it never happened." She gazes at me. "Are you sure you need to see her?"

"I am. I need answers, and she's the only person left who can give them to me. Please try to understand."

I hold my breath as I wait for an answer.

"I'll call and speak to the detectives and my lawyer. Have you put on her visitor's list," she says finally. "But, Piper? Don't ever run away like that again, do you understand?" She finds my hands. "I would have taken you here. You don't have to hide these things from me. You don't have to hide *anything* anymore."

My eyes burn. "Thank you," I whisper.

Jeannie tries to smile. "Let's go home."

46. AFTER

Last Warning. Do Not Stand Up.

Cas drives us to the prison from my house. A razor-wire fence surrounds the sprawling brick building.

When I release my seat belt, it recoils from me.

Jeannie gave me a list of rules for my visit. No halter tops or short shorts. No skirts above the knee. No spandex. No weapons. Nothing flammable.

I'm here in a dirty sweatshirt, nothing in my pockets. But I still worry something will go wrong, and I won't be allowed to see her.

Cas takes my hand as we walk through the parking lot. "You don't have to go in if you don't want to. We can always come back another time."

I swallow. "I need to see her. I need answers."

We enter the lobby, and the officer asks for my ID.

Jeannie's lawyer got me an ID that says Piper Haggerty; it's sweaty from being stuffed in the back pocket of my jeans. I don't look at it as I give it to the officer. He checks me in. Everyone is staring at me like they know me.

Cas is not on the list. "You'll be fine," he whispers. "See you in a bit."

"Do you want me to tell her you're here?"

He looks away. "Better not."

The officer takes me into a room jammed with tables and chairs. Inmates in jumpsuits sit across from family members, talking quietly.

"You're not in here," the officer says.

We move deeper into the prison, to a room with hunter-green brick walls. A wall of glass separates the room into two. Metal stools are bolted to the concrete floor. Two lawyers introduce themselves to me—one represents Mother, the other, Jeannie. I ignore them.

And there she is.

Seated on the other side of the glass.

Dressed in orange.

Flesh and blood.

Hair dull, no makeup. She is smaller than I remember, shrunken.

"Mother," I whisper.

When she sees me, she gasps. "Piper!" An officer on her side tells her to keep her voice down.

I rush toward the glass, pressing my hands against it, getting as close as I can. The stress of being at the compound, finding the blankets—all of it melts into the edges and blurs.

She presses her hands against mine. Two inches of glass can't keep us apart. "My baby," she says, tears drowning her cheeks. "I've missed you so much."

I gulp, trying not to cry in front of all these strangers. "I've missed you, too." I lean my forehead against the glass, and she hums the same lullaby she's been singing to me in my dreams. I wish I could smash through this glass to be with her.

"Why are you here, Mother? Where's Father?" The questions spill over themselves. "When is this all going to be over?"

"I'm so sorry, Piper. I never meant to leave you, or for any of this to happen. You know that, right?"

"Of course I do."

"Good, good." She looks behind her. "I never know who's listening," she whispers.

"Who's listening?" I ask. "*Who* is listening?"

A fluorescent light flickers above her. Her blond hair has started to grow out. She has dark roots.

Her hair was dyed. All this time.

"The government, the cops. Unbelievers. I wish I could tell you everything, sweetheart. But I can't. Your father—" She cuts herself off. "Have you seen him?"

"No one has."

She shakes her head. "No, he's gone underground. He'll surface for you and the others when the time is right."

"What do I do until then?" I ask. "I feel like I don't know who I am anymore."

"You stay strong and resolute in your beliefs. You're being tested, sweetheart. We all are."

"Cas took me to the compound today."

The color drains from her face.

"You and Father were so near, all that time," I continue, my voice losing strength. "Why did you pretend it took hours to come see us?"

"It wasn't a lie, Piper. It was a strategic decision, to keep us all close but separate." Her eyes are too bright. "The adult Community members and our children were better off apart. It kept you safe. You were too beautiful, too pure to live around adult men. Sometimes they can't control themselves."

"But you still could have told me, or come to stay with us more. We needed you." I exhale. "*I* needed you. Did you know I was all alone the first time I got my period? I thought I was dying. The Aunties laughed at me."

"But look at how strong you are now, Piper. We raised you to be a strong woman. And you are. Because of us."

A chill brushes over my skin, pimpling my arms in goose bumps. "I don't feel strong, Mother. I feel like you and Father lied to us and then just...left us behind."

"That's not true!"

"Isn't it? Look where you are. You're in a prison."

"And I shouldn't be! A mother loving her child is not a crime!"

"Caspian told me something else today."

The words sit on the tip of my tongue, teetering. I could swallow them down, keep the peace like I always have. But I can't. Not this time.

"He said you took me from my birth parents. Am I your biological daughter?"

"How *dare* you ask such a question!" she spits, taking her hand away from the glass, away from me. "Of course you're my daughter. Why would you even think such a thing?"

"That's not what I asked you, Mother," I say, through clenched teeth.

A clock ticks on the wall, and time slips through my fingers like wind through the trees. I lick my lips, trying to find a way to ask my next question.

My future sits on the other side of this glass, and it scares me.

"Did you buy me my pink swim cap, or did Jeannie? Not the one with flowers on it—the all-pink one." I tense. "Did you take me to swim lessons? Did you take me to the park for ice cream? *Or did Jeannie?*"

Her lips tremble, but she doesn't answer. She won't meet my eyes.

"Tell me!" I demand.

She shakes her head. "I don't remember, Piper. Don't you let them get inside your head. We *are* a real family. You, me, your father, and all your brothers and sisters. I love you more than anything, even myself. I would give up my *life* to protect you."

"But I remember them. Jeannie and Rich. You can't explain them away."

"No," she says. "You only *think* you do. Those hospitals, psychotropic drugs—it's all an effort to brainwash people. Remember your teachings!"

The clock ticks louder now, and the officer's boots thud behind me as he walks back and forth. "Cas told me the truth, Mother. He's never lied to me. Not once."

She leans forward. Her pupils are big and black, almost erasing the blue. "You were born to us on a spiritual level, Piper. The only way that matters. We did what we had to do to save you."

"Save me from what?" I ask breathlessly.

"From the abuses of the Outside world, from the coming war. From *everything*." She rubs her temples. "You believe me, don't you?"

I stare at her face: her chapped lips, her dirty hair. Without her makeup and dresses, she's so...ordinary. "I think everything I've heard about you and Father is true. That you're liars and frauds."

"No. No, darling. Please don't give up on us," she says, her voice shaking. She puts her hands back on the glass, and the little girl I used to be wants to mirror it, wants to be her perfect daughter again. But the person I am now can't stomach it.

"Don't give up on *you*?" I ask. "The way you didn't give up on me?" I laugh, and the bitterness poisons it, turns it into a stone. "The way you withheld your love, your time, even food? Was that you *not* giving up on me?"

"Ugly things will be said about me and your father, but don't believe it. We love you. Everything we've done is out of our love for you."

"Five minutes left," the officer says, his voice slamming against my back, pushing at my skin, at all my sore spots. Sweat rolls down my neck, and my stomach roils. I can hear the lawyers murmuring.

"I was *starving*, Mother. You let that happen. You and Father. Not the Outside. Not the government. You!" She shakes her head and covers her ears. "Listen to me, goddammit!" When I pound at the glass, an officer places a hand on my shoulder.

"One more outburst, and you're done," he says.

"I'm done anyway," I say, and rise from the stool. Mother drops her hands and looks up at me, eyes as wide as Millie's, as if she's surprised I'm leaving. As if I'm hurting her. But I can see now that she left me a long time ago.

That prick of pain in my chest returns. Because somehow, I know our relationship is over.

There will always be a
before
and an
after.

"Don't you dare give up on me!" she shouts as I turn and walk back to the officer, hands pressed into my stomach. I won't let her see me cry. "Piper! Turn around, my darling! Piper! Piper, please, I'm speaking to you! I'm your mother! *I am* your mother! *Piper!*"

✘

Cas stands when I enter the waiting area.

"How'd it go?" he asks earnestly. "What did she say?"

"Not much."

"Are you glad you saw her?" He touches my cheek, wipes away the tears I hadn't realized I'd shed.

"Ask me later," I say, plopping down in one of the chairs. He sits next to me. For a while, we let the silence wash over us. "Cas, I was supposed to marry Thomas," I admit.

"I know you were."

I look at him. "You knew? How?"

"Thomas told me. After. When we were back with our parents." He puts an arm around me. "He said he knew it was wrong, Piper. That he never would have made you go through with it. That it wasn't Father's choice to make."

"He did?"

Cas nods.

Thomas is a better person than either Father or Mother.

"I wish I could go home with you," I say, finally. "I miss you and Thomas so much."

"Piper, you already have a home. You should try to make the most of it."

"That isn't my home. This isn't my life." I smear tears away. "I don't have a life anymore. I'm alone."

"Hey. No. I'm only a couple of hours away. We'll visit each other on weekends. Maybe Jeannie will even let you get a cell phone now. We can text. Some of my school friends showed me this thing, Snapchat. We can use that, too."

"It's not the same. We used to see each other every day. I have no one left."

"You have Jeannie and Rich and Amy. And me. Always me."

"I'm scared, Cas."

"I'm scared, too."

He pulls me into him, and our bodies curve together.

He is mine, and I am his.

✖

Jeannie is waiting for me outside the prison. She insisted on driving me home, and I'm too tired to argue. I say a quick goodbye to Cas. Jeannie thanks him for bringing me.

She puts her arm around my shoulders and walks me toward her car. My legs are a little rubbery, so I let her. "I brought juice boxes," she says. "Apple or orange?"

"Apple," I say. She gets one from the trunk. I gulp it down, which helps everything come into focus. "Thanks, by the way. For letting me see my mother. I mean . . . for letting me see Angela."

"How was your visit?" she asks as we get into the car.

Some answers are impossible to shrink down to syllables and words.

"It was okay."

"Are you hungry? I could order pizza when we get home? Or we could go out. Whatever you want."

"Pizza sounds good."

When we get home, she calls the delivery place and asks for extra green olives and mushrooms.

My favorites.

I am six again, sitting on the couch, biting into a slice. She and Rich are both there.

If they were always there, why didn't I take them with me? How did I forget them?

When the pizza arrives, Jeannie hands out paper plates, and we watch a movie. Amy snuggles in next to me. She drops a green olive on her shirt and laughs. Everyone smiles at me, and we chew mostly in silence. The movie is about two dogs and a cat who get lost and try to find their way back to their family.

I already know how it ends. No one can really go home again.

Not the same as when they left.

47. BEFORE

"Piper."

My eyes burn. When I open them, my lids rip off the top layer of my eyes, and I am certain I am blind.

"Piper."

I lick my lips, blink again, and the room comes into focus. The ceiling tiles are stained. The fluorescent lighting hums.

A man in a white coat peers down at me. He smiles and touches my arm, gently, as if the slightest bit of pressure will break me.

"Piper, I'm Dr. Okonkwo. Can you hear me?"

I run my hands over the blankets pulled over my body. They're rough, nothing like the soft comforter at home. When I bring my hand to my face, my right arm jerks back.

"You have an IV in your arm," he says. "You're receiving fluids."

The room speaks to me now, shares its secrets. The beeping machines. The blackened TV mounted to the wall across from my bed.

A tear slides down my face. And then another. I swallow them away. I think of Father's strong face, of Mother's expert hands.

The doctor listens to my heart, takes my temperature.

"Your vitals are strong, Piper."

When I try to speak, no sound comes out.

"Don't try to talk now. Just get some rest."

I'm fading again. A woman stands in the corner, silently crying.
Someone please help me.

Voices whispering.

"*How long will she be here?*"

"*It's too soon to tell.*"

"*This is my fault. I shouldn't have left her alone that day.*"

"*It's no one's fault.*"

"*I love her so much.*"

"*I know you do.*"

Father stands over me, blocking out almost all the light.

"*It's for her own good,*" he says. Then he throws a bucket of
ice-cold water into the cramped room, soaking me.

I can't stop shivering.

Mother's face flashes before me, and for a moment, I'm warm.

Father stands aloof while I shiver, drenched from head to toe.

48. AFTER

I rest my forehead against the window. Jeannie is driving us to the house Father and Mother took me to after they stole me.

Stole me. I still can't believe it.

The road whips by, and my eyes jump to the random pieces of garbage tossed into ditches. Jeannie is taking me farther and farther from Father and his teachings. I can feel his disappointment on the back of my neck.

"How much longer?" I ask.

"It's pretty close," she says, checking her phone.

How can you be so weak? Father asks.

I roll down my window, and the air blasts my face. I stick my hand outside, let it skate on the currents.

He doesn't get to decide for me today.

We travel through small towns, each indistinguishable from the one before. I'm disoriented. I have no idea where we are as she takes us down a long driveway that disappears into a grouping of trees.

She slows the car.

Up ahead is a dirty white mobile home. It leans away from us, as if about to fall backward.

"Does anyone live here now?" I ask, breathless.

"No one's lived here for years." She turns off the car. "Are you ready?"

"I guess so."

She opens my door for me, and I take her hand. "I have candy, granola bars, and water in the car. If you feel dizzy, tell me."

Rust has annihilated a lot of the trailer. But the windows and doors are intact.

"Are you sure you want to do this?" she asks softly. "There's no shame in changing your mind. You've taken a huge step just by coming here today."

"I'm ready," I tell her. "I need to see it. I'll go crazy if I don't."

The front door is locked, so Jeannie kicks out the glass. Heat rolls out as the door swings open, like we're opening an oven that's been left on too long, and I hesitate.

Collecting myself, I push inside.

The home is narrow and dark, with paneled walls and angry brown carpeting. It stinks of mold and neglect. There is no furniture.

Light can't get through the dust-covered windows. Jeannie gasps and puts her hand over her mouth.

The kitchen waits to my left, and I open a cupboard door. Running my hands along the shelves, I find nothing but dirt and cobwebs and curled-up cockroaches. No notes from my parents. No dishes that belonged to them. No nothing. I knew there wouldn't be.

There's a narrow hallway on the other side of the living room that leads to two bedrooms, each empty. I wonder which room I slept in.

No one, not even Father, has been here for years. The dead pill bugs and animals' nests are proof of that. Wherever he is now, it's far away.

"Let's go outside," I say. "I can hardly breathe in here."

The breeze dries the sweat on my skin, and I shiver. The Santa Anas remind me of the coolness of the lake. In the yard, I look for signs I was here. A swing set maybe. A sandbox. Weeds and wildflowers crowd the lawn.

"Are you sure I lived here?" I ask her. She stands next to me, mouth set in a stiff line.

"Yes. Angela gave this location to the police, and there's proof of rent paid. The police and FBI have already been here."

The police.

"You can't always trust the police," I tell her.

"Is that what Curtis told you?"

"Yes."

"He's right that some police can't be trusted. But some can. It can have a lot to do with what you look like, I'm afraid. We'll talk about it more."

We walk around the back of the trailer. A pile of wood rots under a line of trees. I wonder if Father cut that wood, if we roasted marshmallows and hot dogs, if we laughed here.

A deck sinks into the ground. I put my hand on the red-stained wood, its color preserved by the trees' shade. Did I hold this railing with my small hand? Did Mother read to me on this deck under the stars?

I peer underneath it, looking for lost toys, an old tricycle, anything to show I was here. I rummage through the brush until I find something: a rusted hinge lock attached to a plywood hatch.

Last Warning. Do Not Stand Up.

I heave up the rudimentary door.

"Piper," Jeannie warns.

A room.
A white six-by-six-foot crawl space.
Water splashing my face.
The last bit of sunlight gone as Father closes the door.
I open my mouth to scream, but my voice doesn't work.
Memories tumble forward, fighting for my attention.
I drown in them.
My cheek skids into the dirt as I fall.
Falling down.
Into the past.
The trailer and deck and door spin around me.
I squeeze my eyes closed, trying to make it stop.
I remember it all.

49. BEFORE

When I wake up, I'm lying in a small bed with rails on either side.

A thin blanket covers my legs and chest. A TV hangs on the wall opposite me. A clear plastic tube is taped to the back of my right hand, a needle imbedded in my flesh.

Something beeps next to me, a machine. A cord runs from it to the pointer finger on my left hand, which is clamped inside a piece of plastic. I slip it off my finger.

It's dark outside. The lights are off in my room, the door closed. A window in the door shows a lit-up hallway. Someone walks by, and I shut my eyes.

"Father," I whisper, as if he can hear me and materialize here.

I remember the car ride, the strange people in our house. I try to remember if it really happened or was only a dream, but the fact that I'm here, alone, must mean it's real.

Where are the others?

Pushing myself up onto my elbows, I brace for a dizzy spell, but it doesn't come. I ease back the covers, drop my feet to the floor. My clothes are gone, replaced by a thin nightgown.

When I move toward the door, the needle in my hand pulls at my skin. Anything could be dripping from that bag into my blood.

The label says SALINE, but I don't know what that is. I pull back a piece of tape over the needle and then back the needle out.

Blood oozes from the hole, and I press down on it with my other hand.

I open the door and poke my head into the hallway. It's beige and smells faintly of bleach. A police officer stands down the hall to my right, talking to someone. I move left down the hallway, passing by more closed doors, toward some furniture. A man in a sweatshirt sits on a couch facing me. He doesn't look up, just presses buttons on a small plastic box, head down.

A TV is on. A woman talks, but no sound comes out. Then the scene flicks to something else.

A face on the screen stares at me. It's a drawing of a young girl, and I know without a doubt who she is.

She's me.

I move closer. The drawing is gone, replaced with a man and woman. They stand with their arms wrapped around each other. The woman is crying.

"I can't hear what they're saying," I tell the man. He looks at me and shrugs.

Standing on my tiptoes, I try to find a volume button. I pound on the sides of the screen. "Come on," I say, sweat slicking my forehead.

A woman in a white uniform approaches me. "Let me help you to your room."

I back away. "Don't touch me."

The man on the couch is gone.

"It's okay. I'm not going to hurt you."

"Where's that man?" I point to the couch. "He was right there a second ago."

She holds her arms out toward me. "Come on, Piper. Let's get you to bed."

"How do you know my name? Where're Father and Mother?"

The woman motions to a man dressed in the same uniform. I try to run, but he pulls me into him, holds down my arms. The woman jabs something into me, and I can't fight anymore.

50. AFTER

I was at a store with Jeannie.

Mama, as I called her then.

She went into a dressing room, told me to stick close. I was eating a strawberry sucker the teller at the bank had given me on our way to the store. I was so happy, walking around the racks, looking at the clothes, lost in color and daydreams.

Then Angela was there. She whispered for me to come closer. She told me she knew Mama. They were friends. It was okay to follow her through the store to the parking lot.

She told me Mama said we could go for ice cream. She said it was okay for me to go for a ride in her car.

We never went for ice cream.

"Piper? Sweetheart?"

I open my eyes. Jeannie kneels next to me, brushing the hair off my face.

"I remember," I say. Bits of dirt and dead grass stick to my tongue.

She is quiet.

"I remember," I repeat.

"It's for her own good."

Father stands above me while I lie in the white room. I can't stop shivering and crying and wondering where my mom and dad are. I wet my pants, I'm so scared.

He locks me inside.

The bile is molten as I retch into the dirt. Into the battleground of a war I didn't want to fight.

"They took me from you," I say. "It's real."

She sits in the dirt and gathers me into her lap, rocking me gently as she rubs my back. "Yes. When you were six." Her voice catches as she kisses the top of my head. "We never stopped searching for you, Piper. We never gave up."

I know it's true.

Mother would open the hatch, climb in with me. She brought me food, held me as I cried. She said things would be better soon, I'd see. And she was right.

We were a family. They loved me. They said they would always take care of me. Keep me safe.

"*They* can't keep you safe," Father would whisper before locking me inside. "*They* did this to you. *They* keep you on the Outside to be poisoned and killed."

My brain is on fire.

"Piper?" Jeannie's voice is muffled and far away. But I can't answer.

She somehow carries me to the car, gingerly sets me inside.

I don't look back.

I can't look back.

✖

Days pass, I think. Mostly I sleep. Jeannie brings me soup and sandwiches, and I eat what I can.

"When will I feel better?" I ask her one afternoon.

She sits on the edge of my bed and smooths my hair. "When you're ready."

"I want to be ready."

"I know you do. You will be."

"But how do you know that?"

She smiles and touches my chin. "Because you're the strongest person I've ever known, that's why."

"Is it okay if I don't hate them yet?"

"You don't *ever* have to hate them, Piper."

I think it took a lot for her to say that. She picks up dirty clothes from the floor and an empty glass.

"The littles were all kidnapped, weren't they?" I ask. I need to know.

She nods. "A few members of the cult gave their children to Angela and Curtis to raise. But Carla and Millie were taken. The police are still trying to find their parents. Henry was their only biological child."

"When can I see them?"

"I'm speaking with their social workers to figure out when and how to best reunite all of you. I'm not sure when, but soon, Piper, I promise you'll see your brothers and sisters again. You're still a family, and nothing will ever change that."

I think of giggly Millie, of sensitive Beverly Jean, of sulky Carla, not sure of who she was supposed to be. Of Caspian's kindness and Samuel's quiet confidence and Henry's innocent laughter. I think of Thomas, and how brave he was to speak up. I'm afraid if I think about them too much, I'll be pulled under again.

"Mama?" I ask.

The word feels strange and right at the same time.

"Yes?" Her voice is barely more than a whisper.

"I'm sorry I forgot you."

She takes my hands. "Don't you ever apologize to me for that, Piper. Not ever. You did what you had to do to survive. Do you understand me? You're a *survivor*, Piper."

I sit up, and her arms are already open, waiting for me. She rubs my back, and I want to tell her everything I can't say, everything I don't fully understand yet, but all I can do is cry.

I love that she lets me.

"Can we have more pizza?" I say once my tears dry up. "I'm pretty hungry."

Her grin is so big. "That sounds awesome."

"Mushrooms—"

"And extra green olives," she laughs. "You were chowing down green olives the second your baby teeth grew in, I swear."

She shuts the door, and I stretch, then slip into a clean T-shirt and jeans. Something claws at the door, and Daisy pushes her way inside. I drop next to her and rub her neck and kiss her nose.

The bed.

The window seat.

The chipped desk with daisy stickers on the drawers.

This was my bedroom, and then it wasn't for a long time.

Father is out there somewhere, the wind at his back, the sunshine on his face. He's probably recruiting new people to brainwash and control. New people to worship and admire him.

He is free, and I am not.

I'm still that girl swimming laps, climbing the roller coaster, mixing clove oil to treat rotten teeth.

I'm still that girl afraid to look past a fence.

Even from a million miles away, I'm still the liar's daughter.

I take the pills from under my mattress and line them up. They stretch from my door all the way across the floor to the window.

They look like candy, sugary and innocent.

I think of the barracks and the box of forgotten blankets. Mother's refusal to answer any of my questions.

I scoop the pills up in my hands and drop them on the bed. How many antidepressants would it take to make me forget?

To let me go to sleep and never wake up?

We have a staring contest, the pills and I.

But I could never do that to my parents. Or to Cas or Amy.

Dr. Lundhagen said my feelings are valid. That they're mine. I have time to make sense of them now.

I don't want to die.

For the first time, it's like I'm seeing the world through my own two eyes instead of Mother's and Father's.

I sweep all but one of the pills into my wastebasket and take it into the bathroom. They swirl around the toilet bowl, and then they are gone.

Then I swallow down the remaining pill, the newest one, given to me this morning.

I think it's time I took care of me for a change.

51. AFTER

Jeannie gave me the combination to the shed outside. She says there are a bunch of papers and articles about my life and my kidnapping in a plastic tub. She offered to look at them with me, but this is something I need to do on my own.

Tonight I'm ready.

The others went to bed an hour ago, but I'm still wide awake. I pull on a sweatshirt and grab a flashlight, go outside to the shed, and enter the combination. It's an ordinary garden shed. Tools are set on a wooden bench. Bags of dirt and mulch lean next to a lawnmower. Something scurries on the ground near my foot. A mouse. It reminds me of home, and the feeling of homesickness is so sudden and painful that I'm afraid I'll fall over.

Easing onto the ground, I find a shelf running along the underside of the wooden table. I shine the flashlight under it, hoping to scare away any other critters. Mostly it's jars of nails and buckets of paint.

There's a plastic bin, just like the ones I found in Jeannie's closet.

I slide it out, carry it into the yard, and remove the lid. Inside is a thick accordion folder.

Father kneels next to me, but I refuse to look at him.

I unwind a loop of string keeping it closed, dip my fingers inside, and pull out a rectangle of paper.

It's a birth certificate.

Jessica Lynn Haggerty, 7 pounds, 4 ounces. Born at 5:59 P.M. on October 22.

I have celebrated my birthday every year on January first. Mother said I was a New Year's baby, an omen of happiness and luck for the following year.

But I wasn't.

Two tiny black footprints are stamped on the certificate. I trace a finger over them. Ten toes, impossibly small.

I set it on the grass.

The next piece of paper shows hospital discharge papers for Jessica Haggerty, age two months. Surgery to repair pyloric stenosis.

I touch the scar on my belly, instinctively knowing I never had a burst appendix.

Flipping through the doctor's notes, I learn it's a condition where food can't pass from the stomach to the small intestines because the muscle separating them is too big. There's still so much I don't know about myself.

The rest of the folder is filled with newspaper articles. I remove them all and fan them out on the grass, slowly shining the light over them, more afraid to read the words than I was of the mouse in the shed.

The headlines seem unreal, like I'm reading a story of someone else's life. But this *is* my life, or would have been if I'd been around to live it.

One Year Later, Still No Sign of Jessica Haggerty

Jessie Haggerty's Family and Friends Hold Candlelight Vigil

It's Been 10 Years Since Jessica Haggerty Was Abducted: Mother Wishes Jessie a Happy Sixteenth Birthday

There's a letter to me, from Jeannie, in this article. A letter hoping I was still alive and safe somewhere. Hoping that I was eating my favorite pizza, olives and mushrooms, on my special day. Hoping that I'm still swimming laps like a champ. Hoping that someday we'd be together again.

I switch off the flashlight.

I don't know how to reconcile the real Piper with the ghost of Jessica. I don't know how to stitch them together into one, whole person.

I shove everything back in the folder and set it on the front porch. There's no point hiding it away anymore.

At the gate, I stare at the keypad. I type in the date from the article, my real birthday, and the gate clicks open.

Father stands in the middle of the road, all dressed in white. He holds open his arms, waiting for me.

"You were never there," I whisper, and walk away from him.

I don't look back, and he doesn't follow.

When I arrive at Holliday's house, I sit outside. Her light is off, and I don't want to bother her. I'm not even sure why I came, but I think she's the closest thing I have to a friend.

Finally I rise and toss pebbles at her window, afraid she won't open it.

I wouldn't blame her if she didn't.

The light flicks on. When she sees me, her eyes widen, and she opens the window. "Piper?" she yell-whispers. "What are you doing here?"

"Can I come in?" My voice shakes, and my head spins.

"Of course you can! Hold on."

I shiver in the dark, and soon Holliday's at the sliding glass door, pulling me inside. "You're freezing." She takes me by the hand and drags me upstairs into a bedroom. It's so bright, it makes me dizzy. Twinkle lights are strung up the walls and on the ceiling. Cascades of silver discs stand in for curtains.

"Holliday," I choke. "I remember everything."

She tugs me against her and hugs me so hard.

"I'm so, so sorry," she says. "You've had a shitty time of things."

At first I just stand there, but when I can't stop remembering everything, as the pieces of my life start to fit together, it's all too much. I cling to her, the tears hot and fast, soaking into her pajamas. I can feel her crying, too.

"I remember this room," I whisper once the tears subside. "Did it used to be pink?"

"I wanted to be a ballerina. Turns out I have no grace. I'm planning to be a poet instead. Or an anthropologist. You know, either, both."

I sit on her bed and wipe my eyes. "We were friends, right?"

"Let me show you something." She digs through a shelf, then sets a book on my lap. "This is our yearbook from first grade. Turn to page seven."

Black-and-white photos are arranged in rows down the page, and I find Jessica Haggerty.

Only she's not alone. A young me is cheek to cheek with a young Holliday. She has two poofs of dark hair atop her head, while mine is long and yellow. Thin, like Amy's.

"We had our picture taken together? I vaguely remember."

"Our moms thought it was a cute idea, and the school was fine with it. We were pretty much joined at the hip." She points to another photo. "There's Jakob."

I recognize him from the swimming video, the kid who stuck his tongue out at the camera.

I touch my photo again. I look so happy with my cheesy grin. Or Jessica did.

"It still doesn't quite feel like *my* life. I'm missing big chunks of my past."

"Yeah. I've been trying to see this from your point of view, Piper. It must be weird and scary."

"Weird and scary doesn't begin to cover it."

I give her the yearbook, but she pushes it away. "You keep it," she says. "Look at it when you feel lost. You're still Jessica, and you're still Piper. Maybe you should start calling yourself Pessica?"

"Pessica," I repeat, and it sounds so stupid that I can't help but laugh.

"And we'll call you Pessie." She lowers her voice. "Why does Pessie seem so pessimistic today?"

"Pessie!" I exclaim. We laugh until tears stream down our faces.

The good kind of tears.

Tears that start to heal something I always knew was broken, but never wanted to admit to anyone, least of all myself.

"What about you?" I ask. "What has this been like for you?"

She looks at me for a moment. "Do you really wanna know?"

"I really do."

She exhales forcefully. "It's been hard. I've always been the girl whose best friend went missing. No one knew me as anything but Jessie Haggerty's friend for a long time. And then you came back, and it was a miracle, but you were a totally different person. I really wanted to know you, Piper. I've missed you so much, all this time. We were supposed to grow up together. I used to stare at your bedroom window, wondering where you were, if you were ever coming back." She exhales again. "But it's been a hard shadow to live under. That's horrible to say, I know."

I touch her arm. "It's not a horrible thing to say. And I understand…or at least I'm trying to."

"Maybe we can figure this shit out together. Deal?" She holds out her pinky, and I hook mine around it.

"Deal."

The next morning, the accordion folder rests on the kitchen table along with a feast of blueberry pancakes and bacon. When I enter, Jeannie sets a jug of apple juice on the table.

"You read the papers," she says.

"Why didn't you tell me everything when I first got here?"

She motions for me to sit, then joins me at the table. "A few days after you were rescued and taken to the hospital, Dr. Lundhagen and I told you everything that happened. Do you remember that?"

I have flashes of Jeannie standing in the room, crying. But nothing else. "No."

"After we told you, you went into some kind of shock. Dr. Lundhagen says you dissociated, as a way to protect yourself from the trauma. You lay in bed for days, staring at nothing. You stopped eating or drinking." She reaches for my hands. "It was so scary. I thought we'd lost you again. So we decided to ease you into the truth. I'm sorry if we made the wrong choice. I just didn't know what else to do."

"I guess that makes sense," I begin.

A tear rolls down her cheek. "I'm so sorry I didn't keep you with me that day, at the store, when I was trying on clothes. If I had, none of this would have happened. It's all my fault."

"It's not your fault." I swallow. "And not all of it was bad."

She wipes her face. "Would it be all right if I hugged you now?"

I consider her, the way her eyes crinkle when she's worried. She's lost something, too.

We all have.

"Yes," I say. The word is barely out of my mouth before she is around the table, wrapping her arms around me. Her body shudders, and I remember the feel of her hugs. I hug her back, and the muscle memory slams into me. She's my mother. It's like I can really feel it for the first time since I came here.

"Mama," I say.

And then I think of Mother's hugs, and the guilt sits on my throat like a stone.

"I need some air," I whisper, pulling away. I go outside and sit on the porch steps.

The door opens, and I assume it's Jeannie. But Amy steps outside instead, carrying a wicker basket filled with dolls. Daisy trails behind her, racing into the grass to chase a squirrel that scurries up a tree just as Daisy jumps onto its trunk. "Wanna play Barbies?" Amy asks. "We can make houses in the grass."

"Houses in the grass?"

She lifts a scissors from the basket. "When the grass gets real long, I cut out little rooms, and I make streets sometimes, too. Come on." She wanders onto the lawn, and together we cut square patches for a bedroom, a living room, a bathroom, and a dining room. She picks leaves from the trees and uses them for beds and a couch.

"This is actually pretty cool," I say as she sets a big rock in the dining room.

She sprinkles grass on the rock, tells me it's the doll's table and food. She arranges a doll wearing a pink ball gown next to one wearing a fur coat and no pants. She looks up at me, squinting into the sun. "We're sisters, you know."

"I know."

"I like it." She smiles.

"Me too," I say. Amy's joy is infectious. She might be the best thing to come out of all this.

"Mama says it's okay now, to tell you we're sisters. She said not to at first. She said you were afraid."

"I was. I still am sometimes."

"I get scared sometimes, too. Then I go in my closet fort. You can use it anytime you need to feel better, okay?"

"It's a deal," I tell her, and before I finish the sentence, she leaps into my arms.

"I love you, Piper." She presses her cheek against mine.

"I love you too, Amy," I answer, and it doesn't feel like a lie.

But for so long, the truth and I have been strangers. Father made sure of that, and I don't know if I can ever believe in anything again, least of all myself.

I hate him for that.

I look at Amy again, at her easy smile, her blue eyes that look like mine.

"Want me to braid your hair?" I ask.

"Yes!" She sits in the grass before me, and as my fingers work through the soft strands of her golden hair, our truth—the truth of me and Amy—slowly begins to solidify.

Her small shoulders, rooms for dolls cut in the grass. A peach sunset and a dog chasing a squirrel up a tree.

I think this is a truth I can believe in.

52. AFTER

Three months later

"How far is this place?" Holliday asks.

Since I don't have a license, she drives us in her mom's car. Rich was teaching me, but I crashed into a rosebush and haven't tried since.

"Not much farther."

"You're brave as hell, did you know that?"

"Not really."

She grins at me. "You need to learn how to accept compliments."

"Oh, yeah? How's this: I think you're probably the prettiest girl I've ever met in real life. Definitely the smartest, getting into Stanford," I tell her. "And just as brave as I am."

She rolls her eyes and doesn't answer.

"Mm-hmm. And you think *I* suck at taking compliments?" I tease.

She laughs.

The unlocked driveway appears up ahead, as if it only exists in my imagination and I wished it into being.

I have to acknowledge the truth: I haven't missed my life at the lake as much lately.

The world is so much bigger than Father's version.

Curtis. I have to get used to calling him Curtis.

Old habits are hard to break.

There's a FOR SALE sign out front. A SOLD sticker is plastered across it.

You can't go home again.

But sometimes, somehow, for a moment, you can.

Holliday slowly drives up the lane to where the house once stood. After the police and FBI finished their investigations, it was bulldozed. All that remains is a huge square of raw dirt like a freshly turned grave. Caspian stands next to it, staring off into the void.

Once he sees me, he meets us in the yard, running his hands through my hair, a shoulder-length cut I got a few days ago. We haven't seen each other since our movie date with Holliday and Dev a week ago, and it feels like an eternity.

"You are so sexy with shorter hair," he mutters before kissing me.

"Get a room," Holliday moans. She shoots off a text, probably to Dev.

"Very funny," Cas says, grabbing my hand. I can tell he's just as scared as I am to be back here.

"Thomas didn't want to come?" I ask, disappointed. I still haven't seen him since we were split up.

I found out from Jeannie's lawyer that the Aunties had been trying to push me and Thomas together for years. That's why they never let Cas watch TV with us.

Father gave them orders to do it. It was sick.

"He said he's not ready yet. But he wants to grab breakfast tomorrow if you're up for it. He misses you."

I smile. "I'd love that." I turn toward where the house used to stand. "It's weird that the house is gone. It's like our life here never existed. Or doesn't count, somehow."

"But it does count," he says seriously. "I don't care what anyone else says about us. It counts."

This used to be Curtis's kingdom.

The king is gone. The police haven't found him yet, but somehow I know they will eventually.

He said to have faith, and I do.

Faith that he will answer for what he's done.

"I hate them now," I whisper, and Cas squeezes my hand. "But I still miss them. How fucked up is that?"

"What would you say to them if you could? If they were standing here?"

They hover in front of me, Angela wearing one of her gowns, Curtis with his bare feet and shaggy hair. It was all a façade. They were bad actors on a makeshift stage.

Only their game of make-believe was my whole world, and they stole it from me. Sometimes I can't feel the ground I'm standing on.

"I wouldn't say anything," I answer. "I'm done giving any power to them."

They fade but don't disappear completely.

Maybe they never will.

"I can see why you liked it here." Holliday tilts her head to the sky and slowly spins in a circle. "It's kind of magical. The woods. The water."

My heart fractures.

Something new will grow from the remains of this place. Maybe a new family will put down roots, or nature will fill in all the empty spaces. Evil things happened here, and the newspapers and doctors and lawyers all chronicled them. There were photos at

Angela's trial of the bruises on Carla's body, the burns on Thomas's arms, my cracked tooth, all inflicted by the Aunties. Samuel and Henry were painfully underweight. Beverly Jean's scalp will never heal right.

But there was goodness here, too. In me and Cas. In the children. The laughter and the dreams. The way we picked each other up, protected each other.

The love. This place was bursting with it.

I'll take the best parts with me.

I gather up a bunch of wildflowers and lay them where our front door used to be.

Flowers for Millie, Henry, Samuel, Beverly Jean, and Carla.

Flowers for Thomas and Caspian.

For Piper. For Jessica.

Flowers for me.

"Let's go home," I tell my friends.

And we do.

AUTHOR'S NOTE

When I was a kid, religion was never a big part of my household. We celebrated Christmas and Easter and attended a Methodist church a few times a year, but my Sunday school class was so poorly attended that our teacher bribed us with gum and pop to show up.

My family's relationship to religion changed when I hit junior high. Some people in nice suits and dresses knocked on our front door and invited us to worship with them.

These people and their beliefs were unlike anything I'd ever experienced before. They mentored my family closely, supplying us with pamphlets, magazines, and books. We were expected to read everything.

They encouraged us to associate only with other members of our group. Outsiders were to be avoided. "Bad associations spoil useful habits," they warned us.

Services lasted for hours, and there were several other meetings each week. We were never on our own for long.

It was all in preparation for the end of the world. God's holy war, they told us, was imminent. Anyone who wasn't prepared would die when God unleashed His wrath on the world.

We believed it.

I was scared, for myself, my parents, and my sister. What if my whole family died during the end of the world? What would I do without them?

And what if I were killed? Would it hurt? Would I suffer?

But I was also relieved. It felt like we'd been singled out, *chosen* to be saved. We were special. I felt sorry for those who weren't.

Armed with this feeling of self-righteousness, I jumped feet first into the exhilarating new world of being one of God's chosen people. I had just started junior high, and I turned down a lot of social invitations. I had new rules: Dating without a chaperone was forbidden. Sports were forbidden. Holidays were forbidden, including my thirteenth birthday. Sure, I may have been a little disappointed, but I had no choice.

I didn't want to die.

Once, when our bus broke down on its way to school one winter morning, I honestly thought it was the beginning of the end of the world. I told other children on the bus that this breakdown *had* to be a sign that God's war had begun.

Every event was loaded. A scary news story sent my anxiety into overdrive. Would *this* be the day fire rained down from the sky?

I don't remember the exact moment I began to question our belief system. Maybe it was when I was told that I shouldn't go to college, because education would take my focus away from salvation. Maybe it was when my family's mentor told me that she'd be my new grandmother, since my actual grandmother wasn't in the group. Or maybe it was when I started to notice that everyone in positions of power were men. Only men were allowed to preach; only men could create and enforce the rules; only men could lead a family.

Doubting the group, they said, meant that Satan was whispering in your ear.

But I still began to doubt. Slowly. Gradually.

By the end of junior high, I was angry and fed up. (And listening to a lot of Green Day.) I'm grateful that my parents, unlike Piper's, respected me enough to allow me to leave. They eventually left, too. They had grown tired of this cultish community and its fear-based grip on its members. They were tired of waiting for the end of days.

When I first started writing *The Liar's Daughter*, I didn't plan to tell a cult story. But as I wrote draft after draft, that's the story that emerged. I saw myself in Piper—in her desire to please others, to be the "good" girl, and, ultimately, to navigate a situation she didn't choose. Writing about her has been cathartic for me.

I also read a lot of first-hand accounts of people who escaped cults as I wrote her story—cults like Scientology, the People's Temple, Buddhafield, and even Charles Manson's The Family. I read memoirs by and interviews with former cult members, including children raised in cults. It was truly heartbreaking research.

People may wonder: How could anyone be sucked into groups that seem so clearly dangerous? But the truth about cults is that no one is immune. They attract people of all ages, genders, races, and economic and educational backgrounds. They prey on our human need to belong and feel seen. They are powerful.

Even though I left the group that dominated my family more than twenty years ago, my experience of spiritual abuse has stuck with me. I continue to struggle with my views on religion and God. I have a hard time trusting churches and organized religion in general.

But something good did come out of this strange and painful experience: I learned that adults and other people in authority don't automatically deserve trust. It must be earned. That lesson goes against what a lot of us are taught as children—listen to your parents and your teachers, obey your elders—but it has served me well.

Now, I question everything. If something doesn't feel right, I trust my gut. I ask questions. I dig deeper. Most importantly, I respect beliefs different from my own.

It can be really scary to grow up and realize that you don't have the same beliefs and worldview as your family, your friends, and even your church. But it's not a betrayal of anyone—not your family or your chosen god—to question or to doubt.

The only betrayal is ignoring that voice inside you that says: "This doesn't feel right."

ACKNOWLEDGEMENTS

Writing is often a solitary endeavor, but it takes many, many people to make a book. It has been an absolutely wonderful experience working with my editor, Mora Couch. Her love for this book and these characters, and her keen editorial insights, have been invaluable. Thank you to the rest of the Holiday House team for their incredible work on this book. I could not have asked for a better publishing team. And thank you to my agent, Margaret Sutherland Brown, and the rest of the team at the Emma Sweeney Agency.

I've been blessed with many writer friends who have been there for me throughout the years: Cheyenne Campbell, my dear friend and critique partner, who has read everything I've written, even the terrible first drafts; Megan LaCroix, who reads pages when I need an extra set of eyes; and Fiona McLaren and Dionne McCulloch, my mentors during Pitch Wars. Their feedback and guidance have helped me grow as a writer.

Thank you to Katy Clay, Mandy Robbins, and Erika Shores, who read the very first words of this story. They told me I had something special and to keep going. Thank you to Jess Ehrgott, who reads everything I ever send her, including the terrible short stories I wrote about us when we were in college. Thank you to all my dear friends who have supported this crazy dream of mine.

This book could not exist without my family. My parents, Randy and Lori, were my first readers, and they always told me I had what it took to be a writer. Thank you, Mom and Dad. I'm so proud to share this moment with you! Thank you to my sister, Adrien, for believing in me and for threatening bodily harm against anyone who's ever rejected me. You are the best sister in the world! To my daughter, Molly, who inspires me to be the best version of myself.

And finally, to my husband, Dale. Thank you for believing in me, even when I sometimes didn't. Thanks for all those extra loads of laundry you did and those extra grocery store trips you made so I could write. I love you.